WEST OF WHITE CHAPEL

Jack the Ripper in the Wild West

Wayne D. Dundee

WOLFPACK
PUBLISHING
— EST 2013 —

WOLFPACK
PUBLISHING
— EST 2013 —

Text copyright © 2021 Wayne D. Dundee

Published by Wolfpack Publishing
5130 S. Fort Apache Road, 215-380
Las Vegas, NV 89148

Paperback IBSN 978-1-64734-728-4
eBook ISBN 978-1-64734-727-7

WEST OF WHITE CHAPEL

Silvercliff Mining Camp
Colorado Rockies Front Range
Monday, second week of Spring,
10:30 PM

*The man in the flowing coat stood calmly smok-*ing his pipe just within the shadows at the mouth of the narrow alley. From time to time he held the pipe away from his face, tipped his head back, and breathed deeply of the crisp night air. He'd forgotten how chill the spring nights could be here in the mountains, even down at these lower elevations. But that was okay, he was getting used to it again, finding it fresh and clean, invigorating.

Even this ramshackle, hastily-thrown-together mining camp with its handful of tilting, raw-cut wood buildings and numerous mud-spattered tents was an improvement over the fog-shrouded squalor he'd recently experienced in one of the world's so-called great cities. The rage and bitterness that churned inside him had been born out of that filth and squalor and now, despite his outwardly calm demeanor, this current setting nor any other could ever tame those demons. They could be quieted from time to time, for brief periods, but never completely. And as he stood there, puffing his pipe once again, the man admitted to himself with a thin smile that he'd grown to *enjoy these times when he could let the demons in him run loose.*

As the pipe smoker watched, he saw two men coming down the middle of the muddy, deeply-rutted street, moving from left to right in his line of sight, staggering and lurching in their drunkenness. He'd seen the men pass by a short time earlier—or maybe two others just like them, it didn't really matter—going in the opposite direction, each with a fawning, gaudily-dressed woman on his arm. They'd been headed toward the quiet, murky, poorly-lighted end of the street opposite the end where lights and music and laughter poured from the cluster of saloons and dance halls. Sluts ridiculously called "soiled doves" soliciting their trade amidst the lights and noise and then taking the simpering fools they'd ensnared down to the row of small, shabby tents that served as whore cribs to conclude their crude, disgusting transactions.

The returning men meant nothing to the watcher except to view them as the pathetic creatures they were—hard-working miners breaking their backs all day to earn money to be wasted on cheap booze and even cheaper whores. It was one among the latter whom the watcher would show interest in. Any who appeared alone, returning from the crib tents to try and drum up her next piece of business. Yes, such a "soiled dove" would interest him a great deal. He'd have some very special business to conduct with her ...

He didn't have to wait much longer.

Here came one now. Not only walking alone, but conveniently hugging this side of the street to try and avoid the worst of the slop out in the middle. The man in the shadows turned the bowl of his pipe upside down and tapped the bottom quietly against the heel of his free hand, emptying its ash and unburnt tobacco before slipping it into a pocket.

"Oh my!" the girl gasped when the man in the flowing coat glided out of the alley just ahead of her.

She stopped short as the man turned to face her. "Pardon me, my dear," he said in a rich, smooth voice. "I'm terribly sorry if I startled you."

The girl placed a hand over her heart, inadvertently (or maybe not) drawing even more attention to the creamy swell of her breasts, both of which were threatening to burst free of the low-cut, spangled dress she was wearing. She was prettier than most. No striking beauty by any means, just not yet hardened by the life she was leading. "Good golly!" she exclaimed. "Sorry or not, you nearly scared the life out of me."

"What a tragedy that would have been," the man said. "Please accept my apologies."

The girl poked out her bottom lip. "Well. I guess you didn't mean it ... What are you doing comin' out of a dark ol' alley anyway?"

"I was out for a stroll, getting some fresh air," the man explained. "When I passed by this alley, I thought I heard something. A whimpering sound. Probably just a cat, I thought at first. But then I heard it again and ... well, it sounded almost childlike. Like a frightened or maybe injured child."

By now the girl's eyes were huge. "Golly!" she said again. "So what did you find back there?"

"Nothing. It's too dark. I was just going to—"

"Wait," the girl cut him off, digging frantically into

the small, beaded purse she clutched in one hand. "I've got a candle in here. I carry it with me for when I'm going back and forth on overcast, especially dark nights."

"Wonderful. I've got some matches right here in my pocket," said the man, his right hand reaching into a deep opening on the side of his coat as he took a step closer to her. And then, with the speed of a striking rattler, his left hand shot out and clamped onto the unsuspecting girl's throat. Her eyes bugged even larger and she made a muted gagging sound as the man jerked her brutally around and shoved her ahead of him into the alley. He rammed his body against her and drove her deeper into the shadows. Just ahead of both their shapes being swallowed by the blackness, the man's right hand swept out of his pocket holding a surgeon's scalpel that gave off a quick glint of reflected light before it too disappeared into the dark.

Moments later, a single desperate whimper truly did escape from the alley ...

Chapter 1

I hadn't seen Russ Wheeler in nearly twenty years. That had been back in Washington D.C., where I'd gone from the Army to working for the Metropolitan Police Department as part of the covert unit that had been formed to handle presidential security after the assassination of Mr. Lincoln. General Grant was in the White House by then, which made the assignment an honor and a privilege as opposed to the early days of the fledgling detail during which that drunken buffoon Andrew Johnson was in office; but that's a story for a different time.

Russ had made his break with the Army by then, too, and had already begun working as a reporter for one of the New York papers, I forget which one. He was in town chasing a story at the time—"Something big, something really big," he'd claimed in a conspiratorial tone, but hadn't seemed willing to go into it any further. What he *had* been willing to talk about, proudly and excitedly, was his wife and brand new daughter. I'd been happy to listen, mostly because I was genuinely glad for him but also partly because there wasn't much I could say in return due to him now having a nose cocked to sniff out news and my security unit being unofficial and not generally acknowledged to even exist.

Prior commitments by both of us had forced our visit to be short, so we'd left it that I would make a trip to New York in the near future for the sake of meeting his family and having a longer chin wag. But then the years slipped away and, for one reason or another, we never did have that follow-up visit. The closest it came, as a result of him turning into a widely traveled and prolific reporter working for one of the bigger news syndicates, was me spotting his byline from time to time in various publications. No reason to suspect he ever heard my name or had cause to think much about me one way or another during that interim stretch.

But now, out of the blue, in the unlikely setting of a saloon called the Kicking Stallion in Cheyenne, Wyoming, here he was jamming a hip up against the bar right beside me and saying, "Lew? Lew Torrent? By God, it is you!"

The years appeared to have been kind to Russ. Yeah, his hair had thinned some and showed touches of gray at the temples, and maybe he was a bit thicker and softer-looking around the waist. But otherwise he stood tall and straight, perfectly groomed, and was attired in a well cut business suit complete with string tie and brocade vest. In short, the trappings of a man who'd achieved a measure of success and comfortable living as he stood on the threshold of his middle years.

Looking at our side-by-side images in the long mirror behind the bar, I saw myself standing taller and sturdier-looking, but further comparisons didn't exactly fall in my favor. I was definitely a bit more battered around the edges, grizzled beyond just being overdue for a good barbering, and my faded denim trousers and worn corduroy jacket, even when brand new, probably cost less that Russ's vest.

But none of that mattered, really; certainly not to me and I doubted to him, either, not if he was the same old Russ. It was just good for two old friends to run into each other again after such a long time.

We gripped hands and pumped arms enthusiastically. Clapping my free hand onto his shoulder, I exclaimed, "Doggone, Russ, is this ever a pleasant surprise! My only question is, what's a big city, high-toned dandy like you" —here I made a gesture to indicate his attire— "doing in a cowtown dive like the Kicking Stallion?"

He threw back his head and laughed. "Where else would I ever hope to run into an old comrade-in-arms besides a dive like this?"

And that's how the first round of trouble started. With that simple remark.

The Kicking Stallion maybe wasn't the rowdiest saloon in Cheyenne, but neither was it a quiet local tavern where mostly regulars gathered to relax and discuss events of the day. The Stallion was big and gaudy and loud, a fairly new addition to a growing, boisterous town that now had bragging rights as the capital of the newly christened state of Wyoming. Almost every night the Stallion drew an enviable crowd ranging from cowboys, railroad workers, soldiers, miners, drummers, drifters, and various sorts in between—all the ingredients necessary for the stew to occasionally boil over.

One such ready-to-boil ingredient who happened to be on hand this night was a tall, dusty, bleary-eyed cowpoke bellied up to the bar directly behind Russ. Apparently, our enthusiastic hand-shaking and shoulder-slapping must have caused Russ to bump slightly back against this hombre. On top of that the "dive like this" remark was overhead and it added up to enough for the cowpoke to decide it was worth taking issue with.

"Hey!" he grunted loudly, planting a palm on Russ's back and giving him a shove that sent him lurching against me.

"What the hell?" Russ responded, catching his balance and then turning to glare at the cowpoke.

The latter had taken half a step away from the bar and was now standing with his feet braced and fists dangling at his sides, facing Russ full on. "That's right—You tell me 'what the hell'," he growled. "What the hell's the idea of a fancy pants like you comin' in here, crowdin' folks aside, and then callin' the place a 'dive'?"

Russ scowled. "Now just a minute, pal. If I bumped against you, I assure you it was purely an accident. And as far as any comment I made—which was strictly between my friend and I, I'll point out—it was harmless and of no concern to you."

"See? There's that high-minded attitude showin' through all over again," sneered the cowpoke. "In the first place, I ain't your pal. In the second place, bumpin' into a fella and causin' him to nearly spill his drink is plumb sloppy and rude, accident or not. And if I hear a snotty comment bein' made, no matter to who, I can decide to make it my concern if I choose ... Which, in this case, I'm sayin' I do."

Two other men, also rough-edged wrangler types who'd been parked at the bar on the other side of the cowpoke running his mouth, now shifted up close behind him. Both were wearing scowls and aiming them at Russ. One of them, a gawky number in a cowhide vest, wanted to know, "What's goin' on here? What's the trouble, Rafe?"

Rafe, the cowpoke who seemed bent on stirring things up, jabbed a thumb at Russ and said, "This Fancy Dan, he's the trouble. Comes crowdin' in like he owns the place, and then starts bad-mouthin' and runnin' it down."

"If he's bad-mouthin' the place, then that means he's bad-mouthn' folks who like bein' in it," concluded Cowhide Vest in a loud voice.

"That's the way I see it," agreed Rafe.

"Sounds kinda damn snooty to me," spoke up the third wrangler, a barrel-chested specimen sporting a bushy, rust-colored mustache. "And I hate snooty damn Fancy Dans struttin' around feelin' superior to workin' men who sweat for a livin'."

Since Rafe had now acquired some backup, it seemed altogether reasonable for me to edge forward and provide the same for Russ. Glancing around the smoky room, I saw that our little face-off was starting to draw the attention of some other patrons.

"Okay," I said. "Everybody's had a chance to speak their piece, I say that ought to settle it."

Rafe peeled his lip back in another sneer. "Settle it, my ass. Who the hell are you to say anything about anything, let alone call this settled? I say it ain't settled until Fancy Dan here apologizes for slammin' into me the way he done ... Come to think of it, occurs to me he owes everybody in here an apology for then goin' on to bad-mouth the whole place."

"You've got to be kidding," said Russ in a low voice. I recognized the streaks of color, almost as bright a red as his string tie, reaching up the sides of his neck and into his cheeks.

But the three 'punchers were starting to feed off one another now, drunk enough to want to be cocky and try to impress each other as well as anybody looking on, rather than showing the sense to want to tame things down before it got out of hand.

"Hell, he needs to do more than *just* apologize," crowed Cowhide Vest. "He needs to buy a round of drinks for everybody to prove he's sincere!"

More and more people were paying attention now, and the "buy a round of drinks" enticement only drew added interest.

Russ pinned Rafe with a hard, flat stare and said in that same low voice, "You've pushed this far enough, mister ... Call off your hounds and we'll call it an evening."

It was a sincere effort on Russ's part, I'll give him that. But I could see right away, in the alcohol-dimmed eyes of the three cowboys, that it didn't make any difference. They were too primed, viewing this as an opportunity for some added fun on this night away from the rigors of their ranch work. Shove around some fancy-pants stranger who looked soft and probably not able to punch his way out of a paper bag. That added up to two big mistakes on their part. Number one, not knowing what I did about Russ Wheeler's fighting past (unless he *had* grown too soft from too many years of just wrestling with words on paper, which I didn't want to think about). Number two, not giving much consideration to me—something I found kind of insulting and added to my personal annoyance with the trio.

Bottom line on how things stood after Russ made his statement, was that I could plainly see what was coming next. Fists were going to fly. And the way I could recognize this so well was that I had unfortunately been in too many such situations over the years. And something I'd learned from them was that, when fisticuffs are inevitable, only a fool waits for the other side to get in the first lick.

So, heaving a fatalistic sigh, I stepped around and past Russ, saying out the side of my mouth, "Rafe is yours, I got this side." From there, I took a long stride, planted my foot, and uncorked the dandiest left jab I maybe ever threw. It landed square in the middle of Rusty Mustache's face and sent him flying backward, arms windmilling wildly, until he collided with two or three other men who'd moved up for a closer look at what was going on.

As I shifted back from throwing the jab, I saw, out the corner of my eye, a surge of motion from Russ that culminated in the sound of another punch landing solidly. My mouth started to spread in a satisfied smile but, before it stretched too wide, I suddenly had my hands very full of the third wrangler, the gawky one in the cowhide vest. He leaped at me, kicking ahead with his feet and swinging his fists in an unorthodox, flailing manner that momentarily bewildered me as far as putting up a defense against it. He came swarming so suddenly and awkwardly that it took me off balance.

I backpedaled, half-staggering, until the edge of a table jabbed just under my buttocks, causing me to tip back and flop onto it with Cowhide Vest climbing almost astraddle me. The table upended, scattering those who'd been seated around it, flinging glasses and pitchers of beer into the air and then raining them down on me and Cowhide Vest as we were dumped to the floor. Sprawled there, I finally managed to swat aside his flailing arms and fists long enough to create an opening through which I reached and wrapped my left fist around the knot of his neckerchief. This enabled me to hold his bobbing damn head still long enough so I could ram my right fist into his face three rapid-fire times.

Squirming out from under the now limp Cowhide Vest, I rolled onto a hip and pushed to my feet. Standing, I saw that a full-blown brawl had broken out all around. At least a dozen other patrons had joined in, grappling with one another, jerking and shoving, throwing punches at any face that made a tempting target. Somewhere somebody started blowing shrill blasts on a whistle. This apparently was a signal for two burly bouncers to hop down from elevated chairs on either side of the wide room and start bulling their way toward the melee, each wielding a fat billyclub.

I looked around and spotted Russ, still over by the bar. His feet were planted wide and his fists were raised and ready. Rafe was nowhere in sight. The only one of the original three cowboys remaining on his feet was Rusty Mustache who was busy trading blows with the men I had knocked him into.

"Hey!" I hollered over at Russ. When his face turned in my direction, I saw a few strands of thinned hair spilling over one eye and, just like the old days, a corner of his mouth was lifted in a rake-hell smile.

I motioned him toward me and stepped to meet him. On the way, I ducked a sloppy roundhouse aimed at my head, and answered with the point of my elbow to the throat of the slob who threw it.

And then Russ and I were standing together, positioned back to back—again like the old days—welcoming any and all who felt feisty enough to make a try for either one of us. A few did, but none of them had much luck.

Pretty soon a couple of deputy marshals poured through the front door to join forces with the two bouncers and things tamed down in a hurry. Although that meant an end to the fun, it at least also brought an end to those ear-piercing blasts from that idiot with the whistle.

Chapter 2

I watched Russ carefully cup the palm of his left hand over the knuckles of his right and then slowly rotate the wrist, gently massaging said knuckles. "Damn," he muttered. "I don't remember it hurting like this before."

I grinned. "That's because 'before' was twenty years ago. And, in addition to not having those in-between years piled up yet, your hands back then were toughened from soldiering and other physical work a lot more strenuous than lifting pencils and sheets of paper like you currently do."

"Hey, I still do other stuff," he protested. "And even if I don't, these pencil-lifting hands still landed some pretty doggone good punches in case you didn't notice."

"Yeah, I got to give you that," I allowed. "But that don't change you now having to pay the price."

We were still in the Kicking Stallion, though now at a quiet table back toward one corner. It was past midnight, the brawl long since over. The crowd had thinned to just us and a handful of others hunched at scattered tables and a couple drunks holding up the bar.

Nobody had been interested in pressing any charges over the fight, so we'd been allowed to stay after contritely owning up to our part in it. I even confessed to throwing the first punch. It helped that the bartender who'd been working the other side of the stick spoke up and told how the three cowboys had been the instigators. What helped the most, though, was Russ saying he'd pay for any and all damages. (I humbly offered to also pitch in but, since he obviously had deeper pockets than me, I didn't push it too hard.) Since everybody knew that ranch hands tended to barely make it payday to payday, the three cowboys could have stuck around, too, even without paying anything as long as they promised to behave. But they'd opted instead to sullenly take their leave, which was probably just as well.

"What about you?" Russ abruptly wanted to know. "You saying you keep those mitts of yours as tough and hard as in the old days? And that dust-up a little while ago didn't leave you feeling any after effects?"

I held up my right hand, spread the fingers and then clenched it into a fist a couple of times. "Oh yeah, I feel the after effects. A little more each time," I said. "Not even having that kind of thing crop up fairly regular keeps my bones and joints from reminding me they wouldn't miss it any."

Russ regarded me. "I'm not sure I believe that."

"What's that supposed to mean?"

"It means your bones and joints might not miss it, but I bet the rest of you would." He grinned. "Face it, Lew. You leading some kind of quiet life, sitting behind a desk or clerking in a store ... You're no more cut out for something like that than you are for wearing ladies' bloomers. Even though I haven't seen or heard from you in two decades, I always knew if I ever ran into you again I'd find you involved in something rough and tumble. And here you are proving me right, turning out to be the top operative for Col. Sam's detective outfit—the Omaha & Points West Agency."

"Just because I work for a detective agency don't automatically make me some kind of thumper," I pointed out. "Detective work may get rough once in a while, but it also takes wits and brains to figure things out. Haven't you heard of the popular Sherlock Holmes stories by that English author? He's a detective who never resorts to rough stuff and solves all his cases just by puffing on a pipe and looking at clues."

"He's also a work of fiction," Russ came back. "And not that you aren't as smart as anybody, old pal, but when's the last time you got what you were after by reaching a conclusion from studying the mud on somebody's boots or catching the whiff of a telltale perfume lingering in the air?"

"You might be right," I admitted ruefully. "Any time I've followed the whiff of perfume, lingering or otherwise, it often as not resulted in causing me a problem, not solving one."

The bartender who'd spoken up on our behalf earlier came over to our table at that point. He was carrying a pot of coffee, the drink we had switched to by then. As he topped off our cups, he said, "We'll be officially closing in a few minutes. But I'll still be around for a while, so if you want to stay and continue visiting a bit longer, that's okay. I'll keep the coffee hot."

We thanked him and said we'd be out of his hair pretty soon.

After he'd gone, Russ took a sip of his coffee and said, "Getting back to talking about you being a detective and all, are you here in Cheyenne on a case?"

"Matter of fact, yeah."

"Something juicy and newsworthy?"

I grinned. "Whether it is or isn't, anything I had to say about it would have to be considered off the record."

"Hey, come on now. That is downright hurtful, you thinking I might take something you told me as part of a friendly conversation and run a story on it."

"Sorry, but I've dealt with too many news reporters over the years," I told him. "The good ones—and that fits you—are always primed to seize hold of anything they think might make, like you said, a juicy story. You can't help it, it's in your blood."

"Nuts to you, then. I couldn't care less what you're working on."

Like he was fooling anybody with that. But, just to put his mind at ease, I told him, "This is nothing big enough to be of interest to you, anyway. It's old news. I'm trying to get a line on an embezzler, that's all. Some slickster who walked away from a Kansas bank a couple years back with fifty grand. A recent lead suggests he might have ended up here in the Cheyenne area and is reported to be running a good-sized cattle operation."

"Good enough sized to be able to squeeze the fifty grand back out of?"

I shrugged. "Maybe. A considerable chunk of it at least. That's better than the nothing the bank has been left holding until now ... All providing, of course, if the lead pans out and I can pin down the right cattle boss. There ain't exactly a shortage of those hereabouts."

Russ drank some more of his coffee. "Interesting ... But you're right, not big enough to divert me away from the story I'm already chasing."

"Uh-huh. 'Bout what I figured. Bet the chase is after a really big one, eh?" I paused, lifting my eyebrows. "Come to think of it, the last time we traded words over a couple cups of coffee, you were chasing a really big story back then, too."

An odd, almost startled look came over Russ. He gazed at me, unblinking, for a long beat before saying, "You may find this hard to believe, Lew ... But the story I was chasing that time in DC? It's the same one that brought me here to Cheyenne."

That must have brought a startled look out of me, too. Until I figured out, he had to be pulling my leg. "Sure it is," I said. "Except it doesn't quite fit with the whole range of other stories I've seen under your by-line over the years."

"No. No, I didn't mean it that way," he tried to explain. "Certainly this isn't the *only* story I've chased for all these years. The thing is, it's too damn elusive for me to ever wrap up while at the same time being too intriguing to ever go completely away. Just when I think I'm done with it, that it's a lost cause, some new revelation will pop up and I'm running after it all over again. It's like that whiff of perfume we spoke of a minute ago. I keep getting sniffs of it, keep being drawn by it—but I can never reach out and wrap my hand around it."

I studied him. Then said, "You're serious, aren't you? This thing has really got a hold on you."

"Man, you don't know," he half groaned. "It's haunting and fascinating, yet at the same time so damnably frustrating it threatens at times to drive me nuts. Like spotting an impossibly gorgeous woman you can't get out of your mind even though you know you don't have a snowball's chance of ever getting next to her."

"All these thoughts about intriguing perfume and unobtainable beautiful women ... Maybe you just need your ashes hauled good and proper," I said, aiming to cut the intensity a bit.

But that just made him look all the more forlorn. "If it was only that easy. Ironically, the subject of hauling ashes and the women who provide that service fits into this in a way that is shockingly sad and bitter."

I replied, "In that case, maybe you ought to fill me in a little more before I stick my foot even deeper in my mouth."

Russ seemed to consider this a moment. Then, giving a self-conscious little laugh, he said, "No, I'd better not. You might think I was already nuts. You see, after all my chasing and digging, all I've really got is a pile of hearsay, suspicion, and conjecture that, unless I can start tying it together with some pieces of hard evidence, will sound like nothing more than wild speculation." He paused and his eyes brightened with excitement. "But, man oh man, Lew—if I ever pull it off, if I ever *can* make a convincing case for all I've come to believe ... Then it won't be just a big story, it'll be *the story of the everlovin' century!*"

I laughed, glad to see his spirits lighter again. "I'll be sure to keep an eye out for it. Then, when it breaks, I can not only brag that you're an old friend of mine but I can also say I was there at the beginning of the story of the century."

"Align yourself with me at your own risk," Russ advised. Pulling a pocket watch from his vest, he snapped it open to check the time and then said, "As you keep pointing out, neither of us are spring chickens anymore, old friend, and this aging rooster had better totter off to bed. I've got to catch the eight o'clock train to Denver in the morning. My daughter will be waiting to meet me at the station. Bad enough I'll have to report that I came up empty on what I hoped to learn here, I don't want to be late on top of it."

"You said Victoria works with you full time now, is that right?"

"Yes, she does. She's been determined to be a journalist since she was six. Ellen and I had every intention to see she got the proper schooling to pursue it. But then, when Ellen grew ill and passed away five years ago, Victoria insisted she didn't need to attend school but instead would travel everywhere I went covering stories and get what she called the best education possible—on the job training directly from me." Russ couldn't hold back a proud smile at the conclusion of telling this.

I said, "I get the impression it turned out pretty good for both of you."

"You bet it did. Better than I dared hope," he affirmed. "She went from a very competent assistant to an efficient fact-gatherer to being able to knock out a flawless report all on her own. She can take one of those new-fangled writing machines—typewriters, I guess they're calling 'em, like even Mark Twain is using these days to write his books—and clackety-clack away with it until a wad of scribbled notes is turned into polished copy in no time."

"Sounds like you'll need to be sharing a byline with her before much longer."

"Heck, she's already earned it. And she knows it, too." Russ rolled his eyes. "In case I didn't mention it, Victoria's one of those emancipated women—thinks anything a man can do, a gal can do as well or better and damn well deserves recognition for it. Don't worry, when she decides it's time, she'll be *demanding* her piece of the byline."

We stood to leave. Left a tip for the barkeep, headed for the door.

"Where are you staying?" Russ asked.

"Little out-of-the-way hotel down near the livery stable. Sam Horn's budget for operatives out in the field is about as tight as a leather purse that's been wetted down and then shrink-dried in the hot sun ... You?"

"I'm at the Grande Cheyenne only a couple blocks from here."

"I should've figured. La-de-dah. It's on the way to mine, we can walk that far together. I figure they'll let a commoner like me at least pass by, long as I don't get too close or tarry too long."

Russ grinned. "I'll tell them you're my manservant. Confuse 'em long enough for you to make a getaway."

"Big of you. I appreciate it."

Chapter 3

Out front of the Kicking Stallion, everything was quiet and the street was mostly empty. A delivery wagon of some sort, pulled by a single horse with a lone, slump-shouldered man in the driver's box, was clopping slowly by. Catty-cornered across the street, up a ways from the direction Russ and I would be heading, a handful of hanger-ons were clustered in front of another saloon that had just closed. Down the way we were going, some bright light could be seen pouring out of the Grande Cheyenne but otherwise all the stores and shops on either side were dark. I'd heard some talk since arriving in town about Cheyenne, especially now that it was a brand new state capital, installing some of Mr. Edison' incandescent street lamps the way they'd done over in Deadwood a couple years back. But so far that hadn't happened and all the lamps in place through this stretch of the city, sporadically-spaced, were the coal oil style giving off flickering, weak pools of illumination.

The night was still and pleasantly cool. As we walked, I glanced up and saw that the sky appeared cloudless, no sign of the moon yet but filled with thousands of glittering stars. I couldn't help thinking how—out on the open prairie, away from any offsetting man-made illumination—they would appear even more brilliant.

Russ asked idly, "You figure on sticking around town much longer?"

"At least another couple days, by the look of it," I told him. "Long enough to determine if there's any sign of my embezzler actually having settled here, or if the rumor to that effect is a wash-out."

"My hotel has a decent coffee shop just off the lobby. You figure you might be up and about in time tomorrow morning to join me there for some breakfast before I have to catch my train?"

"Reckon I could make it a point to. Long as you can sell me as your manservant."

"Aw, knock that off." He regarded me. "It's been damned nice seeing you and spending time with you tonight, Lew. Even worth the sore jaw and swollen knuckles from that brawl. I hate for it to end. I'd hate even more to think it might be another twenty years before our paths cross again."

"Well, then let' make sure not to allow that to happen," I said.

"Sounds good to me. Although maybe we can skip the brawl next time."

At that point, a man appeared on the boardwalk ahead of us. Average height and build, wearing a dark slouch hat and long, loose coat. His steps were steady and even as he approached. As he emerged out of the shadows between two pools of street lamp illumination, he stopped and lifted a narrow, pale face. "Excuse me.

Are either of you gents Mr. Torrent? Mr. Lew Torrent?"
he asked.

"That would be me," I answered.

"Good. I have a message for you."

"At this late hour?"

The man in the long coat shrugged. "I'm just doin'
as instructed."

Remembering I was on a case and had been asking around for information, I said, "Okay. What's the
message?"

"Only this ... Quit stickin' your nose in where it don't
belong!" So saying, the man threw open the front of his
coat and from inside its folds swung up the long snout of
a double-barreled shotgun.

I shouldn't have been so easily caught off guard. But
I was too lulled by the pleasant conversation with Russ
and too hopeful for some feedback on what I was seeking. I was unprepared for trouble. Damn me.

But Russ reacted amazingly fast. Shouting, "Watch
out, Lew!" he hurled himself forward and over in front
of me, lunging with both arms extended, reaching
to slam the heels of his hands against the side of the
shotgun barrels and knock them aside just as they discharged. The double blast, going off so close and under
the boardwalk's shingled awning, was a tremendous
Ba-Boom! whose discharge tore into the face of the boot
shop we had paused in front of and gouged out a cloud
of shattered glass and pulverized wood splinters that
filled the air like shrapnel.

Feeling a score of these shards stinging my cheek and
the sides of my neck, I dropped into a half-crouch and
stabbed my right hand under the lapel of my jacket to

grab the short-barreled Colt Lightning nestled in the shoulder holster snugged against the ribs on my left side. Jerking the gun free, I swung it in a flat arc over the grappling figures of Russ and the shotgunner where they had toppled together onto the boardwalk. But I didn't dare risk a shot for fear of hitting Russ.

That problem didn't last long, though. Thrashing and cursing loudly, the man in the long coat shoved Russ away and rolled frantically to get clear of him. He made no attempt to maintain his hold on the emptied shotgun. Instead, as he rolled onto his back and then jackknifed to a partial sitting position, he pulled a second weapon from the folds of his coat—a handgun not quite as menacing as the double-barreled long gun, but nevertheless a deadly threat.

I was ready this time, my Colt already drawn. I didn't hesitate. As fast as I could cock and squeeze the trigger, I drilled two .44 slugs into his body mass about six inches below the chin. He flopped back onto the boardwalk, his own handgun dropping unfired from dead fingers.

I straightened up and immediately turned my attention to my friend. "Russ! Jesus, man, are you okay?"

He muttered something in response, but I only caught part of it because the night was suddenly ripped apart all over again by another gunshot, this one from across the street. The bullet smacked into an awning post just inches from my head, once more spitting wood slivers against the back of my neck.

I resumed my partial crouch and twisted in the direction the shot had come from. I saw the muzzle flash of another shot and an instant later that slug clanged off the boot-shaped metal sign cantilevered out from the awning post, advertising the business inside.

It was my turn to go into a dive, aiming to drop in behind the nearest cover at hand—the carcass of the man I'd just killed. As I squirmed into place, pressing my body tight to the boardwalk, the shooter across the way triggered another round. This one whacked against the storefront well above my head. That made me bold enough to rise up and quickly snap off some return fire.

Judging by the sound of the reports, the second ambusher was using a repeating rifle. Meaning if he wanted to drag this out, he'd have me and my Colt outgunned. But apparently the sight of his partner biting the dust and me still alive and throwing lead back his way was enough for the yellow skunk to call it quits. The shooting stopped and in its place, I could hear the slap of feet retreating and then fading into the blackness of an alley.

I relaxed but stayed low for several beats, just in case. My breathing was coming in quick puffs and beads of sweat had popped out all across my forehead.

"I think the coast is clear," I called over to Russ. "But hold tight for a minute, just to make sure."

He gave no response.

I could hear voices starting to jabber from different points up and down the street. The bartender and some other man emerged cautiously from the Kicking Stallion; the cluster of men I'd seen gathered in front of the other saloon edged out into the street and started this way. Some previously dark second story windows on either side began glowing with light.

I was peripherally aware of all this, but what had most of my focus was the unmoving, unresponding lump that was Russ still sprawled in the shadows up against the front of the boot shop. "Russ!" I called again, now with urgency and a premonition of dread ringing in my tone. "Are you okay over there?"

This time I got a response. A weak moan.

I shoved up and scrambled quickly over to him. Up close, even in the shadows that hugged the storefront, I could see his face twisted with pain and could hear the irregular rattle of very shallow breathing.

Turning my head, I hollered out to the street, "Somebody get a lantern over here! Hurry!"

Turning back to Russ, I placed a hand on each shoulder and tried to gently lay him back more comfortably than the way he was wedged up against the building's outside wall. When one hand brushed lightly across his chest, I felt a thick smear of hot, sticky blood.

"I took a bad one, Lew," he rasped. "Ricochet ... hit too close to my heart ... not gonna make it."

"Don't try to talk," I protested. "You didn't survive the carnage at Gettysburg and all those other pieces of Hell we fought through together just to fall victim here in the street to some lousy—"

"Listen to me," he cut me off, his face grimacing. "Just listen ... Room key in my pocket ... My briefcase with notes and files there. Train ticket for tomorrow, too ... Use it. Take everything to Victoria in Denver ... You tell her what happened. Don't let her hear it from some stranger or in a telegram ... I'm all she's got. But she's tough, she won't quit ... So you'll have to help her now, Lew ... Protect her ... This thing is ... is ..."

And then he was gone.

Chapter 4

Measured in miles, the train ride from Cheyenne to Denver is relatively short. But covering the same distance for the purpose of delivering tragic news can seem dismally long.

Naturally, I had to fulfill Russ's request about being the one to contact his daughter. Not only because he'd asked it, but also because of the bitterly personal obligation I felt—the gut-twisting awareness that the bullet he took was meant for me. What was more, he'd taken it just moments after saving my life from the initial shotgun blast intended to cut me in two.

Now I was faced with breaking the news to Victoria that her father was dead, had died heroically but violently, and I was partly to blame.

Jesus.

I had moments of feeling more like throwing myself under the train rather than riding it to deliver such a message. But that wasn't an option, of course. I had to see it through. Two tasks lay ahead: one given to me by a dying friend; a second by the scurvy lowdown bastard who had sent the shooters to take my life but had taken an innocent one instead.

... I'm all she's got. But she's tough, she won't quit ... So you'll have to help her now, Lew ... Protect her ... That was the task set for me by Russ regarding his "emancipated" daughter. What it might entail, I didn't yet know. Not that it mattered; I would see it through to the best of my ability.

For the time being, the task of uncovering and dealing with whoever sent the ambushers would have to wait. The most likely suspect seemed the embezzler I was on the trail of, his alleged cattle operation evidently affording him the ability to hire assassins to prevent me from succeeding. But even that much was strictly a guess. I've made enough enemies over the years, too many still lurking across the underbelly of the West, for it to be possible that one of them might have caught up and decided to try and settle an old score ... Whatever the case, whoever it turned out to be and however long it took, I intended to be the one who settled the final score.

But first I had to shatter the heart of a young lady who'd suddenly been turned into an orphan.

* * * * *

The rocking motion of the passenger car and the fact I'd gotten no sleep the prior night resulted in me nodding off a time or two, despite all that was churning inside me. Following the shooting, it took quite a while for Cheyenne's town marshal, Dick Barton, to finish with me. Even though my actions were fully justified and I had a reasonably good relationship with Barton from prior dealings when I'd passed through town, a shooting in the heart of the brand new capitol city warranted a thorough looking into. Russ being a news reporter of some renown only added to that, not to mention adding to the urgency of me needing to make the morning train for the sake of reaching Victoria before she heard the news elsewhere.

Before the marshal was done with me, he revealed that the shotgunner was one Hal Kraig (the name as unfamiliar to me as his face when I had the chance to check it out more closely after he was dead), a local hardcase known to hire out for gun work and other intimidation tactics. But I didn't have time to dwell on any of that in as much as I had too much else to do before using Russ's ticket to catch the morning train. For starters, I had to make temporary arrangements for holding Russ's body until his daughter had a chance at her say on a funeral and burial. Next I gathered up Russ's gear, including said ticket, from his hotel room. That left settling my own hotel room tab and paying in advance for my horse to be boarded an extended length of time at the livery stable, until my return.

Marshal Barton wasn't crazy about me departing town so soon. But after I explained about needing to notify Russ's daughter and pointed out how I likely would be returning with her to tend details regarding her father's remains—not to mention retrieving my horse—he relented. What was more, I reminded him he could always get in touch with me via the contact information on the O&PW Detective Agency business card I left with him.

So it was I put behind me "the Magic City of the

Plains", as Cheyenne was sometimes called, and, with the majestic Colorado Rockies looming ever closer and higher outside the train car window, rolled into "the Mile High City" of Denver.

Since there weren't very many passengers on the run that morning, it stood to reason there weren't very many people waiting on the arrival platform when we hissed to a stop at the station. Even if there had been, I don't think I would have had any trouble spotting Victoria Wheeler. There was something about the dark-haired, dark-eyed young beauty my gaze fell on that immediately proclaimed: *Here I am. It's me you're looking for.* Despite having never met her mother in order to make a possible comparison and the only description from Russ being how lovely she was (as any proud father would say), I didn't have much to go on. But it didn't matter, I felt sure of who I was looking at as soon as I started down the steps off the train with my saddlebags over my left shoulder and Russ's briefcase in my right hand.

I paused long enough to take a deep breath, let part of it out, then walked toward her. She was looking past me, watching for her father to appear, when I stepped up and said, "Excuse me, miss. Are you Victoria Wheeler?"

Her eyes cut to me and made a quick, cool appraisal before she replied, "Yes, I am. How may I—" She stopped abruptly, her gaze having drifted down to the briefcase in my hand. Then: "What are you doing with my father's briefcase? Where is he?"

Damn it, I should have thought to somehow keep from revealing the case until after I had the chance to try and ease into the news I was here to break. Quickly trying to recover, I said, "I can explain everything, ma'am. But it might be better if we—"

"If you have an explanation, then tell me," she insisted. "Here is as good a place as any. And who are you, anyway?"

"My name is Lew Torrent," I told her. I was hoping that maybe—just maybe—Russ might have mentioned me at some point and, if the girl had any recollection of that, it might help this current situation somewhat.

But it didn't look like it was going to be that easy. Victoria responded, "That means nothing to me. Is it supposed to?"

"I was hoping it might. You see, I'm an old friend of your father's. We served in the Army together. That's why he asked me to—"

"Wait a minute," she interrupted again. "Maybe I do ... Torrent, yes. You're a detective now, right? Father spoke of possibly hiring your services a couple different times in the past, to help with some of our inquiries. Is that what happened? Did he decide to bring you on board now?"

"Well, not exactly. Not in the way you mean," I had to admit. "He did send me here this morning, though, but only because—"

I was halted by her hand reaching out to grasp my arm, the one holding the briefcase, her fingers digging in deep. Finishing a statement with this gal around was proving a mighty hard thing to do. Now as her dark eyes gazed up at me they shone in a different way, no longer annoyed and demanding but rather with a sudden realization and a glint of dread as she asked, "Something's happened to Father, hasn't it? Is he ill or injured in some way?"

Here it was. The moment I'd been hating to think about but now had no way to stall or avoid. Dropping the briefcase and pulling my arm momentarily out of her grip, I then took her hand in mine. "Brace yourself, kid, I've got some tough news," I said, trying to make my voice soft and gentle, but having it come out a bit husky all the same. "Your dad met with a bad accident. He got shot ... and he didn't make it."

Chapter 5

I was impressed by the gutsy showing Victoria made after I more or less walloped with the news about her father. Don't get me wrong, she was plenty rocked. First there was a look of disbelief, then shock, then the welling of tears. But, beyond that, she didn't go all to pieces the way many would have in such a moment.

By the time I led her over and got her seated on a bench near the edge of the arrival platform, she seemed to be pulling herself together even more. I hailed one of the train porters who happened to be passing by and asked if he could bring a glass of water from somewhere. Seeing the lady in distress, he promptly complied.

As Victoria sipped water and fought to stay composed, I sat down beside her and slowly filled her in on the details of what had happened. I badly wanted to skim over the part about me being the intended target of the shooters, not wanting to risk her feeling blame toward me like I was already blaming myself. But I didn't; I told it straight. It was bound to come out anyway.

She said nothing—silently taking sips of water and occasionally wiping a tear from one cheek or the other—as I related how the events of the evening had unfolded. From her father spotting me at the bar in the Kicking Stallion, to our leisurely chat at the back table, to the fatally interrupted walk toward our respective hotels. I left out any mention of the brawl, seeing no point in bringing that up.

Victoria stayed quiet after I was done talking. Not sure what more to say, I did the same for several beats. Then, abruptly, she turned her face and looked very directly at me for the first time. "Because the gunmen were out to get you," she said, "you're heaping blame on yourself for the outcome—aren't you?"

Her directness caught me a bit off guard. I said, "Kind of hard not to, the way I see it."

"Then you're seeing it wrong," she stated firmly. "You're no more to blame for that bullet striking my father than the shopkeeper who put up the sign it ricocheted off of. The only ones responsible and truly to blame are the coward who fired the shot from ambush and the villainous scum who hired him to do it!"

"Hard to argue that much," I allowed. "Still .."

"There's no 'still' to it," she insisted. "It is ridiculous for you to continue harboring any sense of blame or worry I might feel that way. And if my father were here—if he'd only been wounded under those exact same circumstances—he would tell you the same."

I felt the hint of a grin tug at one corner of my mouth. "Yeah, I expect he would ... I guess you knew him pretty well."

"I should. For the past five years we've been nearly inseparable ... Ever since Mother passed away." Victoria paused to take a sip of water. Her gaze appeared to drift off above the rim of the glass, as if seeing something far away. Then, lowering the glass, she said, "Now the separation between the two of them will be closed."

Thinking about that unfulfilled visit Russ and I had planned so many years ago in DC, I said, "I never got to meet your mother. I'm sorry I didn't."

"I had a long period of being nearly inseparable from her, too," Victoria said somewhat wistfully. "When I was growing up and Father was away following the leads to various stories, her and I became very close ... With both of them gone now, I guess I need to try and find consolation in looking back on the time I had being very close with each of them."

"That's a brave attitude for such a sad moment," I told her.

She suddenly squeezed both eyes tightly shut and tears seeped from the corners of each. In a voice that for the first time held a trace of raggedness, she replied, "Don't tell me how brave I am. Right now, down deep inside, I'm feeling more scared and alone than ever in my life."

I fought an urge to put my arm around her. Instead I just said, "This probably don't sound like much coming from somebody you never laid eyes on until only a few minutes ago ... But you're not alone. Not unless you insist on it. I told you what your dad asked of me. Now I'm telling you ... and him, too, since I figure he's looking on and listening ... I mean to honor his request. However, whatever, anything you need, kid, you can count on me."

Victoria opened her eyes again and wiped away the tears with swipes from a couple of defiantly balled fists. "Please excuse this display. I'm really not a bawl-baby," she insisted. "Nor am I one to take advantage of another's generosity. But I have to say it's a great relief knowing I can count on an old friend my father counted on. One thing, though ... will you please not keep calling me 'kid'?"

* * * * *

Later that afternoon, I returned to Cheyenne ac-companied by Victoria. Although I had my own unfinished business there, the main purpose of this trip was for Victoria to make final arrangements regarding her father. After some consideration and the exchange of several telegrams, she had decided on a small, intimate funeral service in Cheyenne and to then have the body shipped back to Boston where it would be laid to rest in the family plot beside her mother.

I was at her side during most of this deliberation and execution and, though I knew she was tormented and grieving down deep, I kept marveling at her gutsiness and steady outward demeanor. If she represented what it meant to be an emancipated woman, I couldn't help thinking, then what could be expected from the fairer sex in the future—especially by more set-in-their-ways men, maybe including me—was going to take some getting used to. I wasn't sure whether the change would be for the better or worse in the long run but, either way, it didn't diminish my admiration for Victoria.

While I stuck close to Victoria through most of the morning and early afternoon, it was nevertheless necessary for me to separate from her for a while in order to take care of some business of my own. This amounted to getting off a wire to my boss, Sam Horn, back in Omaha, to inform him my investigation into the embezzler case had been interrupted and I couldn't be sure how long before I got back to it. Normally sending a message like that would have been more or less equal to laying my neck on a railroad track and waiting for Col. Sam's answer to come roaring back and verbally lopping off my head; in Sam's outfit, nobody gave up on a job unless or until he said so.

But, in this case, I figured he'd find my rationale good enough to spare me. You see, Sam—or "Col. Sam", as a number of us still referred to him—had been mine and Russ's commanding officer back in the war. We'd all served in the 150th Pennsylvania Infantry, the 2nd Bucktail Brigade. Sam had been right there, barking orders and leading us in and out of battles and skirmishes from the get-go. He was absent for a spell after a cannon blast blew off his left hand. But then he was back again in amazingly short order, as full of fight and sulfur as ever, brandishing a steel hook (same as he did yet today) where the hand used to be. After that, the men of our outfit would have followed him unquestioningly straight into Hell and we knew his loyalty to us was just as strong.

It was that loyalty to one of the "boys" formerly under his command—even though more than two decades past—that I figured would gain his understanding for me cutting out on an assignment for the sake of looking after Russ's daughter for a while. It would be understood without comment that me seeking to ultimately settle the score directly for Russ would also be part of it.

O&PW has small branch offices in a handful of cities

across the western states, Denver being one of them. As with most of these set-ups, the Denver office has its own telegrapher and main line link which us field operatives are encouraged to use whenever we can, for the sake of keeping things confidential. More for convenience than anything, I made use of the Denver facility this day.

The officer manager, who also doubled as telegrapher, was a twisted up little runt named Meadely. He, too, had served under Col. Sam during the war and his twisted, permanently hobbled physical condition was the result of getting caught under the wheels of an overturned munitions wagon. His job in the Denver office, with attached living quarters in the rear that provided working/living conditions to accommodate his limited mobility, was another sign of Sam's loyalty to one of his boys.

After he'd tapped out my message, Meadely looked up at me with sad eyes and said, "Another one of our old bunch gone. We keep thinning out more and more, don't we?"

"It's a trip we're all gonna take sooner or later," I replied tersely.

"I remember how close you and Russ used to be. I'm sorry for your loss, Lew ... Sorry for him, too, and naturally for his family."

For some reason trying to appear more cavalier than I truly felt, I said, "At least he went out in a blaze of glory. We should all be so lucky."

Meadely looked sadder than ever before responding, "Yeah. Luck and glory ... For some of us, things like that are gone a long time ahead of the final curtain dropping down."

I got out of there then, telling him that if I didn't stop back by in the next day or so I would wire him from some place he could pass along Col. Sam's response. He grinned and said I might be sorry what I was asking for, but he'd see I got it word for word.

From there I rejoined Victoria at her hotel. In the lobby, she secured her room for the balance of the week, left her father's briefcase and a bundle of other files in the hotel safe, then we made for the train station.

Chapter 6

In a small chapel area maintained at the rear of his building by the Cheyenne undertaker I'd left in charge of Russ's remains, a quiet funeral service was held that evening. In attendance besides Victoria and me was Marshal Dick Barton, which I thought was darned considerate of him. The sermon was given by a fresh-faced young minister who looked barely into his twenties, but his words were moving and sounded appropriately sincere. Present also was the undertaker himself, standing silent and somber off to one side, and a plump middle-aged woman whom I suspected might have been his wife playing soft organ music from behind a gauzy curtain.

Throughout the service, Victoria sat very straight in her chair, chin up, gaze fixed straight ahead on the casket holding her father. Once in a while she would lift her handkerchief to dab at a tear trickling down one of her finely chiseled cheeks.

When it was over and those responsible for putting together the simple yet quite satisfactory ceremony had been properly acknowledged, we all respectfully stood back and let Victoria have a few minutes to say a private goodbye to her father and to give him a final kiss on the cheek before the casket would be closed, sealed, and sent on its way for burial in Boston. Afterwards, Victoria and I retired to the adjoining rooms she had previously arranged for us at the Cheyenne Grande. We invited Marshal Barton to join us and, over a tray of coffee and brandy ordered up to Victoria's room, we sat and talked about some matters still needing to be addressed.

"There's no way to be certain, of course," the marshal was saying, "but the discovery of Mosby Higgins' body and the way he'd been killed sure seems like a tie-in to the attempted ambush on you, Torrent."

"'Attempted' on me," I said bitterly, "but unfortunately successful on the wrong person."

"Yes, of course. That goes without saying." Barton frowned and cast an uneasy glance over at Victoria. "I didn't mean to minimize that part, but I didn't want ... that is, I didn't think ..."

"Please, Marshal, don't consider me—or treat me—as some kind of delicate flower," Victoria was quick to advise him. "I just got done sending my father off to be planted in the cold ground, so it's quite clear we're discussing death and murder here. I not only can handle whatever has to be said, I *want* to hear it if it pertains in any way to running down the wretches responsible for the act that took my father's life."

The sitting area of Victoria's suite was furnished with four high-backed, plumply cushioned chairs arranged around a low, glass-topped table on which the tray of drinks had been placed. We occupied three of the chairs and, from the selections on the tray, Barton had poured himself some coffee while Victoria and I sipped from glasses of the excellent brandy.

Barton was tall and trim, thirtyish, with a clean-shaven face and even features that seemed always set in a deeply serious expression. At the moment he sat forward on the edge of his seat, elbows resting just above the bend of his knees, rolling his coffee cup back and forth between his palms as we talked. I'd wired ahead that Victoria and I would be returning on the afternoon train and he was at the station to meet us. It was quickly evident he was smitten by the dark-haired, dark-eyed Miss Wheeler and he'd been attempting a sort of balancing act ever since, trying to maintain his usual serious expression and not slip into the dazed, admiring look that kept threatening to replace it.

The marshal had no trouble staying serious, however, when he first told us about the death of Mosby Higgins, whose body had been found that morning behind a warehouse in the seedier part of town, not long after I left for Denver. The significance of Higgins was that he was known to be a close pal to Hal Kraig, the shotgunner I'd killed less than twenty-four hours earlier after Russ knocked away the double-barreled gutshredder he'd been trying to cut me in half with. Being pals with Kraig meant that Higgins was also a hardcase wannabe who partnered with Kraig on many of the dirty jobs he hired out for.

Knowing this didn't make it too much of a stretch to suspect Higgins might have been the second shooter from last night's ambush, the rifleman from across the street. The fact that beside his body was found a Henry repeating rifle with three rounds fired and the stink of powdersmoke still present in the barrel indicating the firing had been recent—all jibing with the number of rifle rounds sent my way—only increased suspicion of the man. Trouble was, him and Kraig both being dead threw up a pretty effective block to finding out who had sicced them on me. Moreover, the close range gunshot to Higgins' temple that caused his death made it appear likely he'd been killed by somebody he knew; that somebody, it seemed equally as likely, could have been whoever hired the pair now eliminating any connection between him and the botched ambush.

Reviewing this sequence of events with the goal of determining where everything stood and what our next move should be, was the purpose of the discussion currently underway.

"The embezzler you came here looking to uncover—this Everett Byron, who naturally would have changed his name by now—remains the most logical one to have hired Kraig and Higgins for the sake of getting rid of you, shaking you off his tail permanently. Don't you agree?" Barton said to me.

"Seems like," I allowed. "But, as I told you before, I'm not lacking for enemies. Many of them every bit ruthless enough and dangerous enough to also try for me with something like that ambush."

"But are any of them from around here?"

"Not as far as I know."

"So what are the odds, then, of any of them knowing you'd be working an investigation here in Cheyenne and also knowing where to contact and hire a couple local gun toughs like Kraig and Higgins?" Barton wagged his head. "Sounds like an awful big coinci-dence—especially stacked against an owlhoot you suspect of already being in the area and having a solid reason for wanting to stop you from continuing to nose around aiming to expose him."

"I'm not saying that doesn't make the most sense," I stated. "I'm just saying it's not the *only* possibility for what took place. The only thing for certain is that it was me the shooters were trying for."

Barton sighed. "Yeah, there's always that. And, when it comes right down to it, I don't suppose one skunk being behind that ambush is too much different from another."

"What do you mean by that?" Victoria said, frowning.

"I mean from the standpoint of rooting him out," Barton replied. "With what we've got to go on, seeing as how Kraig and Higgins are both dead, tracing back-ward to who hired them is going to be tough, no matter who it is."

Victoria's frown remained very much in place. "If you consider your prime suspect to be the Kansas embez-zler—Byron, or whatever name he's now taken—then it seems to me you have merely a two-year window to concentrate on. That's roughly the time span from when he walked off with the bank money until these recent vi-olent acts. If Torrent's lead is correct, if Byron *did* settle here and successfully invest his stolen money into the cattle business, how many new cattlemen are there any-where in the vicinity who showed up within that time frame? Focusing on anyone fitting such a description, and I doubt the number is very high, I suggest might be a good place to start 'rooting'."

I've got to hand it to Barton, he took her smug and rather admonishing tone better than I might have in his boots. He even managed a bit of a wry smile as he told her, "Those are some real good points, ma'am. I can see you have a sharp reporter's mind. And it so happens those very same lines of thought crossed the minds of me and Torrent here when he first showed up and told me about this case that brought him to town. And I'm not saying there ain't still meat there to keep chewing on. But I'll go ahead and let Torrent explain to you why some new faces in the cattle business around here ain't quite as limited as you're figuring."

I'd have just as soon stayed out of that bit of push and tug between them but, with both Victoria and Barton cutting their eyes to me, I didn't have much choice but to take up what the marshal handed over. "The thing is," I said, directing my words mostly to Victoria, "three, four years back—just before Byron would have showed up if here is where he came—this whole area got hit by back to back hard winters. Real hard. The bigger ranches managed to hang on, though even some of them just by the skin of their teeth, because they had vast herds that left enough surviving beeves to keep 'em going."

"But, for the smaller outfits, it was a different story. Near half of them couldn't last, went under. Some of the others, however, found an alternative way. They either merged, throwing together what was left of in-dividual bunches of ravaged stock to make combined herds of a size to carry 'em through—or, in some cases, taking buy-in money that gave them new partners and the means to purchase what they needed to build back up. Some of these new partners were out in the open, plain for anybody to see; others, though, for whatever reason, stayed more in the background—what some folks call 'silent partners'."

Barton joined in again, saying, "With Wyoming clearly on the brink of statehood and folks elsewhere wanting to reach and grow westward, there was a beef boom following those bad winters and all kinds of new faces poured in with money to invest in more and bigger cattle herds as well as other businesses."

The smugness had left Veronica's expression by then. When she spoke, her tone was even a bit contrite. "So what I said was not only rude, but short-sighted and sadly lacking in taking time to learn all the facts of the situation. Please believe such traits—as well as my snottiness—are are not things I make a habit of."

Still infatuated and quickly forgiving, Barton said, "You couldn't have known the full picture, and you have every right to be strung pretty tight."

Taking a measured sip of her brandy, Victoria replied, "If Higgins *was* the second gunman, then it was one of his shots ricocheting off the boot shop sign that directly killed my father. If we could be certain he was the culprit, then it would be at least some consolation knowing he'd met his own ghastly end. Nevertheless, that still leaves the underlying motive and the identity of the person who paid for the attempted ambush. Until *that* individual is run to ground, the identity of the second shooter—whether it was Higgins or someone else—will never be known for sure. Until then, I hope you understood that, for me, this matter can never be considered closed."

"All of that goes without saying, Miss Wheeler," Barton told her earnestly. "I assure you me and my deputies will do everything in our power to keep at this—keep rooting—to uncover who was behind that ambush. For your father's sake, and also for Torrent's."

"I hope you understand," I interjected quietly, "that 'Torrent' full intends to do some digging of his own into this. All due respect to you and your deputies, Marshal, but I take getting shot at mighty personal—and I take it even more so when innocent people, especially a close friend, gets shot and killed in my place."

Baron regarded me. "Guess I wouldn't expect anything less from you. In your place, I'd no doubt feel the same. I just hope you keep in mind that your involvement needs to be in cooperation with me and my boys—not some kind of vigilante action."

"I'll keep that in mind."

The marshal drained his coffee cup, stood to leave. "Time for me to check on what else might be going on around town. But before I go, there's this: Since we *haven't* pinned down who was behind that ambush and you're back here in Cheyenne, Torrent ... you considered the possibility of another attempt on your life? Maybe even yet tonight?"

"Crossed my mind a time or ten," I admitted. "Wasn't for the close proximity of Miss Wheeler, I might almost welcome it. If it worked out right, it could answer a lot of nagging questions."

"Hey, don't let me hold up the show," Victoria protested. "I've ducked bullets before."

"Yeah, and so had your father," I growled. "It only takes one bullet that you *fail* to duck—and I don't need any more dead Wheelers on my conscience." I paused, letting Victoria glare at me and sending a flat gaze right back. Then I went on, adding, "But I don't think there's much risk of anything more happening this soon. If we're right about it being the money man who shot Higgins to eliminate him as a connection to the first attempt, then it seems highly unlikely Moneybags would be willing or ready to set something new in motion so quick."

The marshal pooched his lips and nodded. "Makes sense when you say it that way. Still, as long as things stay relatively quiet elsewhere around town tonight, I'll go ahead and have a deputy hang around close out front."

I shrugged. "Suit yourself." Then, patting where my jacket hung over the Colt Lightning in its shoulder holster, I added, "But in case anything does happen, me and this .44 won't be caught off guard so easy a second time."

Taking her glare off me and turning it into a beaming smile that she aimed at Barton, Victoria said, "You offer is extremely generous, Marshal Barton. I'm very grateful, even though it seems rather unnecessary. And I surely wouldn't want the attention of one of your deputies diverted from a more deserving matter."

"Don't worry, ma'am, none of my men would ever do that," responded the sappily grinning marshal. "Besides, it's hard to think of much that could be more deserving than your safety."

Silvercliff Mining Camp
Colorado Rockies Front Range
Tuesday, second week of Spring,
11:30 PM

The man in the flowing coat hadn't ventured out *tonight planning to let the demons in him run loose again so soon. The young whore he'd pushed into the alley last night had pacified them adequately, to a degree that usually lasted for a few days, sometimes weeks. True, the camp's largely indifferent reaction to discovering the whore's dead body this morning had been somewhat disappointing. With no kind of official law officer in the new, barely established community and with the foremost thing on the minds of most "citizens" being the goal of prying silver out of the rocky terrain before someone else got to it first ... well, one dead whore with so many still left where she'd come from didn't rate a big concern. It was far different than recent times when a sliced-up whore left in the wake of the man in the flowing coat would cause great wailing and lament and heightened terror would grip so many who feared they might be next.*

But, by design, those days were past. At least for a while. And though neither the man nor the demons in him craved that much furor in response, experiencing next to none seemed a bit unfulfilling.

Sill, that wasn't what was bothering the man in the flowing coat tonight, causing his demons to stir restlessly again so soon. No, none of that would be taking place if not for the scene of blatant debauchery being flaunted right before his eyes in this smoky saloon he had unfortunately decided to visit for the first time tonight. He certainly knew to expect that, in any of Silvercliff's saloons or dives, he would see the kind of sluts he so reviled making their rounds, trying to entice weak-willed customers fueled by lust and alcohol. But here, in the Mountain Rose Cantina, he was witnessing a display of bawdy enticement like he'd never encountered.

The source for this was a whore called Rosita (her name shouted raucously and repeatedly by the patrons) who pranced and danced about completely naked from the waist up. She was appealing in only the coarsest way, with her cascading jet hair, heavily mascaraed eyes, painted lips, and plump, swaying breasts. But it was an appeal that stirred every man in the place, almost to the total exclusion of other whores who came and went barely being paid any attention to. And all the while Rosita was entertaining a stream of admirers so steady that she had no time to take them to one of the crib tents at the other end of the street, but rather had a room directly in the back where she would disappear at regular intervals with a money-waving fool. In short order, the fool would come back out wearing a satisfied grin and, not long after, Rosita would reappear to a round of welcoming cheers.

It was revoltingly vulgar. The prudent thing, of

course, would have been for the man to leave the establishment as soon as he saw what was taking place. But, somehow, it was all so open and extreme that it was mesmerizing to watch. Seated at a table near the back wall, quietly smoking his pipe and with so many other revelers clamoring for Rosita's attention, the man went largely unnoticed except for the grotesquely fat barmaid who came around at intervals to see if he needed another drink. He finally bought a whole bottle of cheap rotgut just to get her to leave him alone.

By then he had begun to recognize that the demons were stirring too demandingly in him to be ignored. And they weren't going to be satisfied by just any bit of action. For one of the few times since their spawning, it was going to take attention to a specific subject ... in this case, Rosita.

The man knew it would be unwise to do the deed two nights in a row, even in this rugged, loosely knit community. Especially considering the kind of popularity Rosita seemed to enjoy with a certain element. But he also knew he would be moving on the next day and, what was more, he highly suspected that what passed for devotion from the element in question could—after a few drinks hoisted in mourning followed by the first throbs of fresh desire—be transferred easily enough to others of Rosita's ilk.

So the deed needed to be done.

The only thing left was determining the details of how to go about it.

A long standing habit of the man in the flowing coat was to always take quick and careful stock of his surroundings. Entering the Mountain Rose Cantina tonight was no exception. Even before he'd chosen his table and begun to grow fully aware of Rosita and her outrageous display, his eyes had carefully tracked the layout of the place. It was one of Silvercliff's rare wood frame structures, simple in design and rather sloppily constructed. The front door opened to a large central room, the barroom; a short hallway led off the back, with a room on one side where Rosita entertained and a room on the other side where the owner of the place presumably had an office, maybe living quarters. A back door opened to a row of wooden planks placed on the ground, leading to a privy. The man in the flowing coat had noted this from the outside, on his approach to the establishment.

The back door, then—left unlocked for patrons to use the privy—was the detail that would provide the man and his demons the means needed to slip in and pay Rosita a secret visit in those few minutes she remained alone in her room after a session with one of her admirers ...

Chapter 7

"He showed up at the jailhouse office first thing this morning. He's calling himself Evers Bailey these days. Runs a little downtown print shop, has some money invested in the Circle R, a small cattle ranch north of town. Like I said, he's known around here as Bailey. But he brought some personal papers with him that make a strong case for his claim to another identity—Everett Byron."

This was the announcement Marshal Barton didn't waste any time delivering when he joined Victoria and me once again the following morning where we were finishing up a late breakfast in the hotel coffee shop. The same place where, just the previous morning that somehow seemed a hundred years ago, I'd been going to meet up with Russ again before he caught his train for Denver. This realization hit me too belatedly to try and make an excuse to go somewhere else. I didn't want to mention to Victoria what was supposed to have been and cause her to get caught in my moment of melancholy; she already had enough sadness of her own.

Barton's typically sober expression was this morning somewhat offset by the fawning looks he kept giving Victoria and the eagerness that danced in his eyes over the information he was relating. Continuing, as he pulled out a chair and sat down at our table, he said, "This fella further claims he was on the brink of turning himself in not long after he heard you were in town looking for him, Torrent. Said he'd known all along it was just a matter of time before somebody caught up with him and he'd have to pay for his crime back in Kansas. He was more or less resigned to that. But what he is strongly *not* ready for is being pulled into anything involving murder—the attempted ambush, in other words, and the deaths that resulted from it."

Victoria's finely arched brows pinched together. "Wait a minute. Are you saying this individual, this Byron, the embezzler Lew has been after, came forward to readily confess that much but is denying having anything to do with the ambush?"

Barton nodded. "Exactly. That's what nudged him to go ahead and turn himself in. When he heard about the shooting and then that the main suspect was Torrent's embezzler, accused of trying to keep the investigation from continuing, that was too much. He didn't want that notion to build and gain momentum, so he stepped forward to own up to the embezzling but swears he had nothing to do with the shooting."

"Which, in my opinion," I said, "only makes him a more clever weasel than I had him figured for up 'til now. Don't you see? Repent and throw himself on the mercy of the court for a smaller crime that will put him behind bars for a while, while at the same time selling himself as being all sincere and innocent of the bigger crime that has the shadow of a hangman's noose waiting at the end."

"You may be right," Barton allowed. "I had those same thoughts. But when you mention 'selling himself as being all sincere and innocent of the bigger crime'—I gotta tell you, he does that pretty darn convincingly."

Because most of the other guests and customers were done with their breakfasts and had departed by the time Victoria and I came down from our rooms, we ended up having the little eatery mostly to ourselves. So continuing this discussion in reasonable privacy was no problem.

Normally I'm an early riser. But the fact I'd been just short of twenty-four hours without sleep at the point Barton left Veronica's suite last night made me plenty weary when I finally fell into bed. There had also been some effect from the brandy I'd consumed. But even at that I hadn't turned in right away once the marshal was gone. First there was the matter of soothing the tension that had cropped up between Victoria and me.

Addressing this caused her to state once again how she was no delicate flower and then go on to accuse me of acting "overly protective". Which brought forth a reminder from me that protecting her was the main gist of her father's dying request and, unless she was prepared to banish me from her presence entirely, that's what I damn well meant to do. With battle lines thus drawn and acknowledged, it came down to agreeing we would give some consideration to each other's stance and see how it went from there. That left only convincing her to hook a chair under the knob of her hallway door (in addition to throwing the bolt lock) and leaving the connecting door between our room slightly ajar ... then we were ready to retire.

Still, slumber didn't come quite as quick as my physical weariness should have warranted. Too much was still churning in my mind—mainly the conflict going on there between what I saw as opposing obligations. On one hand, I felt duty bound to remain in Cheyenne for the purpose of unearthing the man I'd come here after as well as the individual behind the ambush, who I judged to be the same person. On the other, I felt equally bound to sticking with Victoria for the sake of aiding and protecting her at least through whatever she was involved in, alone now since the passing of her father, who'd made this his dying request. (I had yet to learn any details about this "story of the century" they'd been working on together.)

The only thing that might complicate things worse, I hadn't been able to keep from thinking, was if Victoria decided to forego her big story for the time being and insist instead on also staying involved in this embezzler/ambusher matter for the sake of attaining certainty when it came to running to ground her father's killer. That would solve me wanting to remain in Cheyenne but it sure as hell wouldn't ease my protector burden—not if it meant having Victoria right at my side while a proven killer was stalking me if I didn't get to him first. Like I'd already told her: I didn't need any more dead Wheelers on my conscience.

Somehow, without resolving a damn bit of it, I'd managed to toss and turn to a point where I was finally able to get some sleep.

And now, based on a man claiming to be Everertt Byron, my fugitive embezzler, marching into the marshal's office this morning at daybreak to give himself up, it sounded like a hell of a big piece of the tangle had just resolved itself.

"So what happens from here?" Victoria wanted to know, pinning Barton with a direct, somewhat demanding look.

"From here, like Torrent said a minute ago, Byron - or Bailey, however you want to call him - ends up in the hands of a court. The way it sounds, maybe a couple different courts, not to mention however many lawyers," Barton answered.

When Victoria's look persisted, he went on, "According to our new city attorney—who I called in right after Byron showed up—this has the makings of what he calls a 'high profile case'. That's partly due to your father being better known than just any old person, you see, on account of his name having appeared on stories and articles all over the country. It's also because Cheyenne is a state capitol now and it's important for us to be seen as a place of proper law and order."

"Again, that's according to our city attorney—something we never even had before. But he's here now, and he means to make sure we measure up to the highest standards. That's why, in addition to the Kansas charges Byron has gone ahead and confessed to, our attorney is also charging him with fraud for the businesses he invested in around here with stolen money; plus, in spite of Byron's strong denials, he's hitting him with conspiracy to commit murder for his suspected part in the ambush that killed your father."

"Sounds thorough, you got to give him that," I remarked. "It also sounds like something that's going to get dragged out some, what with two separate states involved and then pulling in lawyers and getting a judge, or maybe two, to set a trial date and all."

"Yeah, times are changing," Barton said almost wistfully. "Lot different than just a few years back when I'd throw some owlhoot in the clink, wait for a circuit judge to come around, then we'd hold a trial in the back of Blackburn's feed store and get a sentence handed down in an hour or so."

"Times change for a reason and usually for the better," Victoria said a bit stiffly. "In this case, I for one want to see it handled as thoroughly as possible so I can know, when it's done, all the villains responsible for killing my father have been accounted for and dealt with."

"Believe me, ma'am, that's what everybody wants," Barton assured her. "And I personally promise to keep a sharp eye on the whole thing until it's settled proper and to your satisfaction."

"I appreciate that, Marshal Barton. That, and all you've already done," Victoria responded.

"Will you be remaining in Cheyenne for a while, then?" Barton asked, his tone both earnest and hopeful.

Victoria looked surprised and suddenly a bit pensive. "I ... I'm not sure. I haven't really had time to think about it before this. With the identity of Father's killer still in question ..." her words trailed off and she tossed a quick glance my way. Then, returning her gaze to Barton, she went on. "However, with Byron now in custody and a trial or trials to determine the depth of his guilt sounding like they're going to take a while to get underway, there really doesn't seem like much I can do here. On the other hand, there's a pending matter in Denver that will remain stalled without my attention." Another pause to glance my way before adding, "It's something—a very important story—that my father and I were working on together. I'm sure he would not only understand but actually demand I make every effort not to let it get away."

If Barton made any effort to hide his disappointment, he did a mighty poor job. Sighing, he said, "Well, I can certainly appreciate you wanting to respect your father's wishes. And it's not like Denver is so far, not as long as we keep regular contact on how things are unfolding."

"Which we certainly will," Victoria told him. "I'll wire you on where you can contact me."

"Please be sure to do so." Switching his focus to me, Barton said, "I take it you'll be accompanying Miss Wheeler?"

"More of her father's wishes," I reminded him.

"You realize you'll almost certainly be called to testify during the murder conspiracy part of the trial."

"In addition to being able to contact me through Miss Wheeler, you also have my O&PW business card."

He rose from the table. "Very well. I'd better be getting back. Be sure to keep in touch ... and good luck with that important story."

Once he was gone from the coffee shop, I looked over at Victoria and commented, "You realize, don't you, that under that marshal's badge there beats a very smitten heart?"

She actually blushed. "Nonsense. He's just proving

himself to be a dedicated lawman."

I grinned. "Whatever you say."

"I say mind your own business ... Unless, that is, it's some other business you're *supposed* to be taking an interest in."

"Like the big story you and your dad were working on, you mean?"

"How much do you know about that?" she said, scowling.

I wagged my head. "Hardly anything. Only what you just told Barton about it being important and what little your dad revealed about it in the short time we were together. He called it, and I quote, 'the story of the everlovin' century' if it panned out."

That brought a hint of a smile to Victoria's lips and it occurred to me what a shame it was that she'd had so little to smile about since I'd known her. "That sounds like Father," she said softly.

I drained the last swallow of now cold coffee from the cup before me. "So if you're going back to Denver to resume working on this story and I'm going along to aid and protect you—in keeping with your father's wishes, remember—am I at some point going to get more of a clue what the hell it's about?"

"You really have no idea?" Victoria's eyes searched my face. "You had Father's briefcase ... you never looked at any of his notes inside?"

"No," I told her flatly. "Came to that briefcase, the only interest I had was getting it in your hands. Otherwise, I was slightly preoccupied with thoughts of seeing a good friend get shot down in front of me and worrying how I was going to break the news to his daughter."

She continued to regard me. Then, after breaking eye

contact long enough to check and make sure no prying ears were close by, her gaze came back and she said in a hushed tone, "Have you ever heard of the Whitechapel Murders ... or Jack the Ripper?"

Chapter 8

It was hard to imagine anyone who hadn't heard of Jack the Ripper at some point over the past year. The grisly Whitechapel Murders, so called because of the London slum district where they occurred, had captured the shocked attention of people throughout England and the United States; probably other parts of the world, too, I suspected. But any who could read English surely found it easy to keep up with the Ripper's exploits from the endless supply of newspaper and magazine accounts that poured forth as a result. The most lurid of these were found in our country's *National Police Gazette* and, from what I'd heard, its UK counterpart that printed even more graphic coverage.

Helping to draw interest beyond just the viciousness of the killings was a series of taunting letters sent by none other than the killer himself to the London police and one of the city's top news editors. The first of these, to Scotland Yard, was signed "yours truly, Jack the Ripper", establishing the name the madman would be commonly known by ever after; even though in a

later letter he would also refer to himself as "Saucy
Jack". And another special touch that upped the horrified fascination of the public was the inclusion in two
of these letters of organ parts carved from the victims,
always women known to be prostitutes.

The Ripper's habit of not just killing his prey but
cutting open their bodies with a degree of surgical
precision led authorities to speculate there had to be
some medical training in his background. For a while
this narrowed their search for the culprit, but in the
end none of it helped. The Ripper's identity was never
clearly established and he was never caught. But this
did little to quell the interest of the public— "copycat"
killings cropped up regularly and there was no shortage of reports that the "real Ripper" was still on the
prowl, just biding his time before he would start a new
killing binge.

In the final analysis, there were eleven murders in
Whitechapel within a six to eight month period. Only
five of these—possibly seven, at most—authorities believed to be the work of the true Ripper. The last one,
before the killings suddenly stopped, had been nearly
four months before Victoria Wheeler said the Ripper's
name to me in the Cheyenne Grande coffee shop. In the
interim, while rumors and speculation to the contrary
ran wild, London's Scotland Yard authorities issued an
official statement that the Ripper's reign of terror was
over. They theorized he was either dead, possibly by suicide, or imprisoned on some unrelated charge keeping
him safely (for the sake of others) behind bars, or perhaps the madness that caused him to kill and mutilate
had driven him into an insane asylum.

I had a pretty thorough awareness of all the forego-
ing well in advance of Victoria bringing up the subject.
Like I said, for most of the past year it was hard to go
anywhere without hearing about or reading about (and
yes, in my case that meant now and then scanning accounts in the *Gazette*) Saucy Jack. I thought I was fairly
up to speed on not only the latest facts but also most of
the speculation whirling around the case. I was about
to find out otherwise. Not only that but, judging by the
fact Victoria was bringing it up in conjunction with
her father's "story of the everlovin' century" claims, it
seemed pretty clear I stood on the brink of somehow
getting pulled into it.

I'm not easily surprised, and even more seldom
shocked. So I don't know what showed on my face in
reaction to Victoria's hushed question, but I suspect it
might have been something halfway in between.

Whatever the case, seeing it caused her to smile
again. This time there was an impishness to the curve of
her mouth. "You never saw that coming, did you?"

"No. That's a very accurate statement for you to
make," I allowed.

"The notes in my father's briefcase were only a small
portion of all he has compiled on the matter," she said.
"But, if you'd looked, you would have seen readily
enough what he was working toward … You being a detective and all, I'm surprised you didn't look in the case."

"Maybe I'm a better friend than a detective," I suggested. "Yeah, I guess it's accurate to think that snooping
goes with my profession. But there's a time and place for
it. With you being close by to hand it over to, your dad's
briefcase was outside those bounds."

Victoria's expression sobered. "I guess I made the mistake of thinking the friendship between you and my father was so long ago it didn't matter that much. I'm sorry. I'll try to understand better going forward."

"The friendship between your father and me was forged during the war. That's something that makes a bond no amount of years can break. It's something nobody who hasn't experienced it can probably fully understand," I told her. "But don't ever doubt the truth of it."

"I won't," she said quickly, firmly. Then she added, "I – I'm sorry the reunion between you and Father ... ended the way it did. But I'm nevertheless glad you at least got to spend some time together again."

I appreciated what she meant. But saying I was glad, too, hardly sounded right, not considering Russ had died as a result of getting back together with me. The best I could come up with was, "The thing we can do with it, then—what your dad asked of me, what you were already involved in with him—is to try and see through this 'story of the century' that meant so much to him ... Your hint a minute ago that it somehow has to do with Jack the Ripper put me a little off balance, I'll admit. But my footing's been regained ... So what do you say? We continue after that story together?"

"I think it's exactly what Father would want and expect from us," Victoria replied. Then, cocking one brow in that way she had, she added, "If you can keep from being too overly protective and I can keep from being too bossy, we might actually have a chance at making it happen."

* * * * *

On the train ride back to Denver that afternoon, Victoria began filling me in on the entirety of what her father had been piecing together, on and off, for the better part of two decades. At the core of it was indeed the individual the world now referred to as Jack the Ripper. But well ahead of the gruesome acts that spawned that name, I would learn, there was a trail of other crimes and killings that reached back over time and distance and left bloodstains on at least two continents.

"His true name, at least as best my father was able to determine," related Victoria, "was Ambrose Tuttle. He would call himself different things at different times and places, but Tuttle is how he started out."

Once again, the passenger car we occupied had few other riders so by sitting well removed from anyone else we were able to talk privately and freely. Nevertheless, Victoria kept her voice somewhat low, at times scarcely able to be heard above the clatter of the steel wheels on the tracks.

"Tuttle's first known appearances were right in this general area," she went on. "The borders of western Nebraska and southern Wyoming, but mostly along the front range of the Colorado Rockies. He was part of one of those traveling medicine shows—you know, built around some kind of miracle snake oil that was supposed to be able to cure everything from a toothache to hemorrhoids. According to some old posters Father managed to acquire, it was billed as Dr. Thunder's Indian Herb Miracle Elixir."

"Before long, Dr. Thunder mysteriously disappeared, you can make a guess as to probably how, and the show became Professor Tuttle's Miracle Indian Root. Apparently, it did pretty good for a couple of years, moving around enough to stay ahead of any disgruntled customers. Then the war broke out and Tuttle's show disappeared."

"Yeah, war tends to take folks' minds off a lot of other stuff," I remarked.

"One other thing, though. Before Tuttle's show faded, reports surfaced about another service he was providing besides miracle medicine ... It seems he developed a reputation for performing abortions that were discreet and well done, not the butcher jobs often practiced by others. This made Tuttle sought after both by families of good standing wanting to hide the mistakes of a daughter gone astray, as well as pimps wanting to keep girls who'd gone farther astray on the job and making money, not taking time out for birthing a little bastard."

I'll admit that, for a moment, I found it a tad unsettling to hear a prim, proper, lovely young woman talk so bluntly. Then I remembered: Emancipated. Plus, Victoria did it in such a straightforward, professional manner that it wasn't all that hard to accept. What was more, I had a hunch I was going to have to get used to it, so I reckoned I might as well start.

"How did Tuttle occupy himself during the war?" I asked.

Victoria shook her head. "That remains mostly a mystery, something Father never could find an answer to. There's no record of him ever having served in the army of either side. It wasn't until the war was winding down that he resurfaced again. This was in the Baltimore and Washington DC area and it was very clear he was a Confederate sympathizer. Leaving no doubt about this was the fact that one of his closest friends and someone he was frequently seen in the company of ... was John Wilkes Booth."

Chapter 9

That made twice in just a few short hours that Victoria unexpectedly spoke a name that hit me almost like a punch. Mention of Booth carried with it a bitterly personal impact that struck even harder.

"That look on your face," Victoria said. "I often saw something similar on Father's, whenever our discussions touched on the subject of Booth."

Through gritted teeth I said, "Booth ranks at the bottom of the lowest form of human. He wounded our nation almost as deeply as the war itself and ended the life of a fine, great man—a healer who had so much more he could have accomplished."

"I know about yours and Father's Bucktail Brigade being so close at the time of the assassination," Victoria said softly. "Your regiment was brought in to protect the city and President Lincoln during his second inauguration but withdrawn again shortly after. From what I understand, the president normally had very little in the way of protection, barely even a bodyguard, even though the war wasn't quite over and it was known there were still many who hated him."

"They hated him right up until it was too late—when everybody started to realize what we'd lost," I grated. "After the inauguration ceremonies were done, our regiment remained stationed out at the Old Soldiers' Home just a few miles from the city. That meant the president was left with just one lousy bodyguard, a personal friend, who was called away on the night of the assassination and replaced by a drunken lout of a city policeman who left his post as soon as the play the president was attending started. The wretch went to have himself a few beers, leaving the approach to Lincoln's theater box wide open for Booth ... I ran into the rotten excuse for an officer a few times afterward, during the period I worked for the DC Metropolitan Police, and it was all I could do to keep from throttling the slob each time I laid eyes on him."

I stopped abruptly, realizing I'd slipped into something of a rant. Taking a quick breath and then expelling part of it, I said, "Sorry. Mention of how things were allowed to happen back then sometimes brings up a bitter taste I can't help trying to spit out."

"As I said, I often saw the same thing in my father."

"Let's get back to what else you said. About this Tuttle being somebody often seen in the company of Booth during the months leading up to the assassination. Are you saying he was part of the conspiracy to kill the president?" I wanted to know.

"There's no evidence he was part of the execution team dispatched that night to kill not only the president but also to carry out the failed attempts on Vice President Johnson and Secretary Steward," Victoria answered. "But there's every indication he was in on the planning. And he was certainly present at Surratt's Tavern when Booth showed up there after he'd shot Lincoln. Tuttle helped outfit Booth and David Herold, who was set to accompany the assassin from there, with guns and supplies for their intended flight into southern Maryland and then Virginia."

"That should have been enough to earn Turret a hangman' noose like the other accomplices got."

"If he'd stuck around Surratt's for very long, that most likely would have been his fate," Victoria stated. "But because he went on the move shortly after Booth and Herold departed, his name barely shows up in any notes from the federal investigation. Same for another man by the name of Royce Eisen who went with Tuttle. They decided they would follow the two fugitives at a distance, in order to be on hand in case they ran into trouble and needed help to make good their escape."

"Real thoughtful of 'em," I muttered.

"Thoughtful in their intent maybe. But it turned out neither Tuttle nor Eisen were very good at following a trail," Victoria reported. "They lost track of Booth and Herold almost immediately once they passed into the Zekiah Swamp region and never really caught up again—or came anywhere close enough to ever be of any help—until more than a week later when they reached the Hughes farm in time to assist with the second attempt to cross the Potomac into Virginia."

"Once across, they again split into two separate pairs. One being Booth and Tuttle, the other Herold and Eisen. They knew that federal troops in pursuit of Booth were closing in by then and they figured they could create some confusion and diversion in this manner."

I suddenly had a wild hunch where this seemed to be headed. I said, "When the boys of the 16th New York Cav caught up with Booth and Herold at Garrett's farm, Herold immediately surrendered. Didn't do him much good, he was eventually hanged. But Booth made a fight of it until he was gunned down in a burning barn. Almost immediately, rumors started circulating that the victim from that barn wasn't actually Booth ... Since you're saying that the real Booth had earlier split off with Tuttle, are you telling me you believe there might be some truth to those rumors?"

"It's what my father came to believe. And it's what he convinced me of," Victoria replied soberly. "When we get to Denver, from the papers I left secured in the hotel safe, I can show you corroborating material that I predict may bring you around as well."

With her eyes boring into me hopefully, I said, "My respect for your father—and you, from everything I've seen—tells me that neither of you would accept such a notion without some pretty solid evidence. But, at the same time, I got to tell you that I talked to a couple of the soldiers who were there at Garrett's that day and they made a mighty convincing case for Booth being the one they caught up with. So I'll look at your papers with an open mind, but I can't make any promises about being won over."

"That's fair enough."

I leaned forward in my seat, resting my elbows above the bend of my knees. "But, for now, let's say Booth *did* get away in the company of Tuttle. What then? With the rest of the country and the world thinking Booth was dead, where did that leave them?"

"Naturally they worked their way south. Their exact progress is rather spotty for a while. Remember," Victoria said, "much of Booth's motive for assassinating the president was to re-vitalize the Confederate movement. Although Lee had surrendered, Jefferson Davis hadn't yet accepted defeat and he had a smattering of stubborn generals still leading troops. Booth believed that news of Lincoln's death would rally support for a Confederate surge from all over the country, even in the North."

"Until he found out just the opposite—that what broke out across the country instead was mourning for the loss of Lincoln and hatred for the yellow dog who gunned him down from behind."

Victoria nodded. "Which is what makes tracking the movement of Booth and Tuttle during those early months after Garrett's farm so difficult. Instead of being hailed as a hero and rejoiced for saving the Confederacy, Booth found himself hated and unwelcome wherever he tried to go. He had to alter his appearance, go by different names, and be very careful about staying in one place for very long. The only one he could fully trust was Tuttle."

"Father was able to determine that eventually, more than a year after the assassination, the two of them settled in New Orleans. Except for one extended trip overseas—primarily to France, a brief stop in England—they remained in the New Orleans area for over half a dozen years."

"Sounds like they weren't hurting for money," I noted.

"Tuttle's skill at performing abortions appears to have been their main source of income. And, apparently, a rather lucrative one." Victoria shook her head as if in wonder. "Booth dabbled at learning the printer's trade and writing political pamphlets. Then, as the decade of the '70s wore on and anti-Reconstruction movements like the KKK and others began to build strength and numbers throughout Louisiana and other parts of the South, he started to rise to prominence in their ranks. Until, at some point, it must have struck him that he was at risk of revealing his true identity. So he and Tuttle abruptly moved west into Texas and spent a couple years laying low in the Galveston area."

"The KKK and outfits like the White League weren't strangers to Texas either," I pointed out.

"Maybe not. But if they were around Galveston, every indication is that Booth steered clear of them while he was there. At any rate, after their time in Texas, Booth and Tuttle went overseas again and this time settled in England. I guess I should mention that much of this was pieced together by Father—as you will see in his papers—from coded letters Booth periodically sent to one of his aunts, the only family member not to disown him after the Lincoln assassination."

"Coded letters?"

"Early on, Booth was a member of a Confederate Secret Service branch active throughout Maryland. He learned to send and receive coded messages during that time," Victoria explained. "Years later, now as a fugitive, he used this system to send messages to another former member whose association to the Confederacy went undiscovered. This confidant decoded the messages and forwarded them secretly to Booth's aunt."

Now I was the one wagging my head as if in wonder,

and I realized that meant a part of me was beginning to accept the incredible sequence of events being laid out. What was more, with the time frame of the tale having progressed into the 1880s and the pair under discussion "settled" in England, it could only mean the Ripper phase would be coming up soon. That's what I was expecting and what I thought I was prepared to hear more details about. But, once again, I was about to discover that Victoria had a fresh slice of the unexpected to serve up.

"It was while in England," she said, "that the relationship between Booth and Tuttle was finally—or perhaps I should say just more openly—revealed. They had become homosexual lovers."

There it was again. Another subject that a man and woman didn't generally discuss. And yet, once more, Victoria's manner was so nonchalant and straightforward that it didn't seem near as unsettling as it might have.

But I nevertheless felt the need to take exception. "Wait a minute. I remember hearing endless reports about how women swooned over Booth the handsome, dashing, widely renowned actor. He had 'em lined up practically every night outside whatever theater he performed at. If I'm not mistaken, he'd even gotten engaged to some high society gal not too long before he went ahead with his attack on the president."

Victoria smiled. "That may all be very true. But it's also true that men who are attracted to their own kind often repress those feelings for many years. Some even marry and have children before the truth comes out. Does that make it surprising, then, that unaware members of the fairer sex who happened to be the 'swooning' type would go ahead and do so over a handsome young man of Booth's renown?"

"No," I allowed, "that's about the *least* surprising part of anything you've told me so far."

"I'm sorry if it makes you uncomfortable for me to talk so freely about these kinds of things. Father should have warned you I can be rather outspoken."

"He did. I'm still working on getting used to it, that's all."

"Well, what comes next doesn't get any less tawdry." Victoria paused a moment, then breathed a faint sigh and went on. "Booth and Tuttle, under the names Stallings and Tremont, respectively, fitted into a niche segment of the London scene and got on quiet well for a number of years. Booth even dabbled in some small theater productions, making sure to curb the full extent of his talent so as not to draw attention or suspicion. Tuttle, not surprisingly, again took up providing abortions."

"After a time, however, things started taking some bad turns for the pair. Though abortion was publicly vilified, Tuttle's practice tended to be tolerated because he once again served many prominent families. Homosexuality, on the other hand, was illegal and given little or no leeway. Not to anyone. So when attention to Tuttle finally led to the revelation of how things stood between him and Booth, they both were nearly arrested and quickly shunned by 'proper' society. This drove them into the most unsavory bowels of the city—the Whitechapel slums."

"The lowest muck anywhere would've been too good for vermin like them," I muttered, and I was in no way passing judgment on their lifestyle.

With cool indifference, Victoria said, "You know what eventually transpired in Whitechapel. What led to it was yet another phase in the relationship between Booth and Tuttle. John Wilkes, it seems, was actually bisexual; not above dallying with women on occasion. And in Whitechapel, where prostitutes were as common as lice, the occasions grew more frequent. This next part is largely speculation," Victoria admitted, "but it fits with all that came before and after."

Thinking out loud and drawing from the reading I'd done about the infamous Whitechapel murders, I said, "One of the most popular theories about why Jack the Ripper did what he did, was that he'd become infected with some dreaded venereal disease from a Whitechapel prostitute and then took out revenge by butchering a series of others practicing the same trade. The disease reaching an advanced stage that either killed him or drove him to suicide could also explain why the murders suddenly stopped."

"That theory is somewhat accurate," Victoria stated. "But Father and I believe there was another component—namely, Ambrose Tuttle. We feel it was Booth who contracted and died of a disease he got from his dalliances with prostitutes. And then Tuttle, in a rage of betrayal and sorrow and vengeance, went on a killing frenzy. When the rage started to cool, he stopped simply for fear of getting caught. He was already a wanted man for the charges of homosexuality and the abortions he'd performed. Getting tagged with even the flimsiest suspicion of being the Ripper would have rushed him to the gallows in record time."

"Way overdue," I grated.

Victoria's eyes took on a brittle brightness. "But, instead, he gained passage back to America. He's been making his way west ever since ... And the continuing slaughter of prostitutes has been traveling west right along with him."

Chapter 10

Upon arriving in Denver, I was kept busy for most of the balance of the afternoon tending to some personal matters. First, I had to see to getting my horse unloaded from the stock car and boarded at a suitable livery stable. Then I paid another visit to the O&PW branch office to find out what kind of response was waiting from Col. Sam as a result of the message I'd sent yesterday. All things considered, it wasn't too bad.

Like I'd expected (and hoped for), hearing that one of his "boys" had fallen to a bullet mellowed Sam to the point of being mostly forgiving of me for taking it on myself to divert away from the case I was assigned to. The closing lines of his wire were: FOR THE SAKE OF RUSS AND HIS DAUGHTER DO WHAT YOU NEED TO – STOP – JUST DON'T TAKE TOO LONG TO GET IT DONE.

I grinned a little as I dictated a response for Meadely to send, informing the colonel that the embezzler case I'd temporarily abandoned was now wrapped up. And along with it—in all likelihood, pending the result of a trial—the matter of the ambush that had taken Russ's life. And then I added how I would still need some time away from any new case assignment, with the "don't take too long" proviso understood to still be in effect.

After he'd jotted down what I wanted him to send, Meadely clucked admiringly. "That makes for some mighty nifty work, Lew. You went back to Cheyenne to help arrange Russ's funeral and end up solving two cases. The old man can't be too sore about that."

"Don't be so sure. If he thinks on it long enough, he'll come up with some reason. You know, to make sure I don't get to feeling too uppity."

"Well, I still say it was darn good work."

"Clean living and pure thoughts, Meadely. That's what I owe it to."

That got a horse laugh out of him. "Now don't go trying to push it too far. I ain't ready to let you lay it on that thick. I knew you when, remember?"

"I ain't forgetting that," I told him. "Like we said before and like Russ checking out is a reminder of—our old outfit is thinning out too damn fast. We owe it to one another to keep track of those of us who are left."

"Yeah. I think about that a lot," Meadely said somberly and with a hint of what I took for sadness.

Telling him I'd stay in touch so he could keep being a conduit between me and Col. Sam, I bid so long then left him to send my wire while I went to meet back up with Victoria at her hotel.

Which, once I got there, I learned was also mine since she'd gone ahead and booked me a room directly across the hall from hers. After depositing my saddlebags and bedroll in my new accommodations, I traveled back across said hall to where I'd been informed supper for two was going to be delivered shortly. Already delivered, I saw when I was ushered in, was a large folding table upon which sat Russ's briefcase and several stacks of papers arranged in a row.

"I laid things out, as best I could, in chronological order," Victoria explained eagerly. "I figured we could start right in going through Father's notes and all the pieces of corroborating material he compiled over the years. You know, stuff to back up the chain of events related to Ambrose Tuttle that I told you about. If you want, you can even read through some of it while we eat. I realize there's a lot here to take in, so absorbing it all will no doubt carry into tomorrow. But the quicker you're convinced—"

"Whoa," I interrupted her. "I'll be happy to look through all this that you and your dad put so much work into. Even looking forward to it some. But whether or not I come away buying in as deep as you two, don't really matter. I'm aboard for running down this Tuttle hombre, regardless. He's obviously a snake who needs to be de-fanged. If we're able to accomplish that, then whatever story you can get out of it or however many legal charges he has to face, that will all come in due course. My buy-in won't make much difference one way or the other."

Victoria frowned. "I guess, when you put it that way, it's a valid point. But I'd nevertheless feel better if you started with a stronger belief."

I tried an ingratiating smile. "I already believe in you and your dad. Don't that count for something? Equally as important, it seems to me, is a plan for finally tracking down Tuttle. Something brought you here to Denver and the front range of the Rockies—where, if I recall correctly, you said Tuttle got his start. Care to tell me more about that?"

"Seems like that's sort of jumping ahead," Victoria said, aiming her frown momentarily toward the row of stacked papers, "but I suppose there's no harm in it."

Before we could proceed, however, a knock on the door announced the arrival of the supper Victoria had ordered. It came in on a rolling table big enough for us to hitch chairs up to and dine directly from. The meals consisted of thick steaks with all the trimmings—potatoes, greens, even a slice of pie for dessert. There was also a pitcher of fresh water, a carafe of coffee, and a bottle of red wine.

"I took the liberty of guessing you for a basic steak a potatoes type, just like Father," Victoria said. "The steak is medium rare. We can send it back if you'd like it cooked more."

"Medium rare is perfect."

"I wasn't sure about the wine. It took me a long time to win Father over, and even then I was never sure if he truly acquired a taste for it or if he was merely humoring me ... If you'd like something stronger, we can order up some brandy or whiskey for afterward."

"The wine will be fine," I told her, although it wasn't something I'd ever acquired much taste for. But the repeated references to her father indicated to me that the fact of having him permanently gone was finally starting to hit Victoria so I didn't want to present any added difficulty. And it was all the more reason to keep her occupied with discussing the business at hand rather than sink too deep into melancholy reflection.

Aiming to get back on the business track, I said as I cut into my steak, "Something, I take it, gave you reason to think Tuttle has returned here to his old stomping ground?"

"Not only returned to the area," Victoria replied, "but also to his old habits. What's worse, he brought his newer habits along also."

I wasn't quite sure what that meant, so I chewed a bite of my steak and waited for her to say more. The steak was delicious.

"Every indication is that Tuttle, under a different name, is once again traveling with a medicine show," Victoria continued. "Father and I have it narrowed down to one of three that, taking advantage of the early Spring, have begun making their rounds through the various towns and mining camps that have grown out of the front range silver boom. That's what I meant by him returning to his old habits."

"Let me guess," I said wryly, "the new habits he bought along are the ones you believe he, er, *acquired* in London's Whitechapel slums."

"Exactly!" Victoria confirmed, stabbing her fork into a cut of meat with extra aggression. "When I said the continuing slaughter of prostitutes has been traveling westward with Tuttle, I wasn't exaggerating. Father was able to track a series of prostitute murders from the approximate time Tuttle arrived back in the states. New York, Philadelphia, Cincinnati, Chicago, St. Louis, Omaha ... by then it was obvious what would come next. Sure enough, he struck here in the Denver area at least once only a little over two weeks ago. And God knows how many other smaller towns in between. Always prostitutes. Always the same. Always slit throats and carved open stomachs, sometimes mutilation of the female region."

This had suddenly become dubious subject matter for mealtime and I was questioning my push to discuss business.

But Victoria seemed unphased. "The Ripper seems to have abandoned the precision of his early carving, especially the removal of internal organs. It's as if he doesn't want to draw attention to his handiwork, not the way he initially did back in London with the taunting letters and the bits of evidence he at one time mailed to the authorities. Yet he can't control his urge to keep killing. And, if you know what to look for, there are still telltale signs that it surely is him and his work."

I wagged my head. "But why cross an ocean and then half a continent in order to get back here just to continue killing?"

"That I can't answer. Not yet," Victoria declared. "Maybe it's as simple as him seeing this as a comfort zone. Back to his old stomping ground, like you said ... Plus, think what the string of small mountain towns and mining camps have to offer. They're remote, they basically have no structured law enforcement, but what they do have plenty of is soiled doves to entertain the miners. And it is sadly not uncommon for those doves to get regularly abused and beaten, sometimes even killed. But, since they're only whores and there are plenty more where they come from, it's nothing anybody is going to spend much time fretting about. Right?"

It was hard to miss the bitterness in her tone, and equally hard to disagree with the accuracy of what she said.

"If you're right and if we don't do something to get in Tuttle's way," I grated, "there's going to be more blood than snowmelt running off those mountain slopes before Spring is over."

Chapter 11

By the middle of the following morning, I reached the decision that I'd spent enough time with the papers Victoria had so carefully prepared for me to go through. Everything I read seemed thoroughly researched, supported by testimony or evidence in most instances, and well presented. Short of going back (several years in some cases, which meant it was impossible) and trying to personally verify certain conclusions, there didn't seem much sense in me reviewing any farther.

Was I convinced everything I read was totally accurate? No, not one hundred percent; but that's the born again skeptic in me. On the other hand, I came across nothing I could say was flat in error other than it contradicted some long held prior beliefs. In short, it came down to two things: One, I had faith in Russ and his daughter, that they would never have pursued this chain of events so long and devotedly if there wasn't something to it; Two, I believed that the individual known, among other names, as Ambrose Tuttle was a murderously evil presence who very possibly had a hand in two of the most audacious crimes of this century—and, from every indication, wasn't yet finished.

I was ready to get on with being part of making sure he *was* finished.

When I pushed away from the tableful of papers and made this announcement, the expression on Victoria's face was a mix of surprise tinged with uncertainty. "Are you sure you've seen everything?" she asked.

"No, I'm sure I *haven't* seen everything," I replied, my eyes making a meaningful sweep down the row of papers. "But, along with what you've told me, I've seen enough. There's nothing in there that's going to tell us where Tuttle, or whatever he's calling himself nowadays, can be found. To my way of thinking, *that's* what we need to start concentrating on. Since you already know what's in the research and I like to think I know a thing or two about running a fugitive to ground, our next move seems plain enough."

Abruptly Victoria's expression shifted, and her eyes brightened. Though it was true she'd been urging me to sift through the papers, it was also true that, while I was doing so, for the past couple of hours she'd been drifting about the room showing increasing signs of restlessness and impatience. She obviously wanted to take up the actual pursuit of Tuttle as bad as I did.

"The guide and tracker Father hired, the man I told you about last night," she said now, "should be showing up before long. I sent a message earlier this morning, asking him to come by around mid-day. I figured you'd probably be ready for a break from the papers by then anyway, so this will be your chance to meet him. He should already have animals all selected and outfitted, ready to lead us up through the string of mining camps just as soon as we give him the word we're ready to start."

The previous evening during supper, before I made my initial dive into the pile of papers, Victoria had first mentioned this guide/tracker Russ had hired to assist them. The plan they had formulated for closing in on Tuttle was to pose, under assumed names, as the concerned father and sister of a young man who had ventured to the mountains a year ago but hadn't been heard from in months. Using this premise, they had intended to visit the different mining camps and scattered small communities of the front range, showing a tintype of the supposedly missing individual and asking for any information that might help locate him. In truth, they would be following in the wake of the suspect medicine shows, meaning to isolate which one—by means of the dead prostitutes they expected to find left behind—contained Tuttle as part of their troupe.

It sounded like a decent enough plan and, with me now filling in for Russ, it was something Victoria and I could go ahead and proceed with. Given as how I had my own reasonable familiarity with the Rockies' front range, the idea of a guide no longer seemed necessary. But, since the fellow was already hired and had presumably made preparations, I had no objection. After all, things had a way of sometimes turning rough up in the high reaches so having an extra set of experienced hands might come in handy.

"If you don't mind taking yet another meal here in my room, I can go down to the lobby and order a room service lunch," Victoria suggested. "That way we won't risk missing Mr. Dundy when he shows up."

That lifted my eyebrows. "Wait a minute. Did you say 'Dundy'? As in Mason Dundy?"

Victoria appeared taken aback by my brusqueness. "Why, yes. That's the name of—"

"The name of a lowlife skunk I wouldn't trust with a bucketful of hog slop," I finished for her, though hardly with the words she would have used. "He belongs behind bars—which is exactly where I put him a few years back."

"You mean you think he escaped?"

I grimaced. "No, probably not. I guess enough time has passed that he more likely served his sentence and got released. Not that he deserves to be on the loose amongst decent folks."

"What did he do anyway?"

"What *didn't* he do? He's a thief, a con man and swindler, and a gun for hire. He backshot a freight hauler up in Wyoming when it was still a territory, stole his load and left him for dead. But the man survived and identified Dundy. The freight company hired my agency and I caught up with the yellow dog in a town called Lusk, near the Nebraska border. Last I knew he was serving time in Laramie prison. Too bad they didn't lose his key and just leave him there."

"I'm surprised my father got taken in by such a scoundrel," Victoria said, frowning.

"Don't blame him too much. Like I told you," I reminded her, "among Dundy's shady talents is possessing the oily tongue of a con man. From everything I heard, he's fooled plenty of good folks."

Victoria's frown turned into a scowl. "Well, thanks to your familiarity with him, it's not going to include us.

Not any longer."

"At least you won't have to bother firing him," I said with a wry smile. "When he sees I'm part of this undertaking now, he won't want to be part of it any more than we want him to be."

"How much of a delay will it cause to find a replacement for him?"

"Unless you're dead set on the idea," I replied, "I don't see where replacing him is really necessary. Not to boast, but I figure I know my way around the front range about as good as most. There may be a couple new mining camps that have sprung up and probably a few that have folded since last time I passed through back in the Fall, but otherwise I expect I can make it from one place to the next without leading us over the edge of a cliff."

A corner of Victoria's mouth quirked up in a half smile. "My. With such a glowing self assessment, there hardly seems the need to look any further."

I nodded. "Good. Then it's settled."

I'd barely gotten that out when a knock came at the door.

I rose from my chair at the folding table and motioned for Victoria to let me get it. She remained where she was, looking somewhat apprehensive.

When I pulled open the door, sure enough, there stood Mason Dundy. He hadn't changed much in the five or so years since I'd last seen him. A little older, a little grayer, a bit more hollow-cheeked. But he was still a big, rugged-looking cuss. A shade taller than my six-one, flinty-eyed, thick through the shoulders and chest. Prison might have trimmed his gut some, but that only made him look more solid.

His lantern jaw dropped at the sight of me and he immediately blurted, "What the hell are you doing here?"

I smiled. "Among other things, I'm here to inform you that you are no longer employed by the Wheelers."

His eyes cut past me and glared at Victoria. "Is that right? Does he speak for you?"

"Yes. He does," she replied promptly and firmly.

Dundy's lip curled into a sneer. "Well, I guess I know for certain he don't speak for your old man. Not from what I read here" —he raised one hand, brandishing a rolled newspaper clenched in his fist— "about dear old dad recently bitin' the dust up in Cheyenne!"

"Watch your mouth," I warned him.

"You go to hell. I ain't behind bars where you got me throwed no more! I got the right to say what I want."

"Please," urged Victoria. "Can we at least bring it in out of the hall so not everyone else in the hotel has to hear?"

Grudgingly, I stepped back and allowed Dundy to enter the rest of the way. He made it a point to brush closer than necessary so he could give me a slight bump. I wanted to belt him one right then and there but held myself in check.

Marching into the middle of the room, Dundy swept his eyes over the array of papers on the table and said, "What's all this? You startin' your own library or something?"

"What this is, is no longer any of your concern," Victoria answered. "I believe it's been made clear that your connection to our business has been terminated."

"Yeah, I got that much. Even with all your high fallutin' words, I understand plain enough that I been fired." Dundy paused, cocking his head to one side and eyeing her. "Where I'm a mite confused is just what kind of 'business' you got goin' that I was almost part of?"

"Since you no longer *are* a part of it," I told him, "that kinda falls right back into the category of none of your concern."

"Maybe, maybe not," Dundy countered. "See, spendin' time in in the pen, thanks to you, gave me a chance to ponder hard on the kind of thing I should and shouldn't make my concern when I got out. So when I spot in this here newspaper the picture of a fella I knew as *John* Wheeler but the story that goes with the picture says his real name was *Russ* Wheeler and he was some kind of hot shot writer for a big news syndicate and all ... Well, it not only makes me curious but it makes me wonder if maybe I should bring to the attention of the authorities that something fishy seems to be goin' on. You know, for the sake of protectin' my own reputation."

That made it my turn to sneer. "You purposely going to any law authorities about something? That'll be the day." I cut my gaze over to Victoria. "In case you didn't recognize that feeble attempt for what it truly was—it was this slob leading up to trying to squeeze some pay-off out of you for him not mentioning you're setting up an undercover investigation."

"Is that true?" Victoria demanded of Dundy. "Did you really think my father and I were up to something I would pay you money not to reveal?"

"You damn right. People don't hide behind fake names if they're on the up-and-up."

"You small-minded fool. You've never heard of a journalist going undercover to get to the heart of a story? There isn't a blasted thing illegal about that. But extortion very much *is* illegal—even when it's without basis."

"There you go spoutin' big words again." Dundy's eyes narrowed. "But that don't change the fact you and your dad—and now this meddling damn Torrent, it looks like—are up to something fishy."

"Alright, then let's call in the law," I said. "Come on, we'll do it together. You can make your accusations and see how far it gets you."

"If that's what I decide to do, you damn bet I will," Dundy declared. "But it will be if and when I say so, not you!"

Victoria emitted a disdainful little laugh. "What a pathetic threat. I'll tell you what … You were paid an advance by my father and also given some expense money to purchase animals and necessary supplies for our trip up into the mountains. Are those purchases complete?"

"I already told you they were."

"Where are they?" I wanted to know.

Dundy glared at me. "Goodling's Livery. Three horses and a mule, ready and waiting. The supplies are there, too, stacked in an empty stall."

I was familiar with Goodling's. It was, in fact, where I had boarded my own horse yesterday. Chet Goodling ran a solid operation. If Dundy had purchased his animals there, I was confident they'd be of good stock. As far as the supplies, I would be checking them to my own satisfaction first chance I got.

"Was the money you were given to make those purchases sufficient?" asked Victoria.

Dundy hesitated a beat, long enough for me to know

he was going to lie. And then he did, saying, "Yeah ... just barely." Which meant he'd had plenty and still had a fair amount left over.

To what extent Victoria recognized the same, I didn't know. But, either way, she said, "Very well. Keep whatever remains and also keep the retainer my father paid you. Beyond that, however, if you pursue this any further or attempt to interfere in my business then I assure you *I* will be the one who brings the law into it—including a highly skilled attorney who regularly represents our news syndicate—and you will deeply regret not dropping the matter here and now."

Dundy's face turned nearly purple with anger. He opened and closed his mouth a couple of times before finally growling, "All right, to hell with you then. I can't afford the risk of gettin' mixed up in your shady dealings anyway." He turned as if to exit but paused to aim a fierce scowl my way. "But that don't let you off the hook, Torrent. Not by a damn sight. You keep findin' ways to stick your nose in my business, so here's what I'm gonna do for you. Your sorry ass makes it down out of those mountains, I'll make it real easy by guaranteein' you ain't seen the last of me."

"Always good havin' something to look forward to," I remarked. "But you put yourself in my way once too often, mister, it won't be a lawyer giving you regrets."

He huffed toward the door then, and I obligingly held it open for him. This placed me slightly behind the edge of the door, to his left as he started through the doorway. Just as I'd sensed he was going to lie about how much expense money he still had, I knew with a cold certainty what he was going to try on his way out.

He didn't disappoint.

When he was in mid stride, centered on the door, he pitched suddenly to the left, putting his full weight behind the shoulder he rammed against the door with intent to drive it into me as hard as he could. If the edge of that heavy wooden slab had struck me like he meant for it to, it would have bit into damn near the full length of me like an elongated, somewhat blunted ax blade.

But my hunch about what he was going to try saved me. As the door slammed back, I twisted out of the way. As a result, Dundy throwing all of his weight against it and then meeting with no impact or resistance got thrown badly off balance. The door swung all the way around until it whapped against the side wall and Dundy was left staggering drunkenly.

He didn't stagger very far, though, before I got hold of him. Once I'd dodged the door, I sprang back forward and halted Dundy's momentum with a left hook to his gut. I immediately followed that with a forearm strike to the side of his face that pounded him against the door where it was pressed solidly to the wall. Twice more I smashed my forearm into him, hammering his head against the door and the wall in addition to the force of the blows. When he foolishly tried to turn his face toward me, I knocked his nose to one side and saw blood gush down over his mouth.

Grabbing him by a double handful of shirtfront, I whirled him a hundred and eighty degrees and shoved him toward the doorway. He hit the opposite side of the frame with a loud clunk and just sagged there. Now I gripped the door and tugged it around as hard and fast as I could, slamming it shut on him. He was sent tumbling into the hallway.

The door, failing to latch due to Dundy's bulk being momentarily in the way, hung ajar, shivering on its hinges. I raised one hand and leaned on the wall long enough to call through the opening between quickened puffs of breath, "Be sure to look me up when I get back in town ... We'll chat some more then."

Chapter 12

A couple hours after sunup, Victoria and I rode out of Denver and began winding our way up into the mountains.

The previous afternoon, following my scuffle with Mason Dundy, had been a busy time for each of us as we made final preparations for this departure. To start with, we'd taken lunch together at a small cafe down the street from the hotel. It was there that we'd reached an agreement not to lose another day before heading out.

During much of the meal, Victoria had eyed me somewhat warily, almost like she was expecting me to sprout horns or fangs or something. It was clear this came from the display of my violent side when dealing with Dundy. I didn't try to explain or make excuses. That's the way it was when I got put in that kind of situation; she'd have to decide for herself if it was something she couldn't tolerate. By the time we were done eating, though, without ever making it any part of the discussion, she appeared to reach some sort of acceptance within herself and her wariness lifted. That's when we settled on starting out first thing the next morning.

My part of making final preparations had consisted mainly of checking out the provisions Dundy had gathered. Somewhat to my surprise, I found them quite adequate. That left the matter of the animals he'd secured. Since I had my own mount and we would need only one more for Victoria, plus the pack mule, that left two of the three horses Dundy had purchased unnecessary. But, like I said, Chet Goodling was a decent sort, so he agreed to buy the two spare horses back at slightly less than he'd been paid for them, giving him a reasonable profit for his time and trouble.

From the livery, I went to a downtown general store where I stocked up on some personal items: extra cartridges; a heavier blanket for my bedroll; a pair of good quality soogans, one each for Victoria and I. It was still early enough in the Spring so that the weather up in the higher reaches could take a sudden, nasty turn.

A final stop took me back to the O&PW branch office where I got Meadely to help me make an updated list and a roughly sketched layout of the towns and mining camps scattered across the front range. I had some familiarity with this already but as stated earlier, hadn't been through there for several months. And Meadely, though limited in his own mobility, has a steady inflow of news on comings and goings and various other happenings all through the front range, western Colorado, and even up into Wyoming.

While I was taking care of these chores, Victoria was taking care of things at the hotel. Seeing to her own personal needs, getting the stacks of paperwork boxed up again and once more secured in the hotel safe, keeping her room booked for another two weeks even though she didn't anticipate being there, and booking my room for one more night.

Over supper in the hotel dining room that evening, the subject of money had come up after I handed over to Victoria the refund, I'd gotten back from Goodling for the pair of no longer needed horses. I hadn't failed to note over the past few days, first with Russ and now with Victoria, that they dressed and lived quite well and seemed not to lack for funds. It made me somewhat curious and also a touch envious, I'll admit, but it really wasn't any of my business so there'd been neither cause nor opportunity to bring it up. Victoria took care of that by being the one to do so.

"I fear I might offend you," she'd started out, "but at the same I feel there's a matter that needs to be addressed."

"I'm pretty thick-skinned," I advised her. "Go ahead and spit it out."

"Well, as you saw, both my father and I were willing to pay for that slug Dundy's time and services. In as much as you've now agreed to provide the same while in the process putting your own job and income on hold—"

I cut her off, saying, "Stop right there or you will offend me. If you think any part of me would be inclined to charge a fee for helping the daughter of one of my closest friends—and that's what your dad was, no matter the years that fell in between us seeing one another—then you're not near as savvy as I figured you for."

"I only brought it up because it seemed fair to at least mention it," she protested. "Father did quite well with his writing, the syndicate paying him top dollar for his exclusives. And he and Mother invested wisely in some real estate back in the Boston area where—"

"That's all well and good," I interrupted again. "But it's got nothing to do with me or this current situation. You mentioned what you felt you had to. So now drop it. You already paid for the supplies, what I do with my time is on me."

"Jeez, you didn't have to bite my head off," she pouted.

I pursed my lips. "Tell you what. If it makes you feel any better, in case we stumble across a silver strike while we're plodding around up there, then I damn well want half."

"Deal," she said with a wry grin.

"That was too easy. I should have pitched for sixty percent," I lamented.

"I'll make you a counter offer. If we succeed in tracking down Tuttle and uncovering him as Jack the Ripper, I'll give you credit on the story I get out of it."

"No, can't go with that," I said, shaking my head. "Your dad told me how you were already overdue for your own byline. This story pans out, it should be all yours ... Except for sharing credit with your old man, since he began chasing it back when you were still in diapers."

Victoria's face brightened. "Did Father really say that? That I was overdue for my own byline?"

"He sure did." I grinned. "He said you darn well knew it, too, and he expected it wouldn't be much longer before you'd be beating him over the head demanding it."

She gave an uncharacteristic little giggle. "That sounds like Father. He called me emancipated and claimed I could be too demanding for my own good sometimes."

"More than anything, he was plumb proud of you ... Though he did mention the emancipated part."

"You and he sure seemed to have covered a lot of ground in just one night," Victoria said.

"Yeah, we did. Russ and I could always talk free and easy about anything and everything." I sighed. "We fell right back into it like it had only been a few days instead of twenty years since last we had a fat chewing session."

Right up to the minute, I couldn't help thinking bitterly, *when he got gunned by an ambushing bastard out to get me.*

* * * * *

The morning was clear and cool as we ascended up above the city on a well worn freight trail. By the calendar, Spring had arrived and the talk of locals was that the previous Winter was an uncommonly mild one. But patches of snow were still visible in always-shaded areas and even heavier accumulations could be seen back deep in many of the crevices that ran between rock formations. Out where the sunlight could reach, though, the grasses and trees were beginning to green nicely. Up higher, on the peaks where caps of snow were permanent, the pure whiteness glistened brilliantly in the sunlight.

Victoria sat on her horse with ease, which shouldn't really have surprised me considering her range of skills; but it was nevertheless a welcome sight. Her attire of a fur-trimmed hat and coat, sturdy trousers, and sensible riding boots was further indication she'd spent some past time on the trail and knew how to dress for it. What was more, the change from long, pleated skirts and shape-flattering blouses such as I'd only seen her in before was welcome in another way. Given the make-up of the rowdy towns and mining camps we were headed into, a young woman too fetching in appearance was practically an open invitation for the kind of attention and coarse remarks apt to lead to trouble. There was no hiding the prettiness of Victoria's face or those striking eyes. But at least, I hoped, the bulky coat and trousers would dull her down somewhat.

By mid-day we reached a little community called Sallyville, which had been in place since before the silver boom swept through the front range. They had a restaurant there in a wood frame building where I'd eaten in the past and remembered as having good food and friendly service. This proved still to be the case.

In a large, steamy, crowded room filled with great aromas, we dined on meat loaf, greens, and fresh cornbread. The lunch crowd packed around us at sturdy wooden tables was loud and gregarious. We joined a handful of conversations, listened in on a number of others.

The numerous newspaper accounts of Russ Wheeler's death had caused Victoria and me to slightly alter the premise she and her father were initially going to use for their inquiries as they made their way through the mining camps. We still went with the story of looking for a missing person, Victoria's alleged brother. But she was now calling herself Victoria *Wilson*. And rather than assume the paternal role as Russ had intended, since I'd previously done investigating work in the area and therefore might be recognized and remembered from that, it seemed wiser for me to simply stick with my true identity as a detective assisting in the fictional search.

In the course of asking a few questions in accordance with this premise and then merely listening to the general flow of the conversations around us, we learned that one of the medicine shows Victoria was interested in—this one hawking a product billed as "Alizi's Amazing Arabian Life-Extender"—had passed through here a few days ago. They'd come and gone without incident, however. No trouble, no dead prostitutes left in their wake.

As to the effectiveness of their product, which promised to add at least ten extra years of good health to any lifestyle, it was too soon to tell. But the good news was that nobody had died from trying it either—which was more than a few medicine show concoctions could claim.

Moving on from Sallyville, we headed for a newer mining camp called Dugan's Dig. It was too far to reach before nightfall, though, so come evening we camped close to a line of fir trees. There was a water seep and graze for the animals, plenty of dry deadfall to build a good fire. While I tended the stock, Victoria brewed a pot of coffee. We drank it as we ate the meatloaf sandwiches we'd purchased at the restaurant back in Sallyville.

With nary a cloud in the sky to hold in any of the day's modest heat, I knew the night was going to grow quite chill, so I stacked plenty of fuel close to keep feeding the flames. But as for that clear, cloudless sky, it was sure a sight to see when the stars, thousands of them minus any appearance yet by the moon, began glistening and glimmering in a vast display.

"It's beautiful up here, isn't it?" Victoria murmured. "So quiet and peaceful. It's hard to believe that a bloodthirsty ghoul like the Ripper is stalking somewhere in such a setting."

"I don't know about any other ghouls," I allowed. "But don't ever think the Ripper is the only life taker—two-legged *and* four-legged kinds—to be found in this deceptive peace and quiet. He's the one we *want* to run into ... Let's hope we can avoid the rest."

"Whatever we do run into," Victoria noted, "you seem adequately armed to handle it."

She was referring, I gathered, to the Colt Peacemaker now holstered on my hip. Though she was aware of the Colt Lightning I wore in a shoulder rig, I hadn't before ever strapped on the bigger iron in her presence.

"I tend never to go unarmed," I explained with a casual shrug. "Some people insist the West is becoming more tamed. Maybe so. But that doesn't reach to every corner, certainly not the ones I sometimes travel to. In more populated places like Cheyenne and cities like Denver, mostly to keep from making folks nervous, I'll settle for the shoulder rig under a coat or jacket. But when I'm out on the trail or headed into more wide open towns—like some of these mining camps we've got coming up—then I figure something a little showier and more readily accessible isn't out of line."

"I was only making an observation, not complaining. Precaution and protection are fine by me. Some of Father's work, remember, also took him to unsavory places. On those occasions, he certainly didn't hesitate to carry a gun. And when I started traveling with him regularly, one of the first things he did was teach me to handle a firearm."

I cocked a brow. "Let me guess. You're a crack shot,

right?"

She smiled. "Adequate."

"Long or short?"

"I'm a little better with a rifle, but I do okay with a pistol."

"I bet you do."

"One of our firm instructions to Dundy when Father and I hired him to put together provisions, was to make sure that each saddle was complete with a Winchester in its scabbard. I see you've maintained that. Further, just to make the point once again that I am no shrinking violet when it comes to the way of things, I also gave some forethought to the rowdy camps we'll be visiting." To demonstrate, Victoria reached a hand into the pocket of her fur-lined coat and withdrew a nickel-plated over-under derringer.

"Belly gun," I grunted.

"True. But effective for close work. Plus, I've got another just like it in the other pocket. If four shots isn't enough to get me out of a tight spot and to my rifle—or for you and your hogleg to join in—then I'd say the situation is probably too far out of hand anyway. Wouldn't you?"

All I could do was wag my head. "Young lady, one of these days I might stop being surprised by you ... But I got a feeling it's still a long way off."

Promise Mining Camp
Colorado Rockies Front Range
Friday, second week of Spring,
11:00 PM

The man in the flowing coat felt uncharacteris-
tically anxious. The demons in him were stirring restlessly, needing attention sooner than normal. The two
whores in Silvercliff should have satisfied them longer,
at least for a couple more days. But the reaction to the
loss of the second whore, the outrageous and wildly
popular Rosita—an extreme opposite response from
the indifference shown for the nameless first whore—
had re-introduced an excitement over their deeds that
neither the man nor his demons had experienced since
the height of their time back in the city hellhole that
spawned them.

A return to that kind of reaction, that much attention
was not something the man wanted. His current reloca-
tion and methodology was carefully constructed to get
away from that kind of thing, that much focus and risk.
Yes, his demons had to be satisfied; there was no escaping that. But in order to do so, that meant continuing to
escape discovery.

That was where the man's anxiety entered in tonight.

The lay-out of Promise was anything but promising for a chance to discreetly do the deed his demons were craving. It was a fairly new community that had sprung up quickly, the way these mining camps tended to do, as the result of a recent silver strike in the nearby hills. The population was meager (though the man's troupe had drawn a decent crowd for their presentation earlier in the evening) with a variety of tents housing businesses and dwellings all clustered close together in a shallow, bowl-shaped hollow surrounded by high, ragged peaks.

There was only one saloon, located in the largest of the tents, with a handful of much smaller tents—the whore cribs—pitched directly behind it. The closeness of these and the limited number of whores working out of them was why the man in the flowing coat was fretting so. It was hard for him to conceive a way he could isolate one of the girls long enough to do what his demons required and still be able to slip away un-detected. For nearly half an hour he'd been standing across the street from the saloon, melded into the shadows of a tall, twisted rock formation, trying to spot something—some pattern, some opening—he might be able to use to accomplish this. But nothing seemed to be presenting itself.

He was on the verge of abandoning any attempt for tonight. His demons were not riled to such a demand-ing level that he couldn't hold them at bay for another night. The problem, however, came with the knowl-edge he wouldn't be able to restrain them much longer than that. So what if conditions tomorrow night were no better—or even worse—for trying to accomplish the deed with suitable discretion? The demons would be fully demanding by then, he'd be pressured to act somehow, no matter the risk. Twice before he'd been put in that position. Both times he had barely managed to escape discovery and near capture, and each had been messy and frightening. He wanted to never go through that again.

Damn it all, there must be a way his cunning and experience could find some means in this mud heap of a town to—

The frustrated brooding of the man in the flowing coat was abruptly halted by the sight of someone exiting the side door of the saloon and, rather than head for the crib tents, instead turned and begin moving across the street directly toward him. In the wash of bright starlight from the clear sky overhead, he could see the someone was unmistakably a woman. Where she came from combined with her short skirt and bare shoulders, even though covered ineffectively by a flimsy shawl, left little doubt as to her social standing in Promise.

Why she seemed to be singling him out—how she had even noticed him—the man in the flowing coat found curious and a bit unsettling. He looked up and down the street to see if anyone else was watching. Everything was still and quiet except for the din coming from inside the saloon.

When she had somewhat daintily picked her way across the muddy street and drawn near, the woman peered up at him and said, "Do I make you nervous? Or are you just embarrassed you might be seen in the company of somebody like me?"

"In truth," the man replied smoothly, "I am always a bit nervous in the presence of a lovely young woman.

But embarrassed by such delightful company? Perish the thought."

The woman emitted a girlish giggle. There wasn't much else about her that suggested girlishness, however. Certainly not her age and certainly not the toll her lifestyle had taken on her. She was fighting it hard with makeup and rice powder on her face and a tight corset under the dress to hold back the sag of her stomach, but the tide of the battle had definitely turned against her. Still, she followed the giggle with a reasonably pleasant smile, saying, "See? I knew you'd speak elegantly, even when you wasn't up on the stage."

The man smiled in return. "I take it you saw our show earlier?"

"Oh, yes. I never miss none of the medicine shows that come through. They're about the only real fun to be had in any of these places. I mean, except for ... you know."

The man glanced past her toward the saloon. Then, returning his gaze, he said, "Speaking of these, er, places ... Won't your presence inside be missed if you tarry out here too long?"

She shrugged. "Naw. Not for awhile. There's a real thirsty drinkin' crowd in there tonight and Ol' Gustav— he's the owner of the joint—he's having to help work the bar himself on account of one of our regular bartenders slipped on some ice and busted a hip. Gustav ain't likely to notice I'm gone any time soon, and if he does he'll figure I went out back with somebody."

"Not to question my good fortune," said the man, "but how is it you came out here to favor me with your enchanting company?"

The woman giggled again. "What if I said it was part-ly to hear more elegant talk like that?" She paused for a moment, then continued, "I'm serious. You can imagine the kind of talk I hear night after night from drunks tryin' to sound like big shots. And Ol' Gustav, he can't hardly speak English a body's able to understand at all ... When I was a little girl in San Francisco, my mama used to take me to stage plays. Not in any of the big theaters, but they were still nice. She's the one who taught me to appreciate elegant speaking, and I never forgot."

"You say you're from San Francisco?"

"Yeah." The woman chuffed. "Mama's little girl Mary lookin' for elegant talk in a dump like this. Hard to be-lieve, eh? That's what bad choices and bad men will get you, honey. Mama tried to teach me that, too. If I had to choose, I wish I would've appreciated that advice and given less of a shit about the elegant talk."

The man realized the woman—Mary, if that was tru-ly her name—was quite drunk. He didn't want to allow her condition to turn into so much babbling it risked causing a scene involving him.

Soothingly, he said to her, "I'll be happy to talk with you for as long as you like, Mary. But tell me, how is you sought me out over here in the first place?"

"There are seams in that old saloon tent that don't close all the way tight," Mary explained. "Some nights when it gets all smoky and close inside, I like to sit near one of them to get a little fresh air. That's what I was do-ing a little while ago when I looked out and spotted you over here. I recognized you when you lighted your pipe."

"Alas, I have a weakness for tobacco."

"But even that—a pipe, instead of stinky ol' cigars

or cigarettes—is kind of elegant," Mary insisted. Then: "I kept watching, hoping you'd come on in so I could get the chance to talk to you, listen to you. But you never did. So, I decided to be bold enough to come over and find out why. It seems hard to believe, you bein' so talented and well spoken and all, but is it because you're shy?"

"On occasion, I suppose. Other times I simply prefer solitude," the man told her.

Mary stepped closer. "Solitude. That's just an elegant word for lonely, ain't it? Nobody really prefers that. And I'm real good at helping fellas not feel lonely, honey."

She placed one of her hands on his chest and began moving it in small, slow circles. The man fought to suppress a shiver of revulsion at her touch. The stink of smoke and cheap perfume lifting off her filled his nostrils. He gazed down into her alcohol-glazed eyes for a moment, then cut his gaze quickly up and down the street and once more over at the saloon. No one in sight, no one noticing them at all. And behind the rock outcrop, he knew from checking it out earlier, the shadows were very deep and there was a drop off into some thick bushes.

He gazed down at Mary again. You stupid cow, he thought. Walking right into it. Making a literal gift of what had seemed nearly impossible only moments ago.

Placing his left hand gently over hers as it continued caressing him and at the same time slipping his right into the deep pocket of his coat, he whispered, "Yes, my dear. I know a cure for loneliness, too—a very permanent one!"

So saying, his left hand shot to her throat, squeezing

viciously so that the only sound she could make was a strangled gasp. Turning his body suddenly, he whirled her around and shoved her into the deeper shadows beyond the rock outcrop. He lunged after her. As he did so, his right hand swept from the coat pocket and the scalpel it gripped thrust forward in a menacing flash!

Chapter 13

On Saturday, Victoria and I made stops in two different mining communities; Dugan's Dig at mid morning, a place called Lost Gulch later in the afternoon. Both had recently been visited by medicine shows, but in neither case had there been any dead prostitutes left behind or any other kind of disturbance associated to the shows.

On the way to Lost Gulch we had entertained the notion of possibly spending the night there since it would be nearing evening before we expected to finish talking to folks. But the condition of the camp was so shabby and the mood of most of the inhabitants we encountered so sullen and unfriendly that any thought of sticking around quickly dissipated. So, we rode on out with only a couple hours left until dusk. Given that the day had been warm and conditions again clear, the thought of another trail camp presented no particular hardship.

With evening shadows thickening, I found a suitable spot to halt for the night on a grassy flat notched slightly back into some jagged, upward sloping rocks.

Once again there was good graze for the animals, shelter from the wind in case any arose later, and a spectacular view of the spray of stars beginning to show against the darkening sky.

After we'd eaten and were stretched out on our bedrolls, propped up against saddles and nursing final cups of coffee, we reviewed what we had learned during our stops that day. Unfortunately, it didn't amount to much. Not yet.

"So the Arabian-themed outfit, the one with the life-extending elixir," I was saying, "put on shows at both Sallyville and Dugan's Dig without any sign of our boy cutting up any of the local soiled doves."

"True. But that doesn't prove anything as far as putting them in the clear," Victoria replied. "I mean, the Ripper doesn't strike *every* night, never has. In some instances, he's gone more than a week between killings. Plus, since we have to figure the other members of whatever troupe he's traveling with don't know about his little hobby, he has to take care to keep them from noticing a string of dead girls left in too many of the places where they've performed."

"I understand all that. I'm just trying to lay the groundwork for spotting a pattern in the hope one will start to form," I explained. "So, the gimmick for Alizi's Amazing Arabian Life-Extender is allegedly some exotic concoction handed down from the land of Sinbad or whatever. But the other show that played recently at Lost Gulch—this Col. Hope's Glory Tablets—what's the deal there? What's supposed to put the 'glory' in the colonel's tablets?"

"In his case, as a former military hero in the Mexican

War and more recently world traveler and explorer," said Victoria, "the tablet Col. Thadeus Hope promotes is a specially formulated blend of natural healing remedies he put together from various far lands where he spent time. His 'show' apparently is in large part a sort of traveling museum displaying artifacts from those far lands as evidence of his actually having been to them. Another man, billed as 'Professor VonBrisling' from something called the Institute For The Study of Natural Healing, is presented as the medical authority who helped the colonel perfect blending the various remedies into a single multi-purpose tablet."

"Sounds like a lot of fancy dressing just to hawk another 'Indian herb' cure-all," I remarked. "And isn't that how Tuttle got started in the first place?"

"Yes, it is," Victoria conceded. "So if you're thinking the Col. Hope show sounds like a logical fit for Tuttle due to his history, the same thing occurred to Father and me. It didn't take much checking, however, to determine that Hope and his presentation have been around for quite a while. Since long before Tuttle ever left England.

"The colonel did in fact make something of a name for himself in the Mexican War and has traveled and explored many far corners of the world. Speculation seems to suggest that his dream of a traveling museum to exhibit his artifacts drew only meager crowds until he dressed it up with the claims of a 'glory tablet' also derived from his exploits. At any rate, there's nothing to indicate Tuttle would have found it easier to fit into this troupe than any of the others ... Though neither does it mean there's anything yet to eliminate the chance he *could* have joined."

After a swallow of my rapidly cooling coffee, I asked, "What does that leave then? What's the story on the remaining medicine show you and Russ identified as one of the possibilities Tuttle might have become part of?"

Victoria sat up straight and twisted at the waist, reaching around to her saddlebags. After a moment of fumbling under one of the flaps, she produced some folded sheets of paper. She turned back with these and shook them open so that what was on them was revealed in the flickering illumination of the fire. "These are recent advertising posters that Father and I gathered," she announced. "There's one for each of the three shows we believed to be the best prospects for attracting Tuttle. If you want to try and spot a pattern somehow most suited to him, let's review all of them again. The blurbs and pictures on these fliers give a pretty thorough run-down on who and what each show has to offer, all except for the behind-the-scenes work crews."

"Tuttle's got to be well into his fifties by now, right? So, he's not likely to be a candidate for much in the way of heavy labor. Especially, from some of the physical descriptions I read of him dating back twenty or so years, he was never big in stature anyway."

"No, he was average-sized at best. Even somewhat on the slight side."

I took one of the posters and held it up. The miracle product being promoted here was something called the Potion of the Gods, and this was the outfit hadn't played in any of the towns we'd yet visited. Its theme appeared to be somehow related to the mythical gods and goddesses of ancient Greece.

"That's the newest of the shows we decided on as a

possibility for Tuttle. It began just last summer up in Cheyenne," Victoria said as I continued examining the poster. "In fact, that's the reason Father made his fateful trip there a few days ago. We heard a report that one of the original founders of the Potion of the Gods show, a man named Fielding, had dropped out this spring. Father went to try and speak with him, thinking perhaps some detail about his quitting might provide a lead to Tuttle ... But in the last entry Father made in the notebook I found in his briefcase, he made no mention of even speaking with Fielding, let alone getting any useful information out of him."

I shook my head. "Something about it washed out. When we were talking that last night, without going into any details about the actual story, he mentioned he came up empty as far as why he made the trip."

Victoria's expression tightened. "So not only did that damnable trip cost him his life, it was all for nothing!"

I searched for a proper response. The best I could do was: "So all the more reason it's up to us—what we're doing here, what we've committed to—to make sure it *does* count for something. To run that murderous snake Tuttle to ground and see to it the world knows the full story that your dad worked so hard laying the groundwork for."

Victoria squeezed her eyes tightly shut for a minute. When she opened them again, they were clear and bright and her jaw was set firm. "Yes, of course. You're right. All the effort, all the years, all the little pieces Father pulled together ... each one counted. We just have to build them into forming the final picture."

I studied the poster I was holding some more. Its

premise seemed to be that the powers enjoyed by the ancient gods and goddesses had somehow been distilled into the potion being pitched so that partaking of said potion by mere mortals could greatly enhance their own stamina and health. To demonstrate the promised benefits, the show featured performers who'd achieved impressive abilities allegedly from regular use of the product. Two of these performers were prominently pictured on the poster. One was a massively-muscled strong man who was of course billed as Hercules; the other a pretty young woman clad in a scanty, short-skirted tunic and posed with a bow and arrow, billed as Athena, goddess of the hunt.

"At least I've got to give this bunch a nod for originality," I grunted. "Strongmen are common enough in these kinds of shows, but an ancient goddess showing off bow and arrow skills is an interesting twist on just another Annie Oakley type of female sharp shooter."

Victoria arched a brow. "Their concept might be somewhat original. But their grasp of mythology is a bit off the mark. Athena was the goddess of war, to my recollection; Diana was the goddess of the hunt. But I suppose that's a minor quibble to the crowds eager for a show, and maybe gullible enough to try the latest brand of snake oil."

"And as far as the male half of the audience," I pointed out, "a pretty gal parading around in a short skirt could call herself Hortense the Harpy and none of 'em would mind too much."

With a smug upturn of her nose, Victoria agreed, saying, "Yes. That is, sadly, an all too accurate summation of most men's attitude toward women."

I let that go. Sighing, I said, "Well, it's for certain Tuttle isn't filling the bill as any of the performers indicated here. He can no more put himself over as a shapely bow and arrow master than a present day Hercules. So, we're left with needing to catch up with these outfits in order to see some actual shows and hope we're able to spot something that way ... Or pin down which one starts leaving behind a string of butchered women."

I winced as soon as that last handful of words was out, my own stomach souring at how it might have sounded. "Jesus," I was quick to add, "I didn't mean for it to come across like I was *hoping* for some bodies to turn up in order for—"

"Oh, stop it," Victoria cut me off. "Of course, you didn't mean it that way. I know you better than that." She paused, scowling. Then: "But the wretched reality is that's exactly what it may come down to. More dead women until the trail finally leads to the ghoul. In the end, though, story or no story, we'll be there to put a *stop* to the string of killings!"

I was glad to hear her say that. I'd been thinking it for some time now. For Russ this had been about "the story of the everlovin' century". I figured Victoria saw it that way too. And, to a certain extent, I suspected a part of her still did. But at least she seemed to realize there also was something much bigger involved. Stopping a demented killer from continuing to kill.

Somewhere in the distant, descending darkness a coyote wailed.

Or maybe, up in these higher reaches, it was a wolf.

Or, reflecting deeper ... maybe a ghoul.

Chapter 14

Due to a cloud cover moving in some time during the night, Sunday morning dawned gray and damp. Tendrils of gauzy fog clung to the lower level treetops while thicker, elongated layers obscured many of the mid range peaks.

Victoria and I had a quick, simple breakfast of coffee and leftover biscuits from last night's supper and then hit the trail for a town called Gilcrest. Though the sooty gray sky showed no sign of opening up, at least some of the lower wisps of fog began to lift as we made our way along an easily navigable freight trail.

A couple hours out of camp, we came upon a fellow traveler headed in the opposite direction. He was a plump, middle-aged man riding a stout mule and leading another mule loaded down with bulging canvas packs.

"Good morning, folks," he greeted cheerfully. "And all the blessings of the Sabbath—albeit a rather gloomy one it happens to be today—upon you."

We all reined up and sat our saddles, facing off from a distance of three or four yards.

I nodded in response to the plump man's greeting. Victoria returned his smile and said, "Good morning and blessings on you as well, sir."

"My name is Eli Culbert," the man announced. He had a perfectly round face, a perfectly round dab of a nose, and a tiny slash of a mouth above a dimpled chin riding on a roll of fat pushed up by the wrap of a knit scarf. A bulky black and red plaid mackinaw and a fur cap resting atop his head with unfastened ear flaps dangling down on either side comprised the rest of his attire.

"My traveling companions are Hector and Ethel," he added, still beaming, indicating first his mount and then pack animal. "They don't say much, but please don't think them rude. I handle conversation for the three of us."

"I bet you do," I remarked, marking him right off for the talkative sort.

Victoria shot me a sidelong glance. Aiming her smile once again at Culbert, she said, "My name is Victoria Wilson. My companion is Lew Torrent."

"Headed for Gilcrest, are you?"

"That's right."

Culbert nodded as if in approval. "You'll make it easy by noon. You'll find it a pleasant little community. I just spent the night there and would like to believe I left it even a bit better off than I found it."

Victoria lifted her brows questioningly.

"I say that," Culbert explained, "due to several of its citizens taking interest in my wares. By trade, you see, I am a Bible and candle drummer."

"Bibles and candles?" I echoed.

"To be sure," Culbert confirmed. "The words of the

Bible to light the way to Heaven and the light of my candles to illuminate those blessed words."

"Not a combination I necessarily would have thought of," Victoria allowed. "But, from a practical standpoint, one I must admit makes a certain amount of sense."

Culbert smiled again. "Either by itself has value, of course. One undoubtedly more than the other. But the simple combination is, as you recognize, quite practical."

All this talk of practicality and Providence was fine but it wasn't moving Victoria or me any closer to Ambrose Tuttle. In an attempt to probe something out of Culbert that might steer this conversation more in that direction, I said, "I gather you're making this combination of yours available to all the different front range mining camps?"

"You bet I am. As many as I can," Culbert answered. "I acquired a supply of Bibles last Fall and then my dear wife and I spent all winter making candles. A variety of sizes and colors, some even scented. All of top quality. With the mild winter and early spring, I began traveling to the camps as soon as the trails started to clear. The Lord has smiled on my endeavor, the results so far quite satisfying."

"Congratulations on your success. It happens that Miss Wilson and I have set about visiting the various camps, too," I told him. "She hired my employer—the Omaha & Points West Detective Agency—to help try and locate her missing brother. The young man came here to the mountains last year but hasn't been heard from in months."

Culbert's expression turned very earnest and sympathetic. "Oh, my dear girl. I can only imagine the kind of worry and stress that must be causing you. Do you know where he spent any amount of time when first arriving here—a starting point of some sort?"

"No, not really," said Victoria, immediately picking up what I was attempting and smoothly going along with it. "The last we heard from him was a wire he sent from Denver just before he was planning to head up into the higher reaches. He had no particular target in mind, said he would know where to try his luck when he saw it. When he did, he said he would send a follow-up wire from the closest telegraph station."

"Those can be hard to find up in these hills. Maybe he wintered at a successful dig and just hasn't had the chance to find a telegrapher yet," Culbert suggested hopefully.

"I wish I could believe that," Victoria replied. "But knowing how worried I would be, he wouldn't hold off making contact this long. Not unless something was wrong."

Meaning to play this far enough to make it convincing, I said, "It's a long shot, but why don't you go ahead and show him the picture, Miss Wilson?"

Victoria produced the tintype of some anonymous somebody that she and Russ had chosen for this ruse and held it out to Culbert. The rotund drummer took it and studied it dutifully.

It didn't take long for him to hand it back, though, saying, "I'm sorry, Miss. I truly am. But I can offer nothing useful about the young lad pictured there. I see faces every day, dozens of them. Too fleetingly, however, to confirm or deny if he might have been one of them."

"Thank you for looking, anyway," Victoria said quietly, slipping the picture back into her pocket.

Now I pushed forward the angle I really wanted to

pursue with Culbert. "Since you've visited a number of the camps up the line," I said, "maybe you can give me some advice about them."

"Not sure what you mean. But I will if I can."

"Normally myself and other operatives for O&PW conduct our inquiries alone. In this case, though," I explained, "Miss Wilson insisted on being a part of it. Can't say as I blame her, the kid being her brother and all, but I'm still left with concern for keeping her safe in some of these places. From what I've heard and seen first hand, things can get mighty rowdy in a mining camp. Don't you agree?"

Culbert rolled his eyes. "Oh my, you can say that again. I struck out on this endeavor with full faith that the Lord would look over me. I have to admit, however, that my faith has at times been sorely tested by events and certain individuals I've encountered."

"Yet you're still here. Appearing relatively un-scathed," Victoria said somewhat challengingly.

"True. But he's not an attractive young woman," I pointed out. Locking my gaze on Culbert, I asked, "How about it, candle maker? You see much in the way of pretty young wives or sweethearts making up the citizenry in many of these camps?"

"No. Quite the opposite. Although there are women present in most all of the camps, they hardly qualify as wife material. That is to say, they ... er ..." Unable to find a description he felt suitable for use in front of Victoria, the Bible thumper's words trailed off and he blushed furiously.

"That's okay. I think we get the picture plain enough," I said, actually feeling grateful to his cutting right to the heart (no pun intended) of what I wanted to touch on more. "It's a sad comment that such unfortunates exist, but the unavoidable fact remains that they do."

"It is nevertheless a delicate and discomforting thing to discuss in mixed company," Culbert insisted, continuing to blush bright red.

"Your gallantry is noted and appreciated, Mr. Culbert," Victoria assured him with a smile. "But please try to put yourself at ease. I am a big girl and, as such, quite aware that life has some ugly and unpleasant sides. Moreover, when I insisted on directly participating in this search for my brother, as Mr. Torrent has explained, I did so fully prepared to run into some of them."

"You are a brave young woman, Miss Wilson," Culbert allowed. "Unfortunately, while bravery is an admirable trait, it is not necessarily an effective shield against harm. Mr. Torrent's concern for your safety should not be taken lightly. Even some of the women I alluded to a moment ago ... those who, er, avail themselves willingly to the men in the camps ... are often treated very poorly in return."

"Oh?" said Victoria with feigned innocence, her quick instincts once again spotting the chance to continue probing deeper without being too obvious. "I'd have expected that anyone providing a bit of even superficial companionship would be highly appreciated by the lonely men in these faraway camps."

"That's a reasonable expectation. But some of those 'lonely men' harbor a mean and menacing nature. And most of that sort seem to have a particularly low opinion of women other than for one purpose." Culbert wagged his head sadly. "Add in freely flowing rotgut whiskey, impatience, and even bouts of jealousy over what can only bluntly be called public property ... well, results can turn mighty ugly. And it often happens that the desperate women caught in the middle end up receiving the worst of it. The poor things, who are referred to as soiled doves, get discarded like broken fledglings dumped from the nest."

"Discarded? You mean they end up dead?" Victoria pressed.

Culbert made a distasteful face. "No, I didn't mean it quite that literally. Not on a regular basis anyway. Although I've seen a few who were so badly battered they might have wished for such an end. But what I meant by them getting discarded was that they find themselves too damaged to attract any customers, for a while at least, in order to keep earning a living. And believe me, in that line of work charity is a mighty scarce thing."

"So is being alive—if you consider how being trapped in that line of work isn't really living at all," Victoria said with a sudden twist of bitterness in her tone.

"Sometimes it's a matter of survival," I countered. "Practically everybody, even the most miserable and lowly in the eyes of others, will fight to take one more breath in the hope that it or the one after might somehow lead to something better."

"I'm sure we can all agree that the poor creatures we're discussing suffer a tragic existence," said Culbert, trying to strike a middle chord. Then, his smooth pink brow puckering under the furry ledge of his cap, he added, "But I'm equally sure that even the sorriest among them would take what they have above what recently befell two of their kind over in Silvercliff."

Chapter 15

After parting ways with Culbert, Victoria and I rode only far enough for him to fade from sight before we reined up again in order to discuss at greater length what he'd revealed about the murder of two prostitutes in a mining camp called Silvercliff.

"A killing on two consecutive nights is a break in the Ripper's normal pattern," Victoria said with excitement flashing in her eyes. "But all the other details Culbert mentioned—the profession of the victims, the slit throats, the carved open stomachs—fit too well for it to be anything else."

"Certainly too close to ignore," I agreed.

"Culbert said that Silvercliff was about a two day ride from here. Right?"

"Uh-huh. But I figure he' reckoning by his pace. If we pushed a little steadier and harder we ought to be able to shorten that." From the inside pocket of my jacket, I pulled the rough map Meadely had made for me. I shook it open and held it up, at the same time nudging my horse closer alongside Victoria's, so we could both examine the sketch. Pointing, I said, "Here's Silvercliff. Following the progression of towns and camps the way we have been, the way they're laid out here, we'd have made two or three other stops before we got to Silvercliff. But based on what we learned from Culbert, I'm suggesting—unless you feel otherwise—we ought to bypass those other places and head straight for Silvercliff."

"Yes. I feel absolutely the same. The sooner we get there, the fresher folks' memories are going to be as far as telling us anything helpful."

"And if we can pin down one of the medicine shows as having been in the area at the time of those killings," I said, feeling some excitement rising in my own tone, "then think how much tighter that could close the gap. It would allow us to concentrate on a single show troupe until we're able to identify the murderous wretch who has attached himself to it."

Victoria said, "That all sounds good. One catch, though, might still be a necessary stop in Gilcrest." She reached forward and patted her mount on his right shoulder. "I've noticed since we started out this morning that my horse feels like he's favoring his right front foot ever so slightly. If Gilcrest has a farrier or blacksmith of some kind, I think it would be wise to let him have a look in order to prevent any risk of lameness later on."

"Sure, we can do that," I said. "Or, if you want, I can have a look now. I've got some tools in my possibles pack. If it's a shoe working loose or something simple like that, maybe I can take care of it right here."

Victoria smiled. "I forgot what a jack of all trades you seem to be. By all means, go ahead and see if you can spot the problem."

I eyed her skeptically before swinging down from the saddle. "I can't tell if that was a compliment of sorts or you were being sarcastic."

"Well, I can't compliment you too strongly on the matter at hand until we see if you have any success," she replied, still smiling. Then, turning more serious, she added, "But I assure you I wasn't being sarcastic. You've proven yourself to be increasingly competent, Mr. Torrent, and I'm genuinely grateful you agreed to stick with me on this."

"Then I appreciate the kind words," I said, lighting down. "But let's not lay it on too thick until we succeed in sending Saucy Jack to bark in Hell."

"That would be a beautiful sound. But in the mean time let me, to use your own words, lay it on just a bit thicker and compliment you on the way you were able to coax such meaningful information out of Mr. Culbert."

"You did your share," I reminded her as I bent over and began rubbing her horse's leg, soothing him so he'd relax and let me lift his foot.

"Yes, but only after you set it in motion. If you hadn't done that, I fear I may have brushed Culbert off as merely a round little man worth a pleasant exchange of greetings but not much more."

"He was the chatty sort. I spotted that right off. You let somebody like him rattle on a bit, there's a chance they'll spill more than they mean to, sometimes more than they realize they even know." I shrugged. "Getting folks to open up is kinda what I do."

"I never thought of it that way, but it's sort of what a journalist does too, isn't it? Get folks to open up as part of their job."

I had the horse's foot up now and was using my pocket knife to scrap away caked-on dirt from the bottom of the hoof for a closer examination. Over my shoulder, I said, "Difference, though, is that journalists like you and your dad turn up stuff for a hopefully large audience of readers to learn about. With me, the stuff I turn up goes to a paying client and having it go any farther is often the last thing he or she wants."

"Sounds rather dramatic."

"That's one word for it. Petty or tawdry are a couple others that enter in more than a body might wish for."

"If you disapprove of some of the things your work involves, why keep doing it?"

"Because it's what I've gotten pretty good at, for one thing. For another, every once in a while, like with this current business, something comes along that's satisfying to help untangle. Let's face it, whether we're able to prove he's Jack the Ripper or not, Ambrose Tuttle is a lowdown piece of crud who deserves to swing by his neck or at the very least be locked in a pit somewhere and kept away from the rest of the world. If I can be part of making that happen, then it will balance running down the next sleazy embezzler who cheats his businesses and ducks out on his family."

"I see your point. The only thing I'd add is that I'm already convinced beyond doubt who and what Ambrose Tuttle is. And I'm increasingly confident we're on the verge of proving it to the world."

"I hope you're right," I said, releasing the horse's foot and letting him place it back down on the ground. "But what you for sure were right about is your horse needing the attention of a smithy. There's a hairline crack in his shoe. It'll be okay to go for a ways but will eventually split all the way and I don't have the tools to form and fit a replacement. So, we'll need to make a stop in Gilcrest after all."

* * * * *

Eli Culbert had referred to Gilcrest as a "pleas-ant little community". That may have been an accurate description a few years back but, judging by its appearance now as Victoria and I approached from the southeast, it was a more charitable one than I would have applied. Like Sallyville, Gilcrest had been a small town in existence well ahead of the silver boom. The latter, however, had clearly added considerable growth—and not necessarily for the better—since the last time I'd been through.

The older part of town, its core, remained a reasonably tidy alignment of wood frame buildings. Crowded in around these, representing the additions stemming from the silver craze, was a scattering of various-sized tents and a few hastily thrown together wood shacks.

It was nearing noon when Victoria and I rode in, passing through a fringe of tents and on into the center part of town. The second thing I noticed, right after the shabby new additions, was the curious lack of activity anywhere in sight. It being mid-day on a Sunday, I would have expected things to be quieter and less busy. But not to this extent. It damned near had the eerie, abandoned feel of a ghost own.

Clearly sensing the same thing, Victoria said, "Maybe they're all at church."

"Only one church in sight," I said, "and it's a far cry from being big enough to hold the whole town."

"Then maybe folks decided to stay home and just read out of all those Bibles they allegedly bought from Eli Culbert. Something sure seems to have everybody occupied."

We came to a halt in front of a tall barn-like structure with corral fencing on one side and a set of double doors in front. Above the doors, one of which was swung back and standing open, some weathered lettering read: BLACKSMITH & LIVERY.

"Here's the fella whose time *we'd* like to occupy," I said. Then, after craning my neck to peer into the open door and seeing nothing but quiet shadows with a few dust motes floating in the air, I added, "But there doesn't seem to be anybody here either."

I no sooner got the words out than a voice responded, saying, "I may not be a fella, but that don't make me 'nobody' by a dang sight." And with that declaration, a woman stepped around the inner edge of the closed door and filled the doorway beside it.

She was a stout number, not much more than five feet high and nearly as broad though the shoulders; hips not far behind. She was wearing a man's checkered shirt and denim pants, with a leather work apron cinched around her waist. A polka dot scarf was tied on her head, medium length blondish hair spilling down the nape of her neck. Her face was plain though not unpleasant, conveying an indeterminate age that could have ranged from thirty to middle forties.

"My name's Janice Drummond," she announced. "I inherited this place from my pa and run it these days with a shiftless critter I have the misfortune to call my husband. Like so many other fools around town, he currently, to use your word, is occupied elsewhere."

Victoria frowned. "Occupied how, if I may ask?"

"Watchin' the fights in that empty lot out behind Birnbaum's General Store, that's how."

"Fights?" I echoed.

"That's right. Dog fights." The stout woman gave a dismal wag of her head. "A 'sport' they call it. A nasty, disgustin' business, says I. But every time those Burdetts come around, they draw a bigger and bigger crowd. Not even today bein' Sunday makes no never mind to none of 'em."

I glanced over at Victoria and then back to the woman in the doorway. "Excuse us if we seem a bit wool-headed, ma'am. I've been through these mountains a few times and have heard about some dog fights being staged here and there. But I never knew they turned into events with such big appeal."

"They've got so they do when those blasted Burdetts come around." Janice Drummond scowled fiercely. "I reckon you probably don't know about them neither— the Burdetts, I mean. They're two brothers, Ivan and Irwin. Ivan's the oldest and the brains of the outfit, though that ain't sayin' much seein's how his younger brother got his boiled by a bad fever when he was just a baby. Left him with no more smarts between the ears than a head of cabbage. He makes up for it some by havin' the size and strength of your average ox. Ivan is as shifty and snake mean as a sidewinder, but I gotta give him credit for lookin' after Irwin all these years."

"Sound like a real charming pair," I remarked.

"Uh-huh. And what makes 'em even more so is the pack of fighter dogs they raise. Claim they breed 'em with mountain wolves to make 'em extra savage and tough. Then they bring 'em around to different towns and camps and challenge anybody who's got a dog they're willin' to put up against one of the Burdetts'. They make bets givin' real favorable odds to any takers, that's how they keep suckerin' in fools willin' to sacrifice their animals. Far as I know, the Burdetts never pay out."

"The whole thing is barbaric!" Victoria exclaimed.

"No argument here, sister," allowed Janice Drummond. "It's a sorry statement on the people involved and damned cruel treatment of the animals. I don't try to stop my hubby from goin' to watch, but if I ever caught him bettin' our hard-earned money or, worse yet, havin' anything to do with enterin' in a dog, he'd find *me* turned into a she-wolf and I'd nail his hide to one of these barn doors!"

If it came to betting on that, without having even seen her husband, my hunch was that I'd put my money on Janice. "How long," I asked, "before you expect your husband will be back?"

"Hard to say. They only got started about an hour ago. All depends on how many fools put up a dog they think has a chance and then how long it takes a Burdette critter to chaw 'em up. I expect it'll drag on to late afternoon or so ... You got a reason for carin'?"

I gestured toward Victoria's horse. "What I got is an animal with a cracked shoe on his right front hoof. Easy enough fix for somebody with the skill and equipment. I was hoping we could get it taken care of fairly quick so we could keep moving on."

"And you figure you need my hubby to get back before that can happen. Is that it?" Before I could answer, Janice slapped one hand against a meaty, leather apron-covered thigh and barked another question, "What the hell do you think I'm wearin' this contraption for—tryin' to keep up with those high fashion dollies in the big cities? I told you I inherited this place from my pa. I can do any smithy work needs doin' as good or better than my hubby or any other man you can name. If you want that shoe fixed, all you need to do is ask."

"Very well," I said contritely. "Would you be so kind as to take care of it for us?"

"Hmmph. I let the forge go cold on account of I wasn't expectin' any business today. It'll take me a few minutes to get that fired up. Go ahead and light down, follow me on inside while I do. After that I'll set about pryin' off that bad shoe and replacin' it."

Victoria and I climbed down out of our saddles and led our horses in Janice's wake as she turned and strode into the working area of the shop. As she began pumping the forge bellows, she abruptly said over her shoulder, "You might as well get it done with. Go on over and have yourselves a look."

"A look at what?" said Victoria.

Janice continued pumping, not looking around. "The dog fightin', what else? You can wrinkle up your nose and call it barbaric and so forth, all you want. But I still seen it in your eyes, the both of you ... Blasted ol' curiosity. Oh I believe you truly find the thought of it nasty and disgustin', yet that don't change the sorry human hankerin' to have a peek just because you know you shouldn't."

Victoria and I exchanged glances, each of our mouths twisting into faintly rueful grins that signaled to one another the stout woman had us accurately pegged.

"Go ahead," Janice said again. "I went and took a couple ganders for myself when it first started up. I hated it, just like I knew I would, but I had to go see all the same. So I understand. Go look, get it out of your system, then hightail it on back ... If you get caught up in it and linger too long, I'll be so disappointed in you I swear I'll jack up my charge for fixin' the shoe."

Chapter 16

It wasn't hard to find Birnbaum's store. It was a block and a half straight down from the blacksmith and livery, a broad two-story building with a big sign out front.

Victoria and I followed sections of boardwalk most of the way. As far as I could see, there was little or no activity taking place in any of the other shops and businesses we passed by. Reaching the store, we turned down a side alley that led to the back of the building. By then we were hearing the raucous, low rumble of an excited crowd coming from the other end of the alley.

The lot behind Birnbaum's was a wide expanse of trampled grass probably used most of the time for parking and unloading freight wagons. Today, under the cloudy, still gloomy sky, it had been turned into a loud, busy showplace. An irregular circle of plywood sheets, each about three feet high when stood on edge and bracketed together with short lengths of two-by-fours, had been erected. It was roughly a dozen feet in diameter.

On the store side of this arena, or "fighting pit" to use the terminology of what was underway, a crowd numbering easily a hundred was bunched in close and eager. On the other side, a horse-drawn flatbed wagon was parked. A row of three sturdy cages with close-set iron bars sat on the wagon bed. One was empty, the other two each held a restlessly prowling, snarling dog—large, heavy-chested, bristly-haired canines that indeed had the look of possessing a bit of wolf in their bloodline. A third, similar-looking beast, obviously having once been contained in the empty cage, was inside the pit.

Looking on, leaning casually back against the wagon, was a massive, vapid-faced man wearing baggy bib overalls and a grungy, once-white shirt with the sleeves torn off at the shoulder. The hair on his head was cropped to a spikey black stubble that ran down to a whiskery growth of more of the same covering his heavy jowls. Judging by Janice Drummond's description, this had to be Irwin Burdett.

That made a second man, who was moving around within the walls of the pit, his brother Ivan. The brains of the outfit. He was above average height, trim and muscular, clad in striped trousers tucked into high boots and a faded denim shirt also with the sleeves chopped off. His hair was long, tangled, and greasy, and a droopy black mustache hung from under his nose. His purpose for being inside the pit seemed to be whipping up the aggression of the uncaged dog. He was doing this by striding back and forth, shouting commands and slapping the riding crop he carried in one hand against the side of his boot so that it made a sharp cracking sound. In his other hand he held a thick, two-foot oak cudgel that I recognized as what dog fighters call a "breaker stick", used for separating a pair of dogs locked in combat when the handler of one calls yield and wants to try and save his defeated fighter from further damage.

As Victoria and I jostled to the front of the crowd for a better look, we could see that the second dog in the pit was a terrier mongrel only about two-thirds the size of the animal Ivan Burdette was so actively urging on. The terrier was torn and battered and clearly had been getting the worst of the exchange for some time. Only his quickness and ability to twist and leap away from the slashing savagery of the half-wolf was keeping him alive. He wasn't fighting back so much as fighting to stay alive. The cheering crowd sounded evenly split, half rooting for the terrier, half for his attacker. Among this throng I could see about half a dozen men clutching other dogs on short chains or leashes, candidates for their own turn in the pit I guessed.

To a bullet-headed, elderly man we were jammed up beside, Victoria wailed, "This is a terribly lopsided contest. What kind of moron would think the little terrier had any kind of chance against that other big beast?"

"Oh this ain't no real fight," responded the bullet-headed man. "This is just sort of a preliminary thing, an exhibition by the Burdetts for how they're training a new fighter, getting him blooded to make him ready for an actual match."

"Blooded?" Victoria questioned.

"That's right," came the answer. "Means teaching a fighter not to hesitate at the taste of another dog's blood, to keep going after more. The natural thing, see, when two animals do battle—wild horses, bear, wolves, whatever—they'll fight until one of 'em has had enough and runs away. The winner accepts victory, and that's that. But what you want in a fighting dog is an animal that won't let up, will keep being aggressive and attacking until what he's fighting is all the way destroyed."

"Dead, you mean?"

Bullet Head shrugged. "Either that, or until the handler of the defeated dog calls for an end to it and they pull the fighters apart."

"Then what is the terrier's handler waiting for?" Victoria wanted to know. "He's obviously beat, there's no way the little dog is going to turn the fight around."

The man gave her a pitying look. "You don't get it, do you? I told you this is like an extra little show, a preliminary exhibition of how the Burdetts train a new fighter. They brought the terrier, too, see. There ain't no other handler for it. And you can bet Ivan don't have no intention of calling this quits until his new fighter has done his job all the way."

Victoria's eyes blazed. "Done his job, you mean, by killing the terrier?"

"That' the general idea, yeah."

I touched Victoria's arm, saying, "I think we've seen and heard enough. Let's get on back to the blacksmith. Your horse should almost be ready by the time we get there."

I could feel the tenseness in her and I could see the fire in her eyes. But I still wasn't ready for what she did next. It came too sudden.

"No, I don't think I'm ready to leave quite yet!" she declared.

And then she was surging forward, springing lightly

over the low plywood barricade, and striding out toward the center of the fighting pit. The volume of the crowd swelled instantly until, almost as fast, it faded to a confused, uncertain, half hushed ripple.

Victoria came to a halt not far from the cringing terrier. Planting her feet wide, she stabbed both hands into the pockets of her jacket and then swung them back out with a nickel-plated derringer gripped in each. She thrust the one in her right hand above her head and triggered a round. It made a loud crack not too dissimilar from Ivan's riding crop slapping against his boot. A moment later, with the left hand gun, she fired a second shot into the dirt about a foot in front of the poised, snarling half-wolf. The animal kept snarling but skittered backward.

"This is over," Victoria announced in a loud, clear voice. "The terrier has had enough, nobody's going to see him get mauled to death merely for whatever sick amusement it might bring some of you!" So saying, she returned the derringer to her left pocket, leaned over and scooped the bleeding, heavily panting terrier up into the crook of her arm.

All this while, ever since Victoria charged into the fighting pit, Ivan Burdette had been standing as if frozen, his mouth hanging open in stunned, slack-jawed disbelief. Now, suddenly, he broke into motion. His mouth clapped shut and he took a lurching step forward, almost stomping on his half-wolf. "Now just a gol-blasted minute!" he howled. "What in holy hell is goin' on here? Who do you think you are, you crazy-ass woman?"

"I thought I made it clear," Victoria told him, holding her ground, feet still planted wide. "I'm ending this bloodthirsty nonsense and taking your sacrificial lamb with me."

"Like hell you are!" roared Ivan.

Victoria twisted at the waist and extended her right arm, aiming the unpocketed derringer straight at the enraged man. "You make a move to try and stop me, I'll feed you a pill you're going to have a real hard time digesting."

Ivan stood totally still. His arms hung at his sides and I could see his fists balling into white-knuckled tightness. "You got one round left in that popgun," he rasped. "You shoot me with it, I'll chew it up and spit it back in your face."

All of a sudden, I felt myself in motion and the next thing I knew I was standing close beside Victoria. I brought the heel of my hand to rest on the grips of the Colt riding at my hip, thumbing the keeper thong off the hammer as I said, "I got a popper here with six more teeth dullers to chew on, if you think your appetite is up to it."

The crowd of onlookers went totally quiet.

Ivan's eyes turned flinty and his lips curled to bare yellowed teeth between the stringy tails of his mustache. Without looking around, he said over his shoulder, "Come put this cur back in his cage, Irwin. Then stick close. Looks like we got a situation buildin' here where our dogs might be the ones left lookin' on while me and you have ourselves a little fun."

"No need to ruin all the planned entertainment for everybody else," Victoria said tartly. "Go ahead and do whatever you want with your caged maulers and whatever the suckers in this audience are cruel enough and stupid enough to put up against them. All we want is this terrier and we'll be on our way."

While she was saying this, Irwin lumbered into the pit area, grabbed the heavily muscled half-wolf fighter by its collar and picked it up as effortlessly as I'd lift an old boot. Then he turned and carried it to the empty cage on the wagon where he hoisted it up and in just as effortlessly.

"I paid good money for that mutt," Ivan claimed in response to Victoria. "I'm supposed to let you just walk off with him?"

"I'll buy him back. How much?"

"Fifty bucks."

"He's barely worth ten. Especially the shape he's in," I said.

"I'm dealin' with her. You keep out of this," snapped Ivan.

Victoria pursed her lips a moment, then said, "Okay. I'll pay fifty just to get this over with."

"You're even crazier than I thought," Ivan sneered.

I was keeping an eye on Irwin, wanting to make sure he didn't return from the wagon with a gun of some kind to try and counter the ones Victoria and I had. But I didn't see any sign of one. He just came back and stood by the plywood barricade, waiting for his brother to tell him what to do next.

"Here. Hold him while I get the money out," said Victoria, abruptly shoving the battered terrier into my arms. While I was suddenly busy trying to hold onto the squirming, confused critter, she began unbuttoning her jacket to get at the money belt I knew she had fastened around her waist.

I should have been paying less attention to the mutt in my arms and more to the human mutt that was Ivan Burdette.

With both Victoria and I momentarily distracted, Ivan sprang forward. Closing the gap between us, he swung the breaker cudgel clutched in one hand, aiming it viciously for the side of my head. At the last instant I managed to twist partly away, taking the impact as a somewhat glancing blow above and slightly behind my ear rather than flush on the temple. Still, combined with my instinctive spinning away motion, it was enough to knock me down. The terrier spilled from my arms and I slammed into Victoria hard enough to knock her off her feet as well.

As soon as I hit the ground, I knew what would come next. Sure enough, Ivan's heavily booted foot whistled through the air, once more aiming at my head. I rolled desperately and his heel hammered the back of my shoulder. I felt a tingling sensation run all the way down my arm.

Vaguely, I was aware of a kind of buzzing, rumbling sound issuing from the crowd of onlookers. I couldn't tell if they were cheering or protesting. I could hear Victoria, too—shouting curses at Ivan.

What I heard most distinctly of all was my own grunts of effort as I kept frantically rolling, trying to clear my head while at the same time dodging additional strikes from Ivan's kicking, stomping boots. A couple of them gouged into my back, a third grazed my ribs. Finally, one of his more aggressive attempts overshot and pulled him off balance so that he had to quickly plant his foot in order to keep from falling forward. This left him teetering astraddle me. I was blocked from continuing to roll. But it gave me another option. Without the slightest hesitation, I balled my right fist and drove it straight up into his crotch as hard as I could.

Emitting a gurgling screech, Ivan doubled over and then pitched to one side. He hit the ground, both hands cupping below his belt buckle and groaning loudly.

The crowd went silent again.

I rolled onto an elbow and then a knee and pushed to my feet. I was sucking for air and throbbing in the places where I'd been clubbed and kicked, yet all in all feeling pretty good knowing Ivan wouldn't be getting back up any time soon.

But then I got a jarring reminder. He had a brother.

From the back side of the pit area came a rumbling voice. "I'll get him, Ivan! I'll take care of that sucker-punchin' rat!"

Chapter 17

I pivoted to the sight of the massive Irwin throw-ing first one tree trunk-thick leg and then the other over the plywood barricade before leaning into a lumbering charge directly toward me! Janice Drummond's description of him as "having the size and strength of your average ox" flashed through my mind and that's exactly what I felt like I was standing in the path of. I'm not a small man and most of the time I like to think I'm capable of going toe to toe with about anybody. But this wasn't one of those times. No way in hell did I intend to risk getting pulverized by the human locomotive bearing down on me.

"*God made man, Samuel Colt made 'em equal,*" I thought cockily as I reached for the Peacemaker on my hip. But then my fingers closed on nothing but empty leather—the big iron had gotten dislodged from its holster sometime during my scuffle with Ivan!

There was still the smaller Lightning in the shoulder rig under my jacket, but I had no time to shift and make a grab for that before Irwin barreled into me. I tried to brace myself at the last second, but it was piti-fully ineffective. A rushing sound filled my ears, partly from the air being driven out of me, partly from the crowd of onlookers.

I was rammed backward a half dozen feet though not knocked down because Irwin threw his arms around me and held me up. My own arms were pinned to my sides under numbing pressure and his bristly head was grinding down on the side of my face. Holding me like that, he lifted my feet off the ground and began shaking me, whipping me from side to side like a puppy play-ing with a sock it has stolen out of the laundry basket. I could feel and hear my bones creaking, threatening to crack. I could also hear Victoria shouting and pleading, all to no avail.

And then the giant made a mistake. For whatever reason, he lifted his face and drew his head back as if to examine my expression for how much pain he was causing me. Another couple seconds I might have blacked out. But as it was, I still had enough in-fighting savvy and fading strength to rare back my own head and then ram it forward, crashing my forehead down on his nose, flattening and smearing it all over his broad, sweat-beaded face.

Irwin released a pig-like grunt, along with a hot gush of blood down over his lips and chin. He staggered some, and the pressure of his crushing arms even lessened for a moment. But he didn't let go. That was alright, though; at least for now. I had more business to conduct right where I was. It amounted to drawing my head back once again and this time slamming it forward down across the bottom half of his face. I felt teeth caving in and more hot blood squirting from the corners of his mouth.

He let go of me then. More accurately, he gave me a final shake and flung me out and away like a tubful of dirty washwater. I hit the ground in a limp sprawl and lay there trying to suck some breath back into lungs that had been squeezed nearly empty. It was all I could do to raise my head and look around.

I saw Irwin looming a few yards away, still standing in the spot he'd launched me from. First with the back of one hand and then the other, he was wiping at the flow of blood running from his mouth and nose. He kept frowning down at the smears on his hands, looking somehow more confused than angry or hurt.

But his older brother, lying not too far away, still grimacing in pain as he propped himself up on one elbow, was only too eager to rekindle the giant's rage. "Don't let up on that bastard, Irwin!" he urged. "Go finish him—go break him into pieces!"

Irwin's dull eyes fell on me again. Slowly the confusion left his face, replaced by a furl of his shaggy brows and a menacing curl returning to his bloodied lips. "Oh, yeah," he mumbled in a thick voice. "I'm gonna finish breakin' him up real bad."

A thick worm of panic crawled through my guts. I didn't know if I had the strength to even stand up ...

And that's when the report of a heavy caliber gun roared across the lot. All eyes swept to try and lock on the source. A second shot quickly followed, and its origin became clear to all.

It was Victoria. She was up on the Burdette flatbed wagon, standing in front of the dog cages. Immediately in back of her, the dogs behind the bars were pacing back and forth in agitation, snarling and growling, eyes blazing. In her right hand, held high for everyone to plainly see, Victoria was brandishing my Colt, which she'd obviously retrieved from where it had fallen from the holster.

"Hear me everybody!" Victoria shouted. "Hear me all you gutless cowards looking on and doing nothing to stop this. And hear me, especially, you Burdetts—most of all you, Ivan!"

She waved the Colt with an extra flourish. "I've got four bullets left in this hogleg. Enough to kill every one of the dogs in these cages behind me. And that's exactly what I'm prepared to do, Ivan, if you don't call this off and let me and Torrent leave here with the terrier!"

"No!" protested a horrified Ivan "Don't you dare hurt my dogs!"

"You've already labeled me a crazy woman. What have I got to lose?" taunted Victoria.

Complete silence gripped the scene. The entire crowd seemed to be holding its collective breath.

Looking somewhat confused again, Irwin said, "You want I should break her to pieces instead, Ivan?"

I lifted my right hand and moved it across my chest, slipping it inside my jacket to touch the Colt Lightning in its shoulder rig.

"I can blow the heads clean off every one of these mongrels and still have a bullet left for him if he tries," Victoria warned.

Ivan jackknifed to a full sitting position, wincing in pain. Holding his hands up, palms out in a take-it-easy gesture, he told his brother, "Don't do anything. Never mind what I said before. This bitch *is* crazy."

"Calling me names isn't giving me an answer, Ivan" Victoria said icily. "Maybe you need the incentive of losing a dog to make sure you believe I'm serious."

"No! No, I believe you!" Ivan's face twisted in anguish and he began shaking his head from side to side. "Don't hurt the dogs!" he pleaded in a ragged voice, almost sobbing as he continued to wag his head weakly. "Whatever you say ... Whatever you want ... Just don't hurt our dogs. Please don't do that ..."

Chapter 18

Having worn out our welcome with a large seg-ment of the town due to disrupting their big dog fighting event, it was plain to see that the best thing for Victoria and I to do next was waste no time getting back on the trail and putting the "pleasant little community" of Gilcrest behind us.

Our departure was unexpectedly slowed, however, by none other than Janice Drummond. The delay didn't come from her not having the horseshoe repair completed—that was ready and waiting for us. What got in the way was the barrage of questions she also had waiting after somehow hearing about our run-in with the Burdetts. How word about the fracas reached her ahead of us I never did figure out.

But reach her it did. And so there was no escaping until Victoria and I related some first hand accounts of what had happened, all of which she drank in with a gleeful smile on her face while repeatedly muttering, "Boy, I wish I'd been there to see that." In the process of this, the battered condition of the terrier who'd been the catalyst for everything caught her interest as well, and she insisted in lending a hand to help treat the critter's injuries. In addition to blacksmithing and running the livery, it turned out, Janice was the closest thing Gilcrest had to a veterinarian (though mainly when it came to doctoring horses). Nevertheless, her practiced touch at stitching up some of the more serious gashes and providing some healing salves and dressings for further care was appreciated and surely beneficial to the patient, even if it did cost us some extra time.

All in all, it was well past noon before Victoria and I left town and set our course once again for Silvercliff. Surprisingly, as we rode out past Birnbaum's store, the sounds coming from the lot in back—shouts of a crowd not quite muffling the fierce snarling, growling noises made by canines locked in combat—signaled the dog fights were taking place after all. I couldn't help marveling somewhat at the apparent durability of the Burdette brothers, humiliated and physically damaged yet forging ahead with what they'd come here to do. Nevertheless, I felt dismayed by the whole thing, by what it said about people who found enjoyment in such a spectacle. In my mind, the question then became: Who were the real animals back there behind the store that day?

* * * * *

The cloud cover grew thicker and darker as the afternoon wore on. Tendrils of fog, heavy with cold droplets of mist, began forming again, tattered fingers reaching down gradually lower.

We'd been ascending slightly each day, ever since

leaving Denver. But now, aiming for Silvercliff in as straight a line as the terrain would allow, bypassing some of the towns as laid out in sequence on Meadely's map and thereby cutting more due north, we were traveling in a flatter line at a relatively stable height. At least for now. We would eventually go on the ascent again, though not until some time tomorrow. I hoped by then the weather would clear. The by-pass route I'd chosen was considerably less traveled, leaving it narrower, strewn with fallen rocks, and made slippery in spots by the damp fog. It was tricky even now; climbing a ragged incline under the same conditions could turn into a real challenge.

Late in the afternoon, I spotted a trapper's cabin a short ways off the trail. It was tucked back into a stand of aspen and pine trees at the top of a grassy slope with a tall rock cliff jutting up behind. Though there was still more than an hour of daylight left, I decided this was too good to pass up as a place to stop for the night. Victoria was quick to agree. The misty fog had turned into an intermittent drizzle by then and though we'd halted some distance back to don rain slickers, the warmth and dryness they provided were no match for the thought of having a roof to spread our bedrolls under.

Reaching the cabin, we found it very basic yet well built and not lacking for necessities. There was a decently stocked food chest, a sturdy table with bench seats, and a fireplace with a pile of split wood heaped beside it. On the outside there was even a small corral area partially covered by a lean-to style roof of untrimmed branches.

"Does someone live here?" Victoria wanted to know.

"Not permanently. Not anymore," I told her. "It was probably originally built by a trapper back in the fur trade days. Now it's maintained as just a haven for travelers, like us, who get caught in bad weather or maybe just want to spend a night in greater comfort than a trailside camp can offer."

"Who maintains it, then?"

"The people who use it. At least that's the way it's supposed to work," I explained. "Anyone's welcome to stay. The generally understood rule, though, is that when you move on you're expected to leave things as good—or better, if possible—than you found 'em. That way, if somebody comes along who's been injured or waylaid by an unexpected blizzard or fallen on hard luck with no food or supplies, this can be a place to help them survive until they're able to continue again."

Victoria looked thoughtful and then said, "That all sounds rather ... noble."

"Guess that's one word you could use," I allowed. "Just plain practical is what I'd call it. Especially in the old days, when there were no mining camps and very few towns up through here. The tough old birds who traipsed these mountains back then needed every survival trick they could think of. And while many of them were loners, setting up a few hardship shacks like this was still a way they could depend on and help one another."

"You almost sound like you wish you would have lived that life," Victoria observed.

"Was a time it sounded intriguing," I admitted. "But that time has come and gone. These days I'm too fond of all the creature comforts I can find."

"Creature comforts," Victoria said, smiling. "You mean like the deluxe accommodations we have about us now?"

"Hey. It might not measure up to your suite back at that Denver hotel," I countered, "but compared to the cold rainwater that was trickling down the back of my neck a few minutes ago, it looks and feels mighty accommodating to me."

Victoria spread her hands. "On that I must agree. However, I trust you'll concede we can make it even more accommodating, starting with a fire in the fireplace. I'll take care of getting that started if you'll see to bringing in our supplies so we can then proceed with an elegant dining experience. Deal?"

I pinched the soggy brim of my hat. "Done and done."

Fresh baked biscuits, ham hocks, creamed corn, and coffee sweetened with brown sugar might not sound like elegant dining to some, but it rated as a mighty fine meal in my book. With full darkness descending outside, rain spattering steady on the roof, and warmth from the fireplace spreading though the cabin, that was the supper Victoria and I sat down to. Once I brought in the provisions, she'd prepared the meal while I went back out and got the horses secured in the corral lean-to. I'm a pretty good trail cook myself, but I never mind handing the chores over to somebody else who knows what they're doing.

As if reading my thoughts, Victoria said around a bite of biscuit, "I've seldom gotten much chance in recent years, what with Father and I so often out chasing stories, but I'm a pretty fair hand in the kitchen when I take a mind. Not to say this is my most impressive work, but I hope it's passable."

"More than. With simple conditions and limited fixings to work with, you did great," I replied, paying her the compliment she'd wanted to hear. And meaning it.

"It was the least I could do ... after nearly getting us both killed earlier today."

That was an opening for just the two of us to talk for the first time at any length about the incident behind Birnbaum's barn.

I paused before pushing a forkful of ham hock into my mouth. "Is that what you were doing—getting us almost killed? I thought the whole thing was about *saving* a life?"

With the last, I cut my eyes over and down to the rescued terrier now lying on the bench seat beside Victoria. He had a blanket draped over his cuts and bandages, but his head was raised and alert, waiting for the next piece of biscuit she kept breaking off and giving to him.

"That's how it started, and thankfully ended," said Victoria, reaching down and gently petting the dog's head. "But for a while there, in the middle, it got kind of iffy. And you were the one paying the price for what I set in motion."

"Don't remind me," I said, chewing. "No need to. I already got a half dozen or so aches that take care of that every time I move wrong."

"God, I hope you believe how sorry I am. I ... I don't know what came over me. I've never done anything like that before in my life."

"Could've fooled me." I grinned. "The way you were popping off rounds first with your derringers and then my Colt—you looked like you were born to it."

A bright pink blush colored Victoria's pretty face. "What else could I do? Seeing the way those two Burdetts attacked you, the damage they'd already done and what more Ivan was urging his giant brother to do ... And worst of all, knowing I was the cause of it ..."

"Hey, take it easy," I told her. "It all turned out okay, right? You saved your little pup, you backed down the Burdetts, and I'm still in one piece. Plus, just for the record, I was on the verge of getting my second wind when you jumped up on that wagon. If big ol' Irwin had reached for me again, I was ready to chop him down to size."

Now it was Victoria's turn to grin. "Oh, I see. I didn't realize that. In that case, hope I didn't spoil your fun."

"Like I said, it turned out okay. I took a couple chunks out of each of the Burdetts' hides, I'll settle for that."

Right about then, the terrier gave an impatient little yip at Victoria, letting her know it had been too long since she'd slipped him a bite of biscuit. Chuckling, she remedied his complaint and said, "Something else that appears to have turned out okay is this little rascal. Leastways his appetite is fine."

I grunted. "I've got to admit, when you first handed him to me back there in Gilcrest, I wouldn't have bet a plug nickel on his chances to survive, given the bloody, chewed-up condition he was in."

"Most of the thanks for him making it goes to Janice," said Victoria. "That, and his own stubborn toughness."

I nodded. "I got to give him that. But how long are you willing to lug him around in that papoose pack you and Janice made for him?"

I was referring the combination sling/pouch Victoria and Janice had rigged up as a means to carry the terrier, whose injuries temporarily limited his ability to move very far on his own. Victoria had slung this contraption over her right shoulder, so that the pouch hung down over her ribs on the left side and had ridden all afternoon with the dog snuggled against her in this manner.

Her answer to my inquiry about it now came terse and firm. "For however long as it takes him to get strong enough to go on his own."

And that's how we left it.

Chapter 19

Come morning, the rain had stopped but patches of fog remained, clinging to the treetops and low peaks like wet gauze. Victoria and I rose early, breakfasted on a fresh pot of coffee and leftovers from last night's supper. While I saddled our mounts and re-loaded the pack horse, she tended to the terrier's injuries, applying dabs of salve and clean bandages where required. As far as fulfilling our obligation to leave the hardship shack in suitable condition for its next visitor, I split a stack of wood to replace what we had burned and Victoria added some coffee beans, salt, and a couple airtights of stewed tomatoes in the food chest.

Before quitting the cabin, Victoria started to shrug into her dog-carrying pouch. I stopped her, saying, "Hold off on that a minute. Step outside, let me first show you something you might want to consider as an alternative."

Once she'd followed me out, carrying the terrier in her arms, I pointed to how I had rigged the bundles on the pack horse so a blanketed pocket was created up in the middle, making a cushiony little nest where the

mutt could ride like some high muckety-muck poten-
tate. "Figured it might save some wear and tear on your
shoulder," I explained. "I know your new pal probably
don't seem like he weighs much. But you have him
hanging on you all day while you rock back and forth in
a saddle, I'm betting it'll take a toll. Your choice, though.
I'm just suggesting."

Victoria studied the riding nest for a moment and
then a smile curved her mouth as she shifted her gaze
to me. "You remind me more and more of my father,
you know that? All gruff and crusty on the outside, but
under the crust a lot of tenderness and sensitivity, too."

"Whoa now," I protested. "I don't mind being compared favorably to your dad, but let's not get too carried
away ... The main thing is, we need to get a move on. So
make up your mind, do you want to try the mutt up there
or do you want to go ahead and strap him to you again?"

"I think his new perch will suit him just fine,"
Victoria said. Then she held the terrier out to me and
added, "Here, you're taller. Will you do the honors of
introducing him to it?"

As she predicted, the dog settled into his nest just
fine and a moment later we were swinging up into our
own saddles.

"You still think we have a chance of making Silvercliff by tonight?" Victoria asked.

I shook my head. "I doubt it. We lost too much time
getting out of Gilcrest and then I cramped our progress even more when I spotted this cabin and called
an early halt last night. It'd help if this fog lifts. But,
even still, I expect it'll be more like tomorrow morning before we get there."

"You mention the fog," Victoria said. "You realize this is the kind of weather the Ripper is used to? I mean, the stories you hear about London is how it's always shrouded in fog. Maybe this is an omen, maybe it's a sign we're closing in on the Whitechapel Murderer."

"I don't know from omens," I told her. "I'll save putting my faith in what I can grab hold of or set my gunsights on."

She smiled some more. "There you go again. Gruff and crusty."

We turned away from the cabin and started down the slope toward the little-used trail we'd been following the previous day. Just as we reached it, I spotted a lone rider approaching from the south. He was wrapped in a long, dark rain slicker and had a hat pulled down low over his face. I didn't recognize him. Not at first. About the time I did, so did somebody else. The terrier, from his nest atop the pack bundles, suddenly perked up his head and emitted a low, steady growl.

Victoria and I reined up. When he got a little closer, so did the rider. Lifting his face and thumbing the brim of his hat back a bit, Ivan Burdett regarded us with no particular expression on his face. The terrier growled some more.

Ivan's eyes dropped to where my right hand had come to rest on the butt of my Colt. Then, his gaze leisurely lifting once again, he said, "No need for that, mister. I ain't here lookin' for trouble."

"Then what are you here for?" I wanted to know.

"Well I didn't come to listen to that mutt dog keep growlin' at me, that's for sure. Can't you shut him up?"

Glaring fiercely, Victoria said, "Seems to me he

has every right to growl. And more, if he was in any condition to come at you."

I gave it a beat, then said, "I don't disagree. But for the sake of hearing what this is all about, will you try to settle him down?"

Continuing to glare, Victoria turned her mount and steered him close alongside the pack horse. Reaching out, she lifted the terrier from his perch and wrapped him in her arms. He stopped growling but never took his eyes off Ivan.

Looking on, the latter gave a faint wag of his head. "Little scrapper has plumb got some toughness to him, don't he? When you two carried him off yesterday, I wouldn't have thought he'd last much past the end of the street."

"You and your pet wolf tried awful hard to make sure he didn't," said Victoria.

"The wolf, as you call him, was just doin' its job, ma'am. What he was bein' trained for," responded Ivan. "You gotta lay blame, it's due me, not the animal."

"Fine. I will," Victoria assured him.

Ivan cut his eyes back to me, grinning. "Looks like you got a *pair* of scrappers on your hands, Torrent. Showin' game. I like that in a person and an animal. What I look for in the dogs I train."

"If that's supposed to be a compliment, you can save it," Victoria said icily. "I hardly find pleasure being compared to one of your savage dogs or anything else viewed favorably by you."

Ivan's grinned widened. "See what I mean?"

"What I don't see," I told him, "is what concern any of it is to you. Are you following us ...? And how do you know my name?"

"Yeah, for reasons I'll get to in a minute, I came meanin' to catch up with you. Call it followin' if you want. As far as knowin' your name, you mentioned it to that ornery old gal who runs the livery and blacksmith back in Gilcrest. But I heard of you some before that, too, the detectivatin' you do all through these parts for that outfit back in Omaha—not Pinkerton, some cut-rate operation."

"You don't work very hard at trying to ingratiate yourself to folks, do you?" I said.

He frowned. "I don't know what big words like that even mean. So no, I reckon it probably ain't something I make a habit of."

"Never mind. Let's get back to you setting out to catch up with us. Now you have ... Why?"

"For your own good, that's why." Ivan squared his shoulders and looked suddenly indignant. "Not that you're actin' very doggone grateful for it."

"I might. If I knew what you're talking about. What good is you catching up supposed to do us?"

"The good of bein' warned. Warned about Cherokee Farrow."

"Who is he supposed to be?" asked Victoria.

Ivan cocked an eyebrow. "By all reports he's *supposed* to be a mighty tough hombre, a halfbreed ... And the truth of the matter is, those reports ain't wrong."

"No argument on that part, not from me. I know Cherokee," I said. "But what about him rates giving us a warning?"

Ivan's mouth curved in a sly smile. "I figure you oughta know the answer to that better than me. All I know is that he showed up in Gilcrest yesterday, not more than two hours after you two rode out. Him and a pair of hardcase pals. They asked around in particular about you, Torrent, but they also knew you was travelin' with a lady."

I didn't like the sound of this at all. I said, "What was it they were asking about me?"

"If you'd passed through. How long ago. Like that." Ivan shrugged. "Seein's how you two put on quite a show for a lot of folks to see, Cherokee and his pals didn't have much trouble findin' answers. Funny thing, though. Once they got 'em, they didn't seem in much of a hurry to take out after you. In fact, they stuck around and did some bettin' on the last couple dog fights. That's when Cherokee mentioned to me himself that he was in no hurry because he knew where you were headed. Said he had plenty of time to catch up with you in Barlow or Delsoro."

"What made him think he knew where we were headed?" Victoria asked.

I considered a moment. Then: "Those would've been the logical next towns for us to go to, based on the sequence we'd been following. Cherokee couldn't have known we suddenly had reason to change course."

"I don't know about all that," said Ivan. "But what I *did* know was that you rode north on the old trapper's trail out of Gilcrest—not on the wagon road aimed toward either of those other places."

"So did you correct him about his mistaken notion?"

"Would I be loco enough to be here now—in his path—if I had?" Ivan shook his head, as if in answer to his own question. "You see, I know all too well what kind of hombre Cherokee is. Mean and dangerous. And it was plain to see those two ridin' with him are cut from the same bolt. In other words, havin' them on your trail can't be good news for you or the lady."

Victoria looked at me. "What interest can they have in us?"

I grimaced. "It's me he's asking for." Cutting my eyes to Ivan, I asked, "He give any idea what his beef is with me?"

"We didn't get into that. But, like I said, I know Cherokee and I saw the heat in his eyes. Whatever's proddin' him, it's a long way from anything friendly."

Regarding him tightly, I said, "Not meaning to sound ungrateful again, but I still don't understand what your stake in this is? Why have you gone to the trouble of catching up to tell us about Cherokee?"

Ivan grunted. "Boy, don't think I didn't ask myself that question a whole bunch of times while I was ridin' half the night through the rain. The long and short of it is this: I don't want to end up accused of bein' part of whatever that halfbreed devil turns out doin'. The reason I know him so well, like I keep sayin', see, is 'cause I used to ride with him for a spell. Long time back, but folks still remember. I was part of some mighty rough doin's, stuff I ain't nohow proud of and didn't want to keep gettin' mixed up in. So I split ways with him."

Ivan paused, looking remorseful. If it was an act, he was pretty good at it. Then, switching to a look of earnestness, he continued. "You saw my brother. He needs lookin' after, and I'm all he's got. I can't afford—for his sake, if no other—to get slung behind bars. What we do with our dog fightin' stuff ain't very high class, I know, and plumb sneered at by many. But it ain't illegal, it's something me and Irwin are pretty good at, and it makes us enough money so's maybe we can settle down to some better life someday. In the meantime, this is what we know, all we have."

"So I ain't here warnin' you about Cherokee out of caring and kindness. Not caring so much about you, anyway. What I care about—on account of so many people seein' the fight me and Irwin had with you, and then seein' me and Cherokee talkin' together shortly after on top of already knowin' about my past with him—is that I don't get sucked into anything that comes from him catchin' up with you. I don't want nobody thinkin' I was gettin' revenge through him. If I wanted that, me and Irwin would take care of it ourselves."

Thinking it the kind of cockeyed logic that just might be the truth, I said, "So you went to all this trouble to warn us in hopes it would put us enough on guard to keep Cherokee from succeeding. That way, you'll stay in the clear."

Ivan frowned. "Yeah. Ain't that what I said? Havin' seen you two in action—and havin' heard about other scrapes you been in, Torrent—I figure if you know Cherokee's comin', you got a chance to hold your own." His frown softening, he focused on Victoria and added, "Another thing is the fact Cherokee ain't known for takin' it easy on women. I know you think I'm lower than dirt, ma'am, but I ain't never sunk to harmin' a woman. I already treated you bad enough, callin' you crazy and all in front of everybody. You didn't deserve that, and you sure don't deserve what Cherokee might have in store if you ain't ready for him."

Victoria was clearly taken aback by this and unsure know how to respond. "I ... that is, we ... your advisement is most welcome. We will certainly take necessary precautions."

"I hope you do, ma'am. I purely hope you do."

There was an awkward pause. Until Ivan broke it by speaking again, saying, "Reckon I'll take my leave now. I got to get back to Irwin. I left him in the care of an old witchy woman who knows the ways of Indian healin'. You left him kinda busted up, Torrent. But she'll see to him okay."

I felt a curious urge to say I was sorry. But held it in check.

Ivan swung his horse part way around but then stopped and looked across his shoulder at me. "This don't mean we're friends, Torrent. Nothin' close. Time passes and our paths cross again, I might remember the lumps you put on me and my brother and decide there's need for some settlin' up. Comes to that, though, you'll see me comin' straight on. No more back swipes like I tried yesterday; not by me, not by Irwin. Figure you got enough worry in that direction from Cherokee and his like."

I nodded. "Fair enough. That's how I'll watch for you then ... Straight on."

A Short Distance Outside of Bright Mining Camp Colorado Rockies Front Range Monday, third week of Spring, 10:00 AM

Sitting in the driver's box of the second of two *wagons rolling together up the rugged mountain road, the man in the flowing coat smiled wryly to himself as he watched the last wisps of fog dissolving from the trees and peaks around him. After weeks of enjoying his return to the clear skies and fresh, crisp, high altitude air, he'd been surprised to find himself reacting the way he had to the unexpected fog and mist that settled in late yesterday afternoon and stayed to envelope the area all through the night. It had felt so familiar, almost comforting. He realized that, in a curious way, part of him must have been missing the murky, slowly swirling, ground-hugging grayness. After all, there'd been a time—not so very long ago—that the fog had been his friend, his accomplice when committing his demon-driven deeds and then eluding notice or capture by fading into the embracing gloom.*

But even though this fresh taste of fog may have felt comforting, the man told himself, his smile flattening to a thin-lipped straight line, there was no part of him that missed the squalor and stench of the urban hellhole where it had been his ally in the past. He had no remorse about being gone from that. Things were working out too well in this new setting ... More accurately, a change in setting, in as much as this was merely a return to an earlier past. But it was a return so far quite satisfying to both him and his demons.

And there was something else the fog had stirred ... the demons inside the man. This was the start of a third day since that stupid cow Mary, back in Promise, had so willingly presented herself. The craving of the demons had been unusually demanding in that instance, coming quicker than normal in the wake of their previous feeding. Yet doing the deed with Mary seemed to sufficiently quell them. They had been still and silent ever since. The man expected it would be the middle or maybe the end of the week before they would require further attention. But then the fog came. As soon as he opened his eyes this morning, the man sensed them. Awake ahead of him, starting to prowl, signaling it wouldn't be long before only another deed would quiet them again.

Giving a slap with the reins in his hands, clucking to the team of horses pulling out ahead, the man tried to remember the name of the next town they were scheduled to stop at. The names of the various settlements and camps were unimportant to him. All that mattered was that they kept coming, that his troupe kept on the move from one to the next in order to provide enough time and distance in between so that when it was necessary for him to do a deed it wasn't piled too closely on top of a previous one.

Carmody, that was it. Carmody was the name of the town they would be stopping at this evening. Christ, the names were as indistinct and drab-sounding as the places themselves. The one they'd just left was called Bright, which it certainly was not; and before that—following Promise, another especially ill-fated name, especially for Mary—had been a tent sprawl dubbed Fordham. But that was okay, the insignificance of the camps and their isolation from one another was all part of his plan. What mattered for the moment was the fact that if the demons got too demanding by tonight and he had to do a deed in Carmody, once again sooner than anticipated, it would still be far enough removed from Promise not to be of concern.

The man glanced up at the patches of blue sky starting to break through and spread wider. The wry smile returned to his lips. Too bad the fog couldn't have stuck around one more night, he thought ... for old time's sake.

Chapter 20

The fog lifted shortly after we parted ways with
Ivan Burdett, allowing Victoria and me to cover ground
at a good pace. The sky cleared and the day warmed
nicely. In stretches where the rugged trail was wide
enough to allow it, we rode side by side and talked.

"Do you believe Ivan's warning about this Cherokee
Farrow being on our trail?" Victoria asked.

"Don't see no gain for him lying about it, especially
considering all the trouble he went to deliver the message," I replied.

"Isn't that awfully peculiar behavior in itself? Him
riding through the rain and half the night just to tell
us, I mean. It would seem extreme for anyone short of
a very close friend—let alone somebody as crude and
hard as Ivan, especially after we beat and humiliated
him and his brother the way we did."

"I've been thinking about that as well," I admitted.
"I believe it comes down to two things. One is the word
he used when he was trying to compliment you and the
mutt. He called you 'game'. To a dog fighter, being game

is just about the best, most admirable thing there is. Means a critter who keeps going forward, never backs down, never gives up."

Victoria lifted her brows. "While those may be admirable traits for a 'critter', human or otherwise, that still doesn't make Ivan Burdett's admiration something I particularly long for."

"Not saying you should or shouldn't," I told her. "I'm just trying to explain why I think Ivan did what he did. I doubt he views very many people as showing the kind of game he rates very high. But in you, me, and even the mutt—each in our own way and even though it meant him and his brother took a beating in the process—he *did* see it. And to his cockeyed value system, it was something worthy."

Victoria regarded me. "The way you explain it implies an understanding and almost a certain amount of admiration in return."

I considered for a minute. Then: "I don't know that admiration is the right word. But understanding? Having a kind of respect for an adversary? Yeah, I've been there ... I looked down a rifle barrel and pulled the trigger on many a man dressed in gray whose cause I rejected and had to fight against, but that didn't mean I didn't respect some of those brave devils and how they fought for their cause, how they kept coming straight on into our bullets."

"Kept coming 'straight on'," Victoria repeated, her voice softer but her eyes still trained one me intently. "That's the term Ivan used when he said he might look to face you again ... It's all part of the same thing, isn't it?"

"Yeah. I guess it is," I allowed.

She went quiet for a moment before saying, "I remember Father making a similar comment once. About respecting the bravery of some of the men he fought against in the war."

"Yeah, he knew. Matter of fact, he and I discussed it a time or two."

"I guess it's something only understood by certain men. Men like you and my father ... and being charitable, perhaps Ivan too. Though I suspect not all of you even truly, fully understand." Victoria paused, her lips forming a somewhat wistful smile. "And I fear, no matter how emancipated we get, it's something women may never comprehend."

I grunted. "Don't sell yourself short."

"Okay. That's one explanation for Ivan showing up the way he did, whether I understand or not. You said you believed there were two reasons. What's the other?"

"His brother," I answered. "You heard him. Whatever his crudeness or shortcomings, Ivan feels genuinely responsible for his brother. He don't see how the big lunk could get along without him. So, just like he said, he saw giving us warning about Cherokee a chance for us to keep from getting harmed and for him to avoid the risk of possibly being blamed either because of our recent fight with him or due to his past association with Cherokee."

"And him getting blamed," Victoria said, trying to make sure she got my reasoning, "might mean being hauled in for questioning or possibly even facing charges. And that would include Irwin, too. Or, worse, leave Irwin on his own."

"That's what I got out of it. Plus he flat don't like—and maybe is a little afraid of—Cherokee."

Victoria frowned. "I hate to think anything positive about that cretin but, no matter his convoluted logic, it's hard to fault his devotion to his simple-minded brother."

"The main take-away, like I said at the start," I grated, "is that I believe he was telling the truth about Cherokee. So that means the 'breed' is on the prod for me and I'm damned if I can figure why."

"Judging by your familiarity with him as soon as you heard his name, I assumed you must have crossed paths with him in the past."

"Oh yeah, we've crossed more than once. And never on friendly terms. Definitely no love ever lost between us, as the saying goes." I shook my head. "But all that was in the past. Done and over with as far as I figured. For him to come charging after me now—especially bringing along a couple backups—can only mean something new has put a burr under his saddle."

"But what? Does that mean we won't know until he catches up with us? That doesn't sound very appealing."

"No, it don't. What's more, if he gets close enough to catch us in an ambush, we may never know exactly why." I scowled. "And an ambush sure as hell fits Cherokee' style. He ain't no 'come at you straight on' kind of hombre."

"So what can we do?"

"The smartest thing would be to turn back and get you to safety in Denver. Have you hold there long enough for me to go 'front Cherokee and find out—"

"Hold it right there, mister," Victoria cut me off, eyes flashing. "No way I'm turning back now, not to run from some old enemy of yours and for damn sure not to let up when we're closing in on the Ripper!"

Through gritted teeth, I said, "I told you once before that I don't want no more Wheelers ending up dead due to trouble aimed at me."

"You don't know that this trouble *is* aimed strictly at you. You don't know *what* it's about," Victoria argued. "And back in Denver—if I stayed put, which I won't— we know Dundy is waiting with a chip on his shoulder. You'd leave me to face him alone?"

I frowned. "All of a sudden now you're a delicate flower who can't hold your own against the likes of Dundy?"

"I darn well can hold my own, and you know it. That also means I can hold my own, at your side, if it comes to trouble with this halfbreed—especially if he tries to get in the way of catching up with Tuttle."

We glared at each other for several beats. Until I said, "You are one stubborn damn female, you know that?"

"I've been called worse."

"I bet you have." I glared some more, then finally heaved a sigh. "Okay, I guess a way we could work it is to keep on the move just as we are. Stay extra alert. Be ready at all times, not let Cherokee catch us by surprise. Him heading off in the wrong direction will buy us some time for now. When he realizes where we *didn't* go, he'll have to backtrack and try to figure out where we went instead. That'll leave him having to race to close the gap again."

"By then, we hopefully will have determined which one of the medicine shows was in or near Silvercliff for the murders there and that will provide the lead for us to narrow our own gap. On the Ripper. If we don't watch out, it might come down to us having to hurry up and get one killer out of the way so we can concentrate on dealing with a second one."

"As long as one of them is the Ripper, that's all I care," said Victoria.

I cocked an eyebrow. "Maybe, while you're at it, you could also care, just a little bit, that you and me both come out of it with our hides intact."

* * * * *

The day remained clear and warm in the sun-shine. As evening approached, though, a chill, gusting wind whistling down through the peaks and canyons cooled things rapidly. For our night camp, to get us out of that wind, I chose a deep, wedge-shaped cut that reached back between two flat cliff faces. There was enough scrub brush for a fire but very little in the way of graze for the horses. So, while Victoria set up camp, I watered, grained, and hobbled the animals.

Later, after we'd eaten, we sat by the fire, wrapped in the soogans I had unpacked, sipping from cups of coffee and listening to the wind whip and howl past the mouth of our notch. The slice of sky we could see directly overhead was clear and shot with brilliantly glittering stars but the night nevertheless had a mean bite to it.

"I thought Spring had arrived," Victoria commented at one point. "The roar of that wind sounds like it's threatening to pull down a blizzard."

"Don't jinx us," I told her. "Early Spring in the mountains could mean anything, weather-wise. You could enjoy fifty degrees one day, then be up to your ears in snow the next."

"You're right, let's not talk about it. We don't want to tempt Fate or Mother Nature or whatever. We have enough obstacles to overcome without the weather turning against us."

I gestured to the terrier who was snuggled up under the soogan beside her, his chin resting on his fore paws. "Your new little buddy don't look too worried. After escaping the jaws of the Burdetts' half-wolf, I expect a chilly wind don't seem like no big deal at all to him."

The mutt had quickly become attached to Victoria. He'd ridden contentedly all day on his perch atop the supply packs. Whenever we put him down on the ground, he would explore within a limited range on his injured legs but make sure to never venture far from Victoria.

She reached down now, stroking his head, a smile touching her mouth. Suddenly, her face lifted and she pinned me with a very direct look, saying, "That's it!"

I froze with my coffee cup half raised to take a drink. "That's what?" I wanted to know.

"Well, we can't just keep calling this little fella 'the dog' or 'the terrier' ... or 'the mutt' the way you usually do ... So all day long I've been fretting over what might be a good name for him. I didn't bother asking you because I figured you had enough else on your mind. Either that, or you'd have come up with something God-awful."

"Thanks a bunch."

"But then you went ahead and did it anyway."

Whatever this was about, it seemed to be going in circles I couldn't keep up with. "Did what?" I said.

"You came up with the perfect name." Victoria scooped up the terrier and held him before her in both hands so that they were practically nose to nose. She was smiling wide, the mutt was looking sleepy and confused. "You called him 'my little buddy', so that's what it's going to be. From now on his name is Buddy." She pulled the mutt closer and actually did rub noses with him. "What do you think, little fella? Huh? Are you ready to be Buddy? Do you like it?"

The mutt—excuse me, make that Buddy—continued to look sleepy and confused.

Me, I just rolled my eyes and finished taking my drink of coffee.

Six Miles Short of Carmody Pass
Colorado Rockies Front Range
Monday, third week of Spring,
9:30 PM

The man in the flowing coat was very distraught.
*A wholly unanticipated turn of events had knocked his
carefully laid plans seriously askew. And the timing and
circumstances could hardly be worse.*

*Instead of his troupe being settled at this hour within
the city limits of Carmody, their evening performance
completed and the opportunity for individual leisure
pursuits left to each member, they were encamped in
mountain wilderness being battered by a cold, fiercely
howling wind. Kropolaus, the founder and owner of
the show, aided by the powerful and devoted Leland,
had positioned the wagons and pulling teams to the
best of their ability amidst a stand of aspens and rocky
outcrops intended to provide as much natural shelter
as possible. And although their two traveling wagons
were each covered by canvas and panels of thin plywood, these were proving quite inadequate at blocking
the shuddering gusts.*

*Except for Leland, the members of the traveling
troupe, rich in showmanship talents, were sadly lacking*

when it came to menial tasks such as setting up a camp
under adverse conditions. They were used to hiring
locals in the various towns where they stopped to take
care of anything more than the basics.

Only four in number, the troupe consisted of founder
and owner "Professor" Alexander Kropolaus, who had
perfected what he called Ichor, the centerpiece of the
whole presentation, a potion allegedly handed down
from the gods of ancient Greek mythology and sold as
a life-altering substance that, when taken as directed,
was certain to improve the overall health and longevity
of all who tried it. As evidence of its effect there was
Leland Gaines, a supremely muscled young man whose
alleged use of the potion enabled him to display feats
of strength comparable to the legendary Hercules. And
then there was the lovely Elise Trent, who claimed it
was her reliance on the potion that gave her the skill
and sharp eye of Athena, Goddess of the Hunt, which
she demonstrated by the amazing feats of archery she
performed. And lastly there was the man in the flowing coat himself, who fulfilled the role of announcer
and narrator, mesmerizing (via no claim of needing
the potion to do so) the crowds gathered for each show
by weaving tales of mythical deeds as they were being
performed by a current-day Hercules and Athena and
then segueing into an introduction of the professor and
his potion promising godlike transformations to any
willing to buy and try.

It was all preposterous, of course. But the show was
an entertaining diversion for the hard-working miners.
And the potion, while it may not have done everything
promised, neither did it (contrary to some other such

products) do any harm. So the money shelled out for an inconsequential product was largely offset by the so-called "free" show.

At the moment, however, anything offering stronger, warmer shelter than a pair of wagons loaded down with harmless potion would have been a welcome trade. And this was true for no one more than the man in the flowing coat.

A landslide in the heart of Carmody Pass, the only wagon access to the town of Carmody just a couple miles beyond, was the culprit. It was what had halted the Potion of the Gods traveling medicine show and forced them to turn back. One of the crew working to clear the blockage had informed them it would be days, maybe more than a week, before the passage was expected to be open. Meaning they'd had no choice but to turn around and head back toward Bright, which they were unable to reach before night and the knifing wind descended on them.

So while the others were enduring simple disappointment and discomfort, the man in the flowing coat was struggling with more ... the demons prowling restlessly, hungrily inside him. When they first stirred this morning as a result of the fog, he had let his speculation flow freely, thinking that in Carmody—reputedly a town of some size—it should be easy to find a suitable target for doing the deed necessary to appease them. With that in mind, he'd figured he might as well plan on getting it over with rather than wait and risk the next town being a harder one in which to navigate. In other words, he'd practically encouraged and promised the demons a feeding.

And now a damned landslide stood in the way.

But the demons didn't care. They were ready, on the prowl. Hungry.

Though it would be miserable, the man knew he could keep them at bay for tonight. He'd have to. But the days and nights immediately following presented a greater concern. In order to get to an alternate wagon route that could take them to new towns, the troupe would have to backtrack through Bright, Fordham, and all the way to Promise again before striking out a different way. Places they'd already put on shows (and where he'd already done a deed, in Promise). Meaning brief layovers, if at all, in order to keep on the move for the sake of reaching fresh money-making opportunities as soon as possible. All of which meant it might be as many as three or four more nights before they made a standard stop in an unvisited town—and thereby possibly as long for a reasonable chance to do the deed.

The man did not want to have to go through holding off for that long. Not again.

By virtue of opiates and sea-sickness he had once managed to hold the demons at bay for eleven days, during the ocean crossing from the fog-shrouded hellhole that spawned them. But he cringed at the thought of repeating that kind of torturous withdrawal. No, he'd have to find a quicker way. Even if it entailed increased risk.

The man leaned his head back against the inside of the wagon's canvas covering and emitted a low groan. None of the other troupe members sharing the shelter space with him noticed, however, due to a loud, howling gust of wind on the outside ...

Chapter 21

Before arriving in Silvercliff, Victoria and I decided to alter our cover story slightly. For the sake of getting directly to questions about any medicine show passing through the area recently, we added that the last letter received from Victoria's fictitious missing brother had included mention of him joining such a troupe in order to earn a grubstake for his own attempt at silver prospecting.

Reaching the town in the middle of the morning and finding it largely deserted due to most of its menfolk out working their claims, we gravitated toward a curl of smoke lifting from the stack of a large tent with a slab of wood propped up in front bearing the hand-painted letters: FOOD – GOOD EATS. We tied our horses to a couple of tent stakes, left Buddy on his perch atop the packs, and went inside. Soon we discovered that the lure of the cookfire smoke had been a stroke of good fortune.

The proprietors of the eatery turned out to be a late middle-aged couple named Hank and Hillary Dale, who were relative newcomers to the camp and seemed very welcoming and friendly. They expected to become busy with a lunch crowd in an hour or so, they explained, but in the meantime were more than happy to take few minutes to talk with us.

Experience had taught me that situations like this usually went smoother if you ordered something. So Victoria and I took seats at the plank lunch counter and said we each would like coffee and a slice of pie. When it came, the coffee was excellent but the pie not so much. For the sake of the Dales, who seemed like a nice couple, I hoped either this particular pie was a mismatch to the rest of their cooking or that they didn't have a lot of competition elsewhere in town. Otherwise, they might be in for a tough go of it.

But for now, for the needs of Victoria and me, the fare they served was satisfactory. The coffee was good enough to wash down the disappointment of the pie, and the information that came along with it was nearly everything we'd hoped for.

"Oh, you poor dear," Hillary said consolingly to Victoria upon hearing the fabrication about her missing brother. "I can only imagine your anguish in such a situation. Wondering and not knowing are sometimes harder to deal with than actual bad news."

"Yes, I suppose," Victoria replied somberly, playing her role to the hilt. "But I hope I don't have to put that theory to the ultimate test. Right now, I can stand more worrying over learning something dreadful."

"Heavens yes! I shouldn't have sounded so fatalistic," Hillary was quick to amend. "By all means, you must hold out hope."

After a lengthy study of the tintype we had passed

to the pair, Hank Dale handed it back to me, saying, "Nice looking young fella, but I'm sorry to say he don't look familiar. Put some beard stubble and some sweat and dirt on him—which is the way we see most of our customers when they come in hungry from their digs—he *could* be one of the miners who've eaten here, but none I can say for certain."

"But if he hasn't got a sufficient grubstake put together yet and is still traveling with one of the medicine shows, he wouldn't necessarily be part of that crowd," I pointed out. "Does it make any difference if you think of it that way? Have any of those shows passed though here, and did you get a look at the people associated with them?"

"Yeah, we've had a couple of those outfits come through." Hank frowned. "Even though the wife insisted we go have a look at their ballyhoo each time, not many of them returned the favor by taking a meal here. Too stuck up, it seemed to me."

"You got no call to think that," Hillary countered. "They were busy people, that's all. Think of the preparation needed to put on their shows and then pack up in order to move on and do it all over again."

"They still got to stop and eat," insisted Hank. "Especially that outfit that stayed in town for two nights. Yet not a meal taken here in all that time."

"Never mind feeling sorry for ourselves for missing out on a little bit of business," Hillary scolded. "This poor child is missing her brother. That's worth considerably bigger concern."

"Which brings us back to the personnel associated with those medicine shows," I said. "Even if none of them did business with you, you indicated you nevertheless went to see their presentations. Does it still hold that there was no resemblance in any of them, performers or otherwise, to the face in this tintype?"

The Dales exchanged glances where they stood on the back side of the plank counter. When her gaze returned to Victoria, Hillary's expression was genuinely sad. "I'm sorry, honey. But the answer is still no, nobody in any of those shows resembled your brother."

"We can say that with even more certainty than we can about him being none of the miners," Hank added. "Truth of the matter, wasn't all that many folks a part of those shows. So it don't leave much doubt."

Victoria sighed. "We've been told there are three different shows working their way through the front range. I guess you've eliminated two of them. That still leaves a third possibility for us to have hope for."

Following up on that, I asked the Dales, "Which were the two that came through here?"

Hank made a face. "The first one wasn't much at all. Some old colonel who was supposed to have traveled the world collecting ancient herbs and healing secrets from the four corners, and some professor fella who put 'em all together into the magic tablets they was hawking. They took turns giving a big spiel about all their adventures collecting the ingredients and then showed a display of pictures and doo-dads from the places where they got 'em ... all in all, about as exciting as watching mud dry."

"Oh, it wasn't that bad," said Hillary, though not very convincingly.

Her husband snorted. "There were times when the snores out of the bored audience were louder than the two fellas doing the jabbering up on stage."

I said, "I take it that wasn't the show that stayed for two nights."

"You can say that again," responded Hank. "If they'd have tried putting on a second show, their only audience would have been each other. But the outfit that came through a few days later—now that was a whole 'nother matter. It's that one there, as a matter of fact" —he stabbed a finger to indicate a poster nailed to one of the tent's support posts, an advertising flyer for the *Potion of the Gods* show— "and if you ever get the chance to catch one of their shows, I recommend you take a look. I don't know about their snake oil being better or worse than any other, but folks enjoyed the presentation they put on so much and word spread so wide they probably could have played a third night and still drawn a good crowd."

Hillary's expressive face looked suddenly mournful. "They might have actually stayed another night, too, if those awful murders hadn't occurred. Who could blame them for taking off after that? If we didn't have everything we own sunk in this place, I might demand we flee such evil as well."

Trying to look troubled rather than elated that we'd so quickly struck what Victoria and I came seeking, I said, "Evil? Murders? What happened?"

"Aye, it was nasty business. Evil is the only proper word," Hank growled ominously. "You naturally expect a certain amount of rowdiness in a mining camp. Fist fights, stabbings, even a shooting now and then. Sometimes death results, though not as often as you might think. And it's usually confined to the saloons and such, so decent folks can live and do business in reasonable safety on the fringes ... But late one night, an exact week ago, one of the soiled doves who are also a natural part of any mining camp met a most gruesome end. Butchered by a fiend, she was. Throat slit, belly carved wide open."

"Hank!" his wife admonished. "You needn't repeat everything in such gory detail. If you can't think of me, then at least have some consideration for our guests."

"Just saying it flat, that's all. Telling only that the gal was killed, don't send the full message of the evil," Hank argued. Then, squinting at me, he added, "You see the difference, right? Like I said, the work of a fiend. And then the same thing happened all over again the very next night."

"You have adequately painted the picture," Victoria said, shuddering slightly.

"Was the second victim also a soiled dove?" I asked.

"Uh-huh. That's the only thing that has kept decent women like my wife from fleeing the way she said. That, and the fact there've been no more killings since last Tuesday."

"Which is only limited comfort, let me assure you," said Hillary. "One more such atrocity, I can further assure you that I *will* be gone from here."

"Nor would I have it any other way," Hank agreed. "We can start over again somewhere else if we have to. But in the meantime, like you told Miss Wilson a minute ago, we need to hold out hope that it's over."

"No clue as to motive or the killer's identity?" I asked, trying to steer talk more directly back to the murders.

"Sure as hell not or you'd see what was left of him hanging from a tree limb somewhere out yonder." Hank scowled. "Far as motive, only guess is that the two gals might have somehow in the, er, performance of, uh, their duties ... well, something must have gone wrong that maybe set off some crazy drunk who blamed the doves and wanted to punish them."

"You're getting rather crude," said Hillary.

"Well, he asked, didn't he?"

"Yes, I did," I cut in. "Don't blame your husband, Mrs. Dale. I guess the detective in me made me probe more than was called for."

Hank's eyebrows lifted. "Hey, there's a thought. You being a detective and all, it's too bad you weren't around when those murders took place. Maybe you could have spotted some kind of clue as to who was behind them."

"Maybe," I allowed. "But my agency usually stays away from murder investigations. We leave that to legal authorities. Besides, I've got my hands full right now trying to help Miss Wilson find her missing brother."

"I'm awful sorry we weren't able to tell you anything more useful on that," said Hillary.

"But you actually did," I reminded her. "Providing her brother is still traveling with a medicine show, it's like Miss Wilson said a minute ago—you were able to eliminate two of the three we know to be working this area. You saw both of them and are able to report that young Wilson was no part of either troupe."

"Which means we can now concentrate on catching up with that third show," Victoria joined in, "and it will hopefully result in finding my brother."

"Well I hope it works out for you. We wish you all the luck," said Hank. "But you'll have to excuse us now, we need to finish getting ready for the lunch crowd that will start showing up before long."

"You might want to stay and talk with some of our other customers," suggested Hillary. "But I doubt they can add anything to what we've already told you."

I rose from my stool. "That's okay. We'll go ahead and get out of your hair. Thanks for sparing us the time."

Victoria rose too. We started to leave but then I stopped and turned back, saying, "One more thing ... Did you happen to notice which way that last outfit rolled out of camp? Reason I ask is, I figure those traveling shows probably try to stagger their routes to different towns and settlements, so they aren't appearing too closely on the heels of where another show has already played. I'm surprised that two of 'em showed up here as close as it sounds like they did. But anyway, if we know which way that Greek Potion show was headed, we can try to go off in a different direction for the sake of maybe having a better chance of running across the third outfit."

"Yeah, I see what you mean," replied Hank. "Way I heard, that Greek bunch headed northwest out of town on the Carmody Pass Trail. That goes up through Promise and Fordham and the like. So, keeping in mind that not all the freight routes passable to wagons are even open yet this time of year, you might consider cutting more east and picking up the lower Loveland Trail. Could be you'll find your third show working that route."

I nodded. "Sounds like a good suggestion. Thanks again."

Chapter 22

Before leaving Silvercliff, Victoria and I spotted a telegraph office and took time to send off a couple of wires. One went to Marshal Dick Barton in Cheyenne, a second went to Meadely at the Denver O&PW branch office. We notified each of our present whereabouts, but that we would be on the move. We reminded Barton to channel any news regarding the Everert Byron trial through Meadely and then advised Meadely that the next time we made contact we would hold in place for a reply with any updates. Since his physical limitations kept Meadely mostly confined to the office and his attached living quarters, this seemed like our best bet for an actual message exchange.

After that, we rode out of town on the Carmody Pass Trail in pursuit of the Potion of the Gods traveling medicine show. The visit with the Dales had been beneficial in so many ways. It isolated our quarry to a specific show, it established a logical route said show would be following, and it gave us a clearer idea of the time gap we needed to close in order to catch up.

This was Tuesday, the Greek show had left here last Wednesday; nearly a full week to make up. The encouraging thing, though, was that they were rolling in cumbersome wagons while we were on horseback. Plus we had a strong determination driving us.

So for the rest of that day and the next two, Victoria and I pushed ourselves and our horses as hard as we could. With the well defined freight road to follow, we rode each evening until nearly full dark and started the following mornings at the first glimmer of daybreak. We stripped the pack horse down to bare essentials, lightening his load so he could keep pace. Breakfast was a quick pot of coffee and some strips of bacon; lunch consisted of jerky and hardtack or maybe a leftover biscuit, eaten in the saddle; only at supper did we take time to prepare a more substantial meal.

The weather cooperated with clear skies, fair days, and crisp nights. As we traveled, we met a couple freight outfits making their return trips with empty wagons after having delivered goods to one or more of the camps. We paused for brief, friendly exchanges with each during which we showed Victoria's tintype as a means to ask about the progress of the Greek Potion show. One of the crews knew nothing about it, the other had seen it in passing but had nothing to offer that was new or different from what we already knew.

On the second day we met a pair of hardluck brothers from Kansas who were on their way back home, having given up on striking it rich in the silver fields either from their own attempts at prospecting or as hired labor on the crew of a larger mining outfit. They had no familiarity with any of the traveling medicine shows, but they did bring up hearing about a "lady of the evening" (their words) who'd been killed in the town of Promise, where Victoria and I would soon be arriving. It was as a precaution for Victoria, they said— "though not to say you're that kind of person or anything," one of the brothers was quick to amend—that they mentioned this.

Before parting, we put together a sack of food from our supplies to help them on their way. They were reluctant to take anything, but it was obvious they were in need so we insisted.

After the brothers moved on, Victoria looked troubled. When I asked her about it, she said, "They said the killing of that soiled dove was last Friday. Today is Thursday. Given how we expect to be arriving in Promise shortly, that puts us still nearly a week behind that Greek show—meaning we haven't gained a darn bit on them."

"That's if the brothers were right about the day. They said they *thought* it was Friday," I pointed out. "And they had no details on the victim other than she'd been killed. If it was the work of the Ripper, seems to me the goriness of his work would have been touched on."

Victoria frowned. "You saying you think that killing might have been something else?"

"You remember what that candle drummer said about how many of the crib girls are mistreated in these camps. No doubt some of them get mistreated to death, and not just at the hands of the Ripper." I shrugged. "All I'm saying is we don't know for sure yet what this Promise thing was. We'll find out more when we get there. No matter, though, it doesn't change the fact we've got to keep plugging on if we ever hope to close that gap."

Victoria heaved a sigh. "Okay. You're right. I guess I'm feeling down and, much as I hate to admit it, maybe a little sorry for myself. I'm tired and achy and it seems like forever since I've had a hot bath or slept on anything but the hard ground."

This was the first sign of any peep of complaint from her, even though I'd been moving us along at a pretty brisk pace, especially these past couple of days. I realized she deserved a bit of a break. For that matter, I could use one too; and the horses probably wouldn't mind a warm stall and some fresh hay and grain either.

"Tell you what," I said to Victoria. "It's going to be fairly late in the day when we reach this settlement of Promise. If they've got anything in the way of a decent hotel, we'll stop for the night. You can have your hot bath and a soft bed to sleep on instead of the hard ground. How does that sound?"

Victoria closed her eyes as if savoring the thought. "Heavenly, that's how it sounds ... They're bound to have a livery. I might even be willing to lower my standards to a horse trough for my bath and sharing a bed of soft, fresh straw with the horses."

I shook my head. "Oh no. No half measures. If we don't find the right set-up, we'll move on until we do."

"Let's not waste any more time finding out, then," said Victoria. "Let's hope Promise holds the promise of having what we're looking for."

Four Miles Outside of Fordham Mining Camp Colorado Rockies Front Range Thursday, third week of Spring, 2:30 PM

Even though he'd been anticipating it, the man in the flowing coat was jolted hard when the wheel finally fell off the wagon. After being pitched sharply to one side in the driver's box, he righted himself and immediately hauled back on the reins of the pulling team. Behind him, the wagon rocked and shuddered, emitting loud groans of wood and metal as its right rear corner sagged down and the axle stub gouged deep into the gravelly earth. The rig scraped to a halt.

"Hey! Up ahead!" the man shouted to the lead wagon. "I've got trouble back here!"

The other wagon rolled to a stop and moments later strapping young Leland "Hercules" Gaines came swaggering back with a concerned look on his face. "What's wrong? What happened?" he wanted to know.

The man in the flowing coat eased himself to the ground on the right side of the wagon. "Something in the back," he answered. "Something broke with a devil of a racket."

Stepping around him, Leland quickly spotted the

problem, exclaiming, *"Holy mackerel! The whole dog-gone wheel fell off!"* Only a year or two past twenty, the brawny lad came from a devout Christian family and still adhered to his strict upbringing of abstaining from habits such as smoking, drinking, or cussing.

Following him to the rear of the wagon, the man in the flowing coat said, *"How in the world did that happen?"*

"I don't know, but there it is." Leland pointed down a shallow slope to where the disengaged wheel had rolled and come to rest amidst a small boulder cluster. *"Luckily, it didn't go over a steeper cliff and don't look like it got damaged."*

He dropped to one knee and examined the end of the axle where it was thrust into the ground.

"Can it be fixed?" the man in the flowing coat asked.

Leland didn't answer right away. He was still examining the situation when Professor Kropolaus and Elise *"Aphrodite"* Trent came up.

"Jesus Christ! How the hell did this happen?" blurted the stick thin, leathery-faced, white-maned professor whose language and other personal habits were about as far removed from Leland's as the gods of Greek mythology were from the singular deity the young man was devoted to.

Brushing dirt back from the threaded tip of the axle's iron shaft, Leland said, *"Appears the lug nut came loose and fell off. After a while, the wheel hub, with nothing to hold it in place, worked its way out to the end of the shaft and then fell off too."*

"So can it be fixed?" The professor repeated the question but in a more demanding tone.

Leland straightened up. *"If the wheel ain't dam-*

aged—and it don't look like it is—then, yeah, we can pry up the axle and put it back on. But without the outside nut to hold it in place, it'll likely start working out again once it starts rolling. Might hold quite a while, might go on the slide pretty quick. Hard to say."

"What if we find the nut?" asked pretty blonde Elise, earnestly wanting to help in some way.

"That'd be great, if we could," Leland told her. "But I'm afraid it probably dropped off quite a ways back before the wheel decided to follow suit. Mighty slim chance of ever being lucky enough to spot it."

"How long will it take you to get the wheel back on?"

"A while, I reckon," Leland responded. "First I'll have to fetch the wheel and make sure its okay. Then we'll need to scour those trees over yonder for some logs or stout branches to pry up and block the axle. Ain't gonna be no five minute job, that's for sure."

Elise pursed her pretty mouth and set her jaw firmly. "Then while you men are doing that, I may as well walk back down the trail a piece and take a crack at finding that nut. Who knows, I might get lucky."

"Worth a try, I guess. But I'm telling you, it's a long shot."

"I don't mind. I could use a good stretch of my legs ... Now, what does a lug nut look like?"

Breathing a mildly impatient sigh, Leland said, "Come around to the other side with me. I'll show you on the wheel over there."

Standing off to one side, quietly looking on and listening, the man in the flowing coat could barely restrain a sly smile. Elise could stretch her shapely legs from now until doomsday, he knew, and she would never find the *missing lug nut. He'd made certain of that. Early that morning, before the others rose, he'd loosened the nut but left it snug enough to still hold the wheel in place for a few hours. Then, when the troupe stopped for its nooning, he had slipped back unseen to remove the nut completely and fling it into a deep ravine. From there it was just a matter of time and distance, rolling over the rugged mountain road, before the wheel worked its way off the end of the axle shaft.*

The purpose for all of this was to ensure the troupe was forced to make an overnight stop in the upcoming settlement of Fordham. The cravings of the demons inside the man were growing too demanding to hold in check much longer. And ever since the forced turn-around due to the landslide at Carmody Pass, Kropolaus had been avoiding layovers in any of the towns through which they were re-tracing their route. He feared there would be those who insisted on a repeat performance but not enough in number to make another show worth-while, money-wise. Because this would waste too much too time for too little return, the professor kept pushing through these towns and halting for night camps only in interim wilderness spots.

The man in the flowing coat desperately needed—or, more specifically, his demons required—a nighttime stopover in a town. A mining camp or settlement that would have available the kind of expendable human filth to once more quell the demons for a time.

By rigging the breakdown of the wagon in the af-ternoon hours, the man calculated that Leland and Kropolaus would find a way to somehow nurse it on as far as Fordham where they would then have to stop overnight for proper repair the next morning. That would provide the man the opportunity he needed. He didn't know exactly how, but he would find a way to do what must be done.

He had to. The demons would not be denied ...

Chapter 23

"Now I ain't, what ya call, one of them high fi-
nance fellers. Not by a long shot," Bart Rucker proclaimed. "But, at the same time, I ain't never 'zactly
been allergic to money neither. Reckon I gotta admit I
can't tell for certain positive, on account of I ain't never
rubbed up against very much of it at one time. But I'm
pretty sure, all the same."

Bartholomew "Bart" Rucker had lived in the mountains all of his adult life. He'd first ventured to the high
reaches as a teenager and had gotten in on the tail end of
the mountain-manning years. When that faded out for
the most part, he'd stayed on, continuing to live the life
strictly for himself because it had gotten in his blood. He
hunted, trapped, fished, and panned scrapings of gold to
survive, visiting nearby settlements two or three times
a year to trade his pelts and meager accumulations of
colored dust for additional supplies.

After the war, as more and more people started settling across the front range, he and his Arapaho wife
Sleek Turtle opened up a trading post on the Poudre

River. That's where I knew them from, having stopped by their post a number of times in the course of my travels.

Now, upon Victoria and I arriving in Promise, I was surprised and pleased to find them in business here. BART RUCKER'S PLACE announced the rustic wooden sign over the front door. It looked like (and was, I would later learn) the same one that had been nailed to the front of their trading post. In its new home, the sign hung above the entrance to a business that had grown from its modest origins to a good-sized, full-fledged general store. The store was one of only two wood frame-fronted structures in Promise, the other being a saloon that sat catty-corner across the main street. Other businesses and dwellings were comprised of the different sizes and styles of tents that were common to most mining camps.

Once I spotted Bart's sign, none of those other places were of any immediate interest to me. I steered Victoria directly to the store where, once inside, I was greeted warmly by the old mountaineer and his wife. In her day, Sleek Turtle had indeed been sleek and very lovely with particularly striking dark, almond-shaped eyes. The years had taken away the sleekness of her body, but her now-rounded face was still quite pretty and her eyes had lost none of their allure. In contrast, Bart was a couple inches over six feet and still as lean and leathery as a strip of rawhide. His bushy reddish beard and wild mop of hair had some streaks of gray in them these days and the crow's feet around his eyes were etched in deeper, but otherwise he'd hardly changed since I first laid eyes on him.

Something else that clearly hadn't changed was his

long-windedness. Once our initial greetings and my introduction of Victoria was out of the way, I had asked about his re-location here to Promise and he was still rattling on with an explanation.

"So it was plain ol' curiosity and maybe a tetch of nasty greed what brung us from the Poudre," he was saying. "The lure of hopin' to rub up against more money in hopes of findin' out if I *did* like it as much other folks claim they do. We was gettin' by at the old place, but never gettin' ahead, see, on account of our customers was mostly simple gettin'-by folks just like us. So when I kept hearin' about fellers gettin' rich off the silver strikes over this way, I finally convinced Sleek Turtle we oughta scooch on over ourselves and try for a share of what they had to spend."

Looking around at the spacious, well-stocked interior of his store, I said, "Looks like things are working out pretty good for you."

He nodded. "It's gettin' there. Winter was kinda slow, as you might expect. But Spring has right along been busier and busier." He turned his head to propel some tobacco juice into a nearby spittoon. Then, when his head swung back around, he eyed me from under a cocked shaggy brow. "So that's my tale. What about you? You still workin' for that detective outfit?"

"Am for a fact," I told him.

His gaze went to Victoria. "Let me do a little detectin' of my own. You introduced this pretty thing as Miss *Wilson*. Reckon that means you two ain't hitched then?"

"Your detecting and reckoning are both accurate," Victoria said.

"Whew! That's a relief," Bart responded. "Woulda

plumb troubled my sleep at night, the notion of a prize like you bein' snared by a scalawag like Torrent here."

"Hey. Thanks a bunch, friend," I spoke up.

Bart held up one hand, palm out. "Aw, now don't go gettin' your feathers ruffled. I ain't sayin' you ain't a good friend and a fine feller in most ways. But you're too ornery and set in your ways and got too many miles on you to probably ever settle down, especially not with a rare, refined beauty like this one."

"You caught a rare beauty when you hooked Sleek Turtle," I pointed out. "She was an Indian princess and you were barely civilized. How do you sleep at night with the notion of that in your head?"

Bart's mouth spread in a wide smile. "I sleep just fine at night, thank you. With Sleek Turtle's warm, plump behind cuddled tight against my belly."

"Before this gets too far out of hand," said Victoria, "maybe it's best to explain that Mr. Torrent is a family friend who is lending his detective skills to assist me with a problem."

Bart turned abruptly sober. "In that case, if you got a spot of trouble, ain't nobody better than Torrent to have in your corner ... Is there any way I can help?"

"Hopefully with some information," I answered. "But we got time to get to that. First, is there any place in this settlement of yours where a couple of weary travelers can bed down for the night, maybe get a hot bath and a good meal?"

"You need look no farther than right here, friend Torrent," said Sleek Turtle. She'd been standing quietly off to one side, as was her way, but stepped forward now to speak in her soft, lilting voice.

"That's a pure fact," Bart agreed eagerly. "We built a loft there in the back, see it? Put a couple rooms up there, each with a nice bed and a wash stand, even a patch of carpet on the floor. Ain't nothing fancy, but it's clean and comfortable and we rent 'em out cheap. Heck, for you there wouldn't be no charge at all."

"And if you wish a bath, we have a private area with a big copper tub in a corner below the loft," added Sleek Turtle.

"Comes to vittles, you're already familiar with Sleek Turtle's cookin', Torrent. She ain't lost her touch none, and I happen to know that venison steak with greens and 'taters is on the menu for supper tonight. There'll be plenty for you and Miss Wilson to join us."

I glanced over at Victoria. "Sounds to me like everything we were looking for, wouldn't you say?"

"No question about it." Then, to Bart: "It looks like you and your lovely wife have a couple of guests for the night, Mr. Rucker."

* * * * *

A little over two hours later, we were seated with Bart and Sleek Turtle at the large kitchen table in their living quarters at the rear of the store. Victoria and I had each taken turns in the bath tub and then re-dressed in freshly brushed clothes; my beard stubble was scraped smooth and she looked positively glowing with her lustrous hair piled intricately high in a way I'd never seen her wear it before. Buddy the terrier was curled on the floor beside Victoria's chair, gnawing on a bone Sleek Turtle had given him. A short distance down the street, our horses were stalled at a livery Bart had recommended.

Outside, evening had turned to night and a low, cold wind was moaning in the darkness. Vaguely, from the saloon out across the street, the frantic strumming of a banjo and occasional bursts of raucous laughter could be heard.

"Every night is Saturday night to some handful of miners who make their way into town each time the sun goes down," Bart observed around a mouthful of venison steak. "But they work hard for their fun, so you can't blame 'em too much. They'll go at it hard and loud for a while, but not too late since most of 'em have to go back to diggin' in the morning. They should start to tame down shortly after your heads hit your pillows, so I don't think the noise will bother you too much."

"Once I stretch out on a soft bed with a real pillow, I can guarantee a little bit of noise won't keep me from a good night's sleep," Victoria assured him. "You could trot a full marching band back and forth outside my door and I'd just sink my head a little deeper into that pillow."

I lifted my eyebrows. "That sounds all well and good until it's time for us to roust up and hit the trail again in the morning. If a marching band isn't enough to raise you, what chance am I going to have?"

Before Victoria could reply, Bart said, "Comes to lightin' out in the morning, hoss, you might find you you won't be in too big a hurry yourself."

"What's that supposed to mean?"

"You hear that wind buildin' up out there?"

"Wind in the mountains is nothing new," I replied.

"We had one just the other night that nearly knocked us out of our saddles. We made it through that, we will again. We've got cause to push on without letting up."

"Pushin' through some wind is one thing. But there's reason to think what's blowin' out there now is bringin' something more with it." Bart tilted his head toward his wife. "Sleek Turtle has been tellin' me for a couple days now that there's a bad turn of weather comin'. I didn't feel it myself, even though I'm pretty sharp at sensin' that kind of thing too. But I've learned better than to question Sleek Turtle's knack for such. And now I'm feelin' it right along with her—there' a mean storm brewin' out there."

"Rain, you mean?" asked Victoria.

Bart gave a slow wag of his head. "Not rain. Snow. And a lot of it, I'm thinkin'. We're comin' off a real mild Winter, see, so I got a hunch Mother Nature finally got around to realizin' how easy she was on us and now has took a notion to wallop us one last time just to show she's boss and not to take her for granted."

"The weather does what it will do," Sleek Turtle added somberly.

Victoria and I traded looks.

To Bart, I said, "If you and Sleek Turtle are right ... and I got no call to doubt you ... then I guess landing here to ride out a blizzard is a stroke of luck for us. But being brought to a halt, no matter where, sure works against our momentum and our whole reason for being up this way."

Bart chewed down a big chunk of potato he'd just popped in his mouth, then responded, "Ain't sure what 'momentum' means. Ain't sure what your cause for bein' hereabouts is neither, come to think of it, on account of you never got around to sayin'. Just like you never got around to sayin' what information I might have that maybe could be of help."

"Fair enough," I allowed. "For starters, let me back up a bit and re-introduce my companion as Victoria *Wheeler* rather than Wilson. We started out using the altered name to avoid anyone connecting her to her late father, who was a pretty well known journalist. As is Victoria, in her own right. Under most circumstances she would be pleased and proud to be connected to her father, but for the time being it doesn't fit the cover story we're using for this matter we're involved in ... Simply put, we're on the trail of a particularly vicious killer."

I paused to let that much sink in. In an earlier side discussion, I had convinced Victoria that, due to my full trust in Bart and Sleek Turtle, it wasn't necessary to hide anything from them. What was more, I pointed out we could probe more directly and thoroughly for any information they could provide about the recent killing in Promise if we didn't have to waste time beating around the bush.

Continuing now, I told our host and hostess, "The killer I'm talking about is, we believe, the same one who struck here in Promise just short of a week ago."

"*Matantu!*" Sleek Turtle exclaimed in a hushed whisper.

Bart stopped chewing and his furry brows pinched together above narrowed eyes. "Sweet mother's milk, hoss! You sure know how to toss a hot coal in the powder barrel, don't you?"

"Hot coals have a way of landing in my lap. I deal

with 'em as best I can," I said.

"Yeah, I've knowed about some of those dealin's in the past. How you've managed to keep your fingers from gettin' burnt to nubs is more than I can figure." Those brows stayed bunched tight together. "What surprises me even more, though, is seein' you this time drag somebody else—a young gal no less—along for the risk with you."

This caused Victoria's brows to furrow. "If you're referring to me, sir, I'll remind you that it was I who dragged Mr. Torrent into this matter. It was my late father who initiated the whole thing and, as I also mentioned, Torrent is a friend of the family who felt bound to help me see it through."

"I keep hearin' about your 'late' father. That mean it was this killer who did for him too?" Bart wanted to know.

Victoria shook her head. "No, he died as the result of a different matter. The killer we're after preys only on women. As you're familiar, he attacks them in a particularly savage way and his bloody trail of victims stretches over at least two continents. We mean to bring his butchery to an end."

"Matantu!" Sleek Turtle hissed again.

I looked at Bart. "What does that mean?"

"It's Injun lingo for a powerful evil spirit. The worst of the worst."

"The man we're after is certainly evil. But he is nevertheless just a man, not a spirit," said Victoria. "We're going to run him down, reveal him to the world, and see that he meets justice for his foul deeds."

Sleek Turtle, her eyes wide and an expression of

deep anguish on her face, rose suddenly and left the table, disappearing into a dimly lighted area somewhere in the back.

Bart's eyes followed her, his own expression conveying concern and what looked like a touch of sadness. When his gaze came back to Victoria and I, he said, "You'll have to pardon Sleek Turtle. Her people take their evil spirits mighty serious. The killing of the girl here in town, the plumb nastiness of it, has had my woman rattled ever since. Way she was raised, anybody with sense don't chase *after* a Matantu, they lay low and perform chants to ward it off."

"I mean no disrespect to her beliefs or practices," Victoria replied. "If anything I said or our being her is too upsetting to her now that she knows our business, we can seek elsewhere to spend the night."

"No, Sleek Turtle don't want that no more than I'd hold for it. You're our guests, you stay our guests. She's gone to spread some seeds and such from her medicine bag and say her chants over 'em, but at the same time she respects your right to do what you need to do." Bart paused, regarding us each in turn. "Now ... Let's talk about the killin' that happened here in Promise, and I'll tell you anything I can that might prove of some help to you."

I nodded. "Sounds good. And afterward, maybe you can speak with Sleek Turtle and ask her to offer up a couple chants for us too. We'll take all the help we can get."

Chapter 24

"Wake up easy, hoss ... It's just me."

No matter how weary, I tend to be a very light sleeper. Especially out in the field in the middle of a case. So it was a testament to Bart's skill at stealth honed by years of hunting and surviving in the wilderness that he was able to enter my room and speak before I had any awareness he was there.

I thrust up on one elbow, right hand slipping under my pillow and curling around the Colt Lightning nestled there. I relaxed after a moment when I recognized who it was looming at the foot of my bed, his shaggy-haired silhouette outlined against a rectangle of pale light coming from somewhere beyond the open door.

"Easy," Bart said again.

It was still night. Full dark. I sensed I hadn't been asleep for very long. Outside, the wind was moaning louder and stronger.

After Sleek Turtle left the supper table earlier, Victoria and I hadn't spent a great deal of time talking further with Bart. We learned a few key things in that short amount of time, though. The details of the killing that occurred here nearly a week back matched the Ripper's usual savagery. Yes, it had happened around the time the Greek Potion medicine show was in town, but the body wasn't discovered for a couple of days so no one had considered a connection to anybody from the show.

The most telling bits of information Bart was able to supply had to do with the specific makeup of the troupe involved in the Greek show. There were four in number and he gave a clear description of each. The brawny young man who fulfilled the role of Hercules; the pretty blonde archer presented as Aphrodite; the eccentric grayhair who passed himself off as a professor who had deciphered ancient Greek formulas to come up with the potion that could provide all who tried it with vitality akin to heroes of mythological times; and the syrupy-voiced narrator who presented all of this so appealingly to the gathered crowd.

It was the latter, described by Bart as a lanky man somewhere in his fifties, who was of particular interest. Victoria had in her closely guarded possession a decades old newspaper photograph taken of John Wilkes Booth at the peak of his acting fame, some months prior to him becoming the world's most despised assassin. Standing next to Booth in the shot happened to be Ambrose Tuttle, the only known picture of him. Holding the newsprint replica folded back so that just Tuttle was visible, Victoria showed it to Bart and asked if it resembled a younger version of the narrator from the Greek Potion show. The sharp-eyed old mountaineer hadn't needed to study very long before stating that yeah, he reckoned they could very well be the same person.

The excitement of that confirmation had stuck with me—and Victoria too, I had no doubt—for quite some time after my head hit the pillow. It took us even past the isolation of the Greek Potion show as our target and narrowed it down to a specific person. The narrator. A lanky man in his fifties ... the elusive Ripper finally given solid shape and form and an identity.

All of this rushed through my mind all over again in the second or so it took me to pass from slumber to full wakefulness. The only reason I could think of for Bart to be here now was that he must have thought of something more he deemed too important to wait.

I was soon to find out that was the case ... Only it had nothing to do with the Ripper.

Pushing to a full sitting position, I said, "What's going on, old friend? Something wrong?"

"Nothing else to make of it. You told me all about the killer you're on the trail of. But either you didn't bother to mention—or you flat don't know—about the other owlhoots who are on *your* tail."

I pushed down the covers and swung my legs over the side of the bed. "Okay. You got me awake and you got my attention. Reckon now'd be a good time to tell me what the hell you're talking about."

Bart stood motionless for a couple beats. I couldn't see the look on his face because it was lost in deep shadow. Then, jerking a thumb over his shoulder, he said, "Little bit ago I went over to the saloon to chew the fat some with ol' Gustav, feller runs the place. I wanted to warn him about the bad turn of weather comin' and to knock down a few stiff jolts to oil my joints against the same. While I was there, three men new to Promise walked in." He paused, seeming to give me time to contemplate that. Then he went on. "One of 'em I never saw before but he had the look of a hardcase stamped plenty clear on him. One of the others was Clyde Mungo—don't reckon I have to say any more than that. Don't reckon I have to say much about the third one, neither, 'cept for his name. It was Cherokee Farrow."

The wind outside suddenly sounded colder and meaner.

"Cherokee recognized me right off, same as I did him. After he got done bein' surprised to see me here in Promise, he remembered how you and me have a standin' friendship. So, he wasted no time askin' if you'd passed by this way lately. Said, him and his boys were lookin' to conduct some real urgent business with you ... and the rabid wolf smile on his face when he said it didn't make no attempt to hide that it was business not slanted in your favor."

"How long ago was this? Are they still over at the saloon?" I asked.

"That's where I left 'em. I told Cherokee I hadn't seen hide nor tail of you in a coon's age, but I don't think he believed me. I had to hang around for a while so's to not make it look like I was hurryin' off to give warnin'. I made sure nobody followed me when I left, but it would've been easy enough for one of 'em to watch out the window and see where I came."

I fumbled for my clothes in the dark, stood up and began pulling on my pants.

"You know they was comin' for you?" Bart said.

"Caught wind a while ago they were on my back trail, yeah. But I thought they were a lot farther off. Figured I had time to take care of this other matter before I'd have to worry about those peckerwoods."

"So, the two sitchyations ain't even connected nohow? Sweet mother's milk, hoss, if you have to pick fights with *every* polecat in the territory can't you at least do a better job of spacin' 'em out some?"

"I wouldn't mind. But either I'm slowing down or the polecats are getting faster at catching up."

I stamped into my boots, pulled on a shirt, buckled my gunbelt around my waist. Next I shrugged into the shoulder holster rig but then paused, considering. Cherokee knew I regularly wore a shoulder holster; he'd seen me use it before, would be expecting it. The thing about shoulder holsters is that they're good for concealment and readiness, but not necessarily for quick access. Unlike those touted as "gunslingers" (to an unwarranted extent, in many cases) I am not especially fast on the draw, no matter how the gun is worn. So in this instance—both to counter any expectations by Cherokee and for a speedier grab should the need arise—I took the Colt Lightning from its underarm leather and slipped it inside my belt at the small of my back.

With that adjustment made, I asked, "What about Victoria? Cherokee say anything about her?"

"Mentioned you was travelin' with a gal. But mostly he seemed interested in you."

"Uh-huh. But if I was out of the way, you can damn well bet he'd show some interest in her." I grimaced at the thought of what kind of interest. Then: "Comes to that, Bart, I hope I can count on you to look out for her."

"Thinkin' you even need to ask that is insultin'," he growled in response. "Almost as insultin' as actin' like you figure I'm gonna let you go brace those rannies all on your own."

"A few days ago, another old friend sided me in a fight he shouldn't have been part of," I said. "I ended up burying him. I ain't ready to risk that happening all over again with another old friend."

"But you're talkin' three to one odds, hoss. And that 'breed and his pals, lowlife scum though they may be, ain't exactly a pack of church deacons."

"So do I hold off and wait to be ambushed at that their convenience?" I shook my head. "No, it's because they *are* lowlife scum who think in those terms that I'm going to go at it straight on. Catch 'em off guard. It'll give me the edge."

"You got a strange notion about what gives a body an edge, hoss."

I started for the door.

Bart said, "What about Miss Victoria? Ain't you gonna let her know what's goin' on?"

"Let her sleep. I'll fill her in afterwards," I said as I brushed past him.

Chapter 25

Listening to the wind from inside didn't quite prepare me for its bite when I stepped out into it. It was strong and cold and damp. Tiny ice crystals, the precursors to snow flakes, stung the sides of my freshly shaved cheeks.

I flipped up my jacket collar, pulled the front brim of my hat down low, and began angling toward the saloon across the way, trudging over the muddy, deeply-rutted street. Soft yellow light glowed in the windows of the saloon's wood frame front. They might have looked like a warm, inviting respite if I didn't know what was on the other side. I saw no movement through the yellow glow, no indication that anyone was peering out watching.

I stepped up on the narrow strip of boardwalk running across in front of the entrance. Paused to slip the keeper thong off the hammer of the .44 riding on my hip. Then I twisted the knob and went in.

It was late enough so that there weren't many customers left in the place. Behind the bar leaned a stout man in a striped vest and a wrinkled white shirt, sleeves rolled up to reveal muscular forearms. His head was shaved clean, the weary but stubborn expression on his bulldog face looked like he'd been working on it for fifty or so years. I took him for Gustav, the owner of the joint as mentioned by Bart. Across the bar from Gustav sat a rumpled stringbean with sunken eyes and a saloon pallor. The banjo resting on the bar in front of him indicated he was the one responsible for the plinking I'd heard earlier.

Off to one side, a pair of staggeringly drunk young men were trying to hold up a billiard table long enough for one of them to finally sink the winning shot. A hard-faced middle-aged woman in an off-the-shoulders dress sat watching from a nearby stool, smoking a cigarette and looking bored.

And last but not least, gathered at a round-topped table on the other side of the room, were the three stalwart, upstanding individuals I'd come expecting to find. Cherokee Farrow, a stringy-haired, halfbreed back shooter who liked to work with a "mare's leg" converted Winchester that he carried in a special holster worn at an angle down across his bony shoulder blades sat with his back to the wall. To his left sat Clyde Mungo, a whip thin individual, reputedly a fast draw with bone white hair and a pair of matching Colt .45s that he wore in silver-studded black leather holsters. The third man, the one Bart hadn't recognized, I knew as Harley Brocus, a swaggering tub with bushy blond mutton-chop sideburns and one blue eye, one brown—both of them squinty and mean and a disposition primed to unload on anybody who commented on the oddity of their differing color.

I took all of this in with a single sweep of my gaze, meeting no return looks. I walked slowly up to the bar but didn't take a seat on one of the stools.

Gustav left the banjo player and sauntered down to stand across from me. "What can I do you for?"

"A beer'd be good," I told him.

While he filled a glass, I purposely kept my back to Dundy and his bunch just to show the slobs they didn't intimidate me. But all the while there was an ice cold knot tightening between my shoulder blades.

When the beer was placed before me, I spread some coins on the bartop and then took a long pull. After that, I turned slowly back around to face the room. I leaned against the bar with the glass of beer gripped in my left hand.

Over at the pool table, the two drunks were taking turns still sloppily trying to get a ball to drop into one of the pockets, neither succeeding. The bare-shouldered woman gave me the once over but apparently decided I wasn't worth the effort of getting up and coming over to see if I was interested.

I let my eyes drift to Cherokee's table. I traded looks with each of his cohorts, then let my gaze settle on the 'breed himself.

His mouth formed a smug grin. "So, the old mountain man was a lying sack after all. Just like I figured. He went running to you and, like I figured the rest of the way, your set of onions wouldn't let you duck and dodge once you found out I was on the hunt for you."

"Sounds like you got it all planned out," I said. "Tell me ... What am I going to do next?"

His grin broadened. "You're going to ask me how we

found you, and then you're going to want to know what we got in mind now that we have. Right?"

"Got to hand it to you. You have a real knack for that figuring business," I said. "Wish I was better at it myself."

"Do tell."

"Uh-huh. Way I had it figured, see, I thought you boys would be off Barlow or Deloroso way about now."

Cherokee's grin didn't falter. "Yeah, I can understand how you're disappointed we ain't."

"If we was dumb enough to go just by words told to us," Clyde Mungo joined in, "you're figuring might be closer. But to anybody who can follow ground sign, the trail you'd been leaving up to Gilcrest all of a sudden didn't show going off that other way at all. Took us a while to pick up where it *did* lead, but we managed."

"And lo and behold, here we are," proclaimed Cherokee.

"Yeah. Lucky me."

Now his grin suddenly faded and his expression turned flat. "No. This ain't gonna turn out lucky for you at all, Torrent. You're about to learn a hard lesson on payback for too many years of sticking your damn nose in other folks' business."

"Now hold on!" Gustav suddenly protested. "Whatever this is about, I won't have no trouble in here. The lot of you, pull in your horns and—"

"Shut your mouth, baldy!" Harley Brocus cut him off. "You don't want trouble, just move away and stay clear."

There was a pause, then I heard the scrape of Gustav's feet easing away from behind me.

I remained very still, keeping my gaze centered on Dundy's table, holding all three men within my focus.

Whether or not any of them realized it yet, that was one of two mistakes Cherokee and his cockiness had made by setting this in motion so quick; they were all clumped too closely together in case gunfire erupted. I could blaze away at them with far more abandon this way than if they were spread out. Their second mistake was that, while I was standing unencumbered, they were all seated with their legs partly under the lip of the table, making it harder and slower for them to clear their shooting irons should they take a notion to try.

I'm not saying this was enough to balance out the lopsided odds, but it tilted things back my way at least a little bit. In a dicey situation, you grab what you can.

Responding to Cherokee, I said, "The only time I stick my nose in anybody else's business is when I'm hired to do so. So let me try my hand at figuring again—meaning, I figure that's sort of the same for why you three hombres have decided to pay me a visit. Somebody must have hired you and sent you after me. How about it?"

Cherokee showed his teeth again. "What? So hard for you to believe some folks just plain don't like you?"

"Pure break my heart, if that was the case," I told him.

"Well I don't like your ass. Never did," snarled Brocus.

"Me neither," added Mungo. "And if that gives you a pain in the ticker, so much the better."

"See? For a detective, you're plumb awful at figuring," said Cherokee.

"So I'm supposed to believe nobody's paying you for this? That you all got together one day and based strictly on your mutual dislike for me, made up your minds to ride all this way just to let me know. Is that it?"

"Believe what you want. What the hell difference

does it make?" Cherokee said impatiently.

I shrugged. "It's just that, if you're going to teach me a lesson like you said, it only seems right that I have all the facts so I can learn thoroughly."

"You got all the facts you need. And you're about to learn your lesson alright—permanent-like!"

There it was. The talking was done. I felt the same sense I'd had that night less than two weeks ago in Cheyenne's Kicking Stallion saloon, when the brawl that would involve Russ Wheeler and me had reached the point of inevitability. Only what was about to happen here—what I'd come more or less expecting— would involve more than mere flying fists. Which made it all the more crucial not to wait for the other side to get the jump.

I let go of the beer glass in my left hand and my right, fingers curled, dropped for the grips of my Colt.

But somebody else was faster on the trigger.

One of the saloon windows—the one slightly off center behind where Clyde Mungo was seated—suddenly imploded inward with a shattering roar of sound and a burst of rolling blue gunsmoke and flying glass shards. Within the glittering needles of glass was also a heavy caliber slug that struck Mungo, who was himself starting to reach for his .45s, just below the base of his neck. The impact lifted the white-haired gunny up out of his chair and hurled him forward across the table, flopping loosely and awkwardly with arms splayed wide and a geyser of bright red blood arcing up from of the gaping bullet hole.

Cherokee, who'd been seated right beside Mungo, was jolted out of his chair by a combination of Clyde being propelled into motion as well as the stinging spray of broken glass. He managed to stay on his feet, staggering, while at the same time clawing desperately for the mare's leg holstered on his back.

But my .44 was already drawn by then, and I had long since chosen Cherokee as my first target if and when it came to throwing lead. I planted my first shot square to the center of his chest. When this turned his sideways stagger into a jerky backstep, I sent a second round slamming about an inch higher than the first. This one knocked him back against the wall where his suddenly limp body went into a slow death slide to the floor.

That left Harley Brocus. Just as Cherokee's reaction had been affected by Mungo, Brocus was jostled in turn by the halfbreed lurching into him. But the heavyset man's bulk withstood the bump with hardly any noticeable response. Luckily for me, he was just plain slow in shoving to his feet and pulling the long-barreled Remington he wore in cross-draw fashion.

Still, I'd spent enough time pumping lead into Cherokee so that Brocus managed to get a shot off. He hurried it, though, and it came as I was already shifting and dropping into a slight crouch after my second trigger pull. I felt the burn of his slug singing the hair just above my right ear. Before the big man had any chance to correct his aim, I set my sights on the ample target he made and rapid-fired three rounds straight to its center. He appeared to crumple a little bit as each bullet tore into him and then, after the last one hit, his knees buckled completely and he toppled into a heap.

Everything went suddenly quiet except for the cold wind rushing in through the shattered window. I straightened slowly up out of my crouch. Without conscious thought, I shifted the nearly spent Peacemaker to my left hand, reached to the small of my back and filled my right with the fully loaded Lightning.

My eyes swept the room. Nothing moved except for the coils of gunsmoke twisting in the wind from the window. Gustav had disappeared somewhere in the back of the bar. The banjo player had ducked down behind the end. Across the way, the bare-shouldered woman and the pool players, even in their drunkenness, had been smart enough to hit the deck behind the billiard table when the bullets started flying.

And then the front door opened and Bart Rucker stepped through with a smoking Sharps buffalo gun cradled in the crook of his left arm.

Fordham Mining Camp
Colorado Rockies Front Range
Thursday, third week in Spring,
10:45 PM

For the first time since he'd started being driven by the demons inside him, the man in the flowing coat was taking measures to conceal the results of having done the kind of deed it took to periodically quell them. In the beginning, back in the fog-shrouded hellhole that had first wrung the demons out of a soul twisted by un-bearable anguish, the hue and cry that ensued after the discovery of each such deed had seemed an important part of it all. The boldness, the audacious taunting of the authorities, it was a way of giving voice to his deep agony and shaking up the hellhole and the malignant forces contained therein; forces so foul and insidious they had betrayed and then robbed the man of every-thing he held dear, leaving him nothing but a torment that insisted on some kind of retaliation.

But now the retaliation had become a force of its own. Something he both wanted and needed to maintain. He'd made his voice heard, he'd shaken things up and caused anguish in return. What remained was a matter of survival. For the sake of that, he no longer craved—

nor could afford—notoriety like before. He just needed to keep the demons fed and, one by one, remove the kind of slatterns who'd been the final and most direct link to all that had been torn from his past life.

These thoughts flooded through the mind of the man in the flowing coat as he knelt on the edge of a shallow depression in a thick stand of evergreen bushes and trees. Stuffed down into the depression was the result of his latest deed—the body of yet another dull-witted prostitute he had lured away from others of her kind and then introduced to his scalpel before dragging her to this remote spot on the edge of town where he was now shoving handfuls of dirt and fallen branches over her.

The man's plan to force tonight's layover of his troupe in the town of Fordham had gone as he'd calculated. Thanks mainly to Leland's muscles and directions, aided a meager amount by the professor and the man himself, they'd gotten the wheel back on the second wagon. From there, rolling along very slowly and stopping twice to pry and force the wheel back in place after it began working off again, they'd managed to reach Fordham by evening. Because the local man who passed for a blacksmith lacked the proper nut for a quick repair or the right equipment for a modification, his alternate suggestion was to send his young son the following morning on ahead to Promise to borrow what he needed from a brother there. With no other choice, that's what was agreed to.

Hence, the Greek Potion show troupe settled in for a night's stay in Fordham. While the other members occupied themselves in more sociable ways among the locals, the man in the flowing coat stayed with the usual routine he'd established of keeping to himself. Until, of course, he'd gotten the chance to slip away unnoticed and single out a sheep for the unique shearing required by his demons.

It was the uncertainty of if and when the wheel would be repaired, combined with an approaching storm threatening to delay leaving Fordham even longer, that prompted the man to take the measure of concealing his most recent victim. If he and the others were forced to stay in town for another night or two, he reasoned, that might very well prove enough time for some amount of suspicion to fall on them over a discovery of the slashed remains of even a lowly soiled dove. If the same merely turned up missing, however—especially if the anticipated blizzard hit with its expected fury—then that wasn't likely to generate as much alarm.

For the time being, the man in the flowing coat thought as he put the finishing touches on his concealing efforts while being flailed by evergreen branches whipping wildly in the cold wind, he'd done the best he could. With the demanding fervor of the demons calmed once again, he felt confident he could deal with anything further that might arise. In fact, if this freak late season blizzard lived up to its expectations, that might actually be a good thing. Getting dug out from under its aftermath would keep folks too busy to worry about much else for a while ...

Chapter 26

I didn't get much sleep the rest of the night. For many reasons.

Chief among them, of course, was the furor that followed the shooting in Gustav's saloon. Above the howling wind and through the thin canvas walls of the tents that comprised dwellings in the vicinity of the saloon, the gunfire had been too loud and distinct to ignore. Several citizens came pouring out to see what was going on, and then the ensuing buzz of voices and activity drew forth even more.

Despite her earlier declaration that not even a marching band outside her door would rouse her, it didn't take long for Victoria to also show up in the crowd. She naturally made a beeline to me, first to make sure I was okay and then to deliver a few choice words (with the promise of plenty more to follow as soon as we were alone) for not letting her know as soon as I found out Cherokee and his bunch were in town.

As far as the fate of three hardcases, Gustav and his banjo player provided all the testimony necessary to establish they'd deservedly got what they came gunning for. For his part, Bart Rucker—whose shot through the window was what had taken out Clyde Mungo—was feeling kind of low for doing what he called "back-shootin' a critter, even if he was a lowdown snake." The way he told it, he'd only just positioned himself outside the window and couldn't clearly tell what was being said inside when he saw Mungo start to reach for his gun. If he was going to be of any help to me, Bart had to quickly decide, eliminating the threat of the gunslinger seemed the most obvious thing to do. I sure as hell couldn't fault his choice (even though I'd tried to dissuade him from joining in), and I made sure nobody else did either. The only one who did have a complaint was Gustav—for his window being blown to bits on the eve of an impending blizzard.

Toward solving that problem, several of the men present gathered up some boards and a heavy sheet of canvas and went to work covering over the damage. The results weren't pretty, but at least the patch was effective.

Some comparably minor patching also called for was the bullet burn I'd received above my right ear as well as a handful of scrapes and cuts on my face and hands from flying shards of glass. Spotting these, Victoria put aside being sore at me long enough to insist on cleaning and tending them. Sleek Turtle brought over some salve to smear on that was supposed to help with the healing. How successful it was I'd have to wait and see, but its initial application to the bullet burn stung about twice as bad as the damn bullet did.

Throughout all of this, I continued to be nagged by the unanswered question I'd been probing to get before the shooting started—what was behind hardcases coming after me? I'd held out hope that the unpleasant task of going through the dead men's pockets and saddlebags might yield something. But it didn't. Not necessarily.

Each man had a pocketful of twenty dollar gold pieces, indicating recent payment for something. Something like a deposit on hunting down and killing me, maybe? This thought harkened eerily back to the gold pieces found in the pocket of Hal Kraig, the Cheyenne shotgunner who had tried for me the night Russ Wheeler was killed. But any connection to that had to be strictly coincidental. Otherwise, these most recent dead men had nothing more in their possessions except for a few standard items like tobacco, snuff, a couple combs, some playing cards, dice, and a half dozen leather-encased pornographic tintypes in the pocket of Brocus.

And one other item found in Cherokee Farrow's shirt pocket; a folded piece of paper with some sketches on it. This I kept to myself, palming it and slipping it into my own shirt pocket for closer examination later on.

After things began to tame down and the bodies had been carried to a wood shed out back where they would stay cold enough not to ripen until burial could be arranged, I suggested part of the gold coins go toward a round of drinks or everyone, double for the crew who had made the temporary window repair. The rest I told Gustav to keep toward the expense of bringing in new glass and whatever else would be needed for a full and proper repair.

It was into the wee hours when I finally took my leave from the saloon and headed back to my room to try and get some sleep.

But two things stood in the way of that happening right away.

The first was Victoria, who had gone on ahead but stayed awake, waiting with the door to her own room ajar so she could hear me coming up the stairs to the loft.

"Is this where you finish chewing me out for not letting you know right away that Dundy's bunch had arrived in town?" I asked when I saw her standing there in the opening.

But even as I said it, I could see that the look on her face was more contemplative than combative. And her tone was softened when she responded, "No, I'm past that. You'll have to forgive my foolish pride and hair trigger resistance to being coddled."

"Emancipation, right?"

"More like that stubborn streak you accused me of before. I don't like being left out of things."

"Even the risk of getting shot?"

"Let's not start that again. Besides, it didn't stop you, did it?"

"It was me they were after," I insisted.

"And so you went to accommodate them ... straight on."

I didn't have a response for that.

Sighing, Victoria said, "Never mind. I didn't stay awake to start an argument about your choices, your own stubbornness. In fact, I want to tell you that I - I admire them ... admire you, what you stand for and most things about you. How could I not, I realized, when you remind me so much of my father?"

"I'm not sure I'm deserving of the comparison, but I surely won't object to it," I told her.

"I further realized," she went on, "that even though I'm usually quite slow to warm to anyone ... Well, I've quickly grown awfully fond of you, you big oaf. And if anything were to happen to you—especially coming so soon on the heels of losing Father—it would be devastating. So you can damn well quit being so eager to risk your neck! You hear?"

I lifted my eyebrows. "I never realized it was something I was being exactly eager about. It may not be the greatest neck in the world, but it's the only one I got."

At which point Victoria stepped out of her doorway, reached up to place a palm on either side of said neck, then pulled my head down to plant a warm daughterly kiss on my cheek. Releasing her hold and drawing back, she said, "I'm serious, darn it. I want you around to help me bring down the Ripper and then for a long time after that."

"So happens that fits my plans, too. Just remember, if that storm hits the way it feels like it's going to, then our Ripper chase might have to be put on hold until it blows over."

Victoria's expression grew stern. "That's okay. If the storm halts us, then it will halt the show troupe as well. When they can move again, so can we. It'll just mean a delay of the inevitable for when we catch up."

"Okay. But just in case it turns out we're able to cover some ground tomorrow after all," I suggested, "we'd best try to catch some sleep so we're ready."

Which led to the second thing that kept me from being able to follow my own advice. I wasn't going to be able to get any sleep, not right away, not until I pondered some things.

After lighting a candle on the nightstand, I sat down on the edge of the bed and pulled two folded pieces of paper out of my shirt pocket. One was what I'd taken off Cherokee Farrow's dead body, the other I'd been carrying in the pocket for some time. I unfolded each and held them side by side before me. Studying, comparing. Together, the papers told a story. Exactly what it was, I wasn't sure. Not yet. After several minutes of rolling things back and forth inside my head, first one way and then another, it came down to only two possibilities. Both were very troubling. More frustrating still was the sorry fact I could do nothing more to sort it any finer. Not now, not anytime soon.

I finally re-folded the papers, put them back in my pocket, blew out the candle and stretched out on the bed to try and get some sleep.

Chapter 27

When Bart called Victoria and I for breakfast the next morning, it turned out he had more to serve us than just the meal Sleek Turtle was preparing.

"If I hadn't gone over to Rafe Blessing's place to buy some of the fresh cream he sells from his milk cow," he started out, "I never would've run into the young feller comn' out of Calhoun's blacksmith shop. I recognized him as Custis, Calhoun's nephew from Fordham. When I saw he was gettin' ready to climb back on his horse and ride off, I asked him where in blazes he was headed with a storm gettin' ready to land on us."

Outside, the blizzard hadn't yet arrived but it showed every sign of being almighty close. The sky was a churning, ugly gray mass and the snow flakes carried by a still-howling wind were growing larger and more frequent.

"So Custis tells me," Bart went on, "that he's headed lickety-split back to Fordham, figurin' he can ride hard enough to beat the storm. He's got this gunny sack of tools that he's borrowin' from his uncle, see, to take back to his pa—that'd be Calhoun's brother, who's a blacksmith over in Fordham—on account of his pa has an important wagon repair to make but don't have the right tools for the job."

Frowning, Victoria said, "That sounds a bit troubling, doesn't it? How old is this boy, and what kind of father would send his son out under threat of such bitter weather?"

"I don't rightly know how old Custis is," Bart replied. "But he's a sturdy, savvy lad. Born to the mountains. He'll make it back okay."

"I certainly hope so."

"The main reason I'm mentionin' the whole thing, though, has to do with the wagon that's broke down in Fordham." Bart paused, let his gaze cut back and forth between Victoria and me. Then: "You see, it's part of that Greek Potion medicine show you two seem so interested in."

I'd already taken a seat at the Rucker kitchen table and was reaching to accept the cup of coffee Sleek Turtle was holding out to me. At Bart's words, my head snapped around so fast my hand jerked and nearly bumped away the coffee. "Whoa. Are you saying that Greek show is right this minute as close as the next town?"

"That's how it shakes out. If one wagon is busted down, I don't reckon 'tother is off somewhere without it."

"But how can that be?" said Victoria. "If the show played here nearly a week ago, they should be much farther along by now."

"Way it was told to Custis," Bart explained, "they got as far as Carmody Pass but had to turn back on account of findin' it blocked by a landslide that wasn't gonna be cleared for a week or more. Ain't no other open wagon road without backtrackin' all the way here to where they can catch the fork what goes off toward Poudre River."

"How far is it to Fordham?" I asked.

"Couple, three hours by wagon. Say half on horseback. Even less, if you spur it hard."

Victoria and I exchanged glances and then, nearly in unison, said, "We need to get there!"

"Now? That's crazy talk. You'd be ridin' straight into the teeth of the storm," Bart protested.

"You said that boy Custis would make it okay," I reminded him.

"Yeah, but—"

I stood up. "No buts about it. Is Custis already gone?"

"Yeah, he took off right after he got done talkin' to me."

"That doesn't change anything. We'll be following along after him, then," declared Victoria.

Bart made a sour face. "I don't understand this big, reckless rush. That show outfit ain't goin' nowhere. Not with a busted wheel and a storm comin'. And when they do roll again, it'll bring 'em right here to catch the Poudre fork. Smack into your laps, in other words. Why not relax, sit tight and wait for 'em to come to you?"

"You're right, old friend, you don't understand," I told him. "This runs too deep and too personal and there's too much behind it for us to hold off now, not when we're this close. We have strong reason to believe Sleek Turtle's *Matantu* is part of that show, and every second his evil continues unchecked is another second too long."

Bart heaved a heavy sigh. "I shoulda knowed. I had a hunch you'd react this way." He sighed again. "All right. At least sit back down long enough to cram in some bacon and swallow down some hot coffee. You'll be glad you did. Then go get dressed in your warmest duds—take a couple parkas off the store shelves if you need to ... While you're doin' that, I'll fetch around your dang horses."

* * * * *

Barely twenty minutes out of town, the storm descended on Victoria and me. It came like a massive, murky white wall slamming over the landscape. A thousand snow flakes, hurtling like arrow tips, stung our faces and heightened gusts of wind took our breath away. Once we'd endured the initial blasts and had ourselves braced against it, though—bundled in the heavy parkas Bart had provided, with thick wool scarves wrapped around our necks and over our mouths and noses—it became a matter of leaning forward in our saddles and urging our mounts to keep going.

"If visibility turns bad, and it no doubt will," Bart had advised, "keep pushin' straight into the wind. If your horses start steppin' through brush or rocks, you'll know they wandered off the road. Rein 'em back quick and hard to where the goin' is clear. Get 'em close enough to Fordham where they start pickin' up the smell of the town on the wind, they'll steer themselves toward it the rest of the way."

Twenty minutes turned into forty, and then more. We kept pushing our horses hard but bucking the wind and the rapidly deepening snow made the going tough. Yet they slugged on, responding bravely to what was asked of them.

Acting on another piece of advice from Bart, Victoria and I had tied a connecting rope between us to ensure we didn't get separated. More than once, when wind gusts whipped up and the snow particles whirled so thick I couldn't even see my horse's ears out ahead of me, I was mighty glad to have the reassuring feel of an invisible Victoria tugging back on the other end of the rope.

And then, at last, as we descended down into a shallow valley, we could make out blobs of yellowish illumination through the swirling whiteness. After that, the irregular shapes of tents and other structures began to be discernible.

We'd made it to Fordham.

Chapter 28

The town buildings lay bunched on the floor of the valley. Some high cliffs to the north blocked out a portion of the wind, though enough of it still swooped down to rattle the smattering of wood frame structures and shake hell out of the tents.

We spotted a livery barn among the first buildings we came to and immediately swung our horses over to it. My calling out and dismounting to go pound on the wide double doors in front raised no one, so I let myself in through a narrow side entrance off to one side. Once inside, I dislodged the wooden bar holding the big doors shut and swung one of them back so Victoria could bring the horses through. After I'd closed it and shoved the bar back in place, the sudden blotting out of the storm was a relief to all. The inside of the barn was dim and smelled of musty straw and tangy manure, but it was quiet and warm and wrapped around us like a welcome embrace.

"Wonder where everybody is," said Victoria, swinging down from her saddle. We'd left Buddy, the terrier, in the care of Sleek Turtle; he'd already taken quite a shine to her table scraps.

"If they're smart, they're probably home with the shutters and doors closed tight around them," I said. "I doubt whoever runs this place is expecting much in the way of business on a day like this."

I'd no sooner got that out than we heard the creak of a door and the slow, uneven shuffle of feet coming from deeper within the barn. Looking around, we saw a low-burning lantern floating toward us, held high in a bony-knuckled fist attached to the long, stringy arm of a limping old man dressed in baggy bib overalls. In his other hand he was gripping a three-tine pitchfork.

"Who the hell is there?" he growled. "What kind of infernal idjit is out and about in weather like this?"

"Reckon that'd be a couple folks with poor judgment, old timer," I answered. "We thought we'd be able to beat the storm here, but we figured wrong."

"You sure as hell did. Coupla lunkheads ... Lucky you ain't stranded out there somewhere, freezin' off your asses and what must be little pea-sized marbles that pass for brains rattlin' between your ears."

He'd reached us by this point and, in the glow of the lantern he was holding up, he could see Victoria as she removed her scarf and hat, shaking the snow off them while at the same time tossing loose the long spill of hair that had been pushed up inside the hat. "Wailin' wildcats—you're a girl!" the old man exclaimed.

Victoria smiled. "Yeah, I noticed that, too. Even with my pea-sized little brain."

In the smoky illumination of his lantern I could see the old timer actually blush. "Aw, man – er, I mean,

Miss – I'm powerful sorry for those words. And the cussin', too ... I never figured in a hunnert years it'd be a woman showin' up at a time like this."

Still smiling, Victoria said, "No need to apologize, sir. Under the circumstances, you have every right to question the wisdom we are displaying."

"Ain't so sure about all those fancy words. But I gotta wonder all the more how anybody smart enough to use 'em is out in this storm." Having addressed that to Victoria, he then pinned me with a glare, saying, "And what in blazes is your excuse, bub, for draggin' a lady out into it?"

Having removed my own hat and shaken the snow off of it, I then used it to swat more accumulation off the front of my parka as I said, "Like I already told you, a matter of bad judgment. I wasn't counting on the storm hitting so hard so fast."

"And it was a judgment I fully supported," added Victoria. "I assure you, I wasn't dragged against my will, sir."

The old man winced. "Quit callin' me 'sir'. It makes me fidgety. My name's Reese. Reese Laberty."

"You run this place, Mr. Laberty?" I asked.

Another wince. "No 'mister' neither. Just make it Reese. And I only work here, for Herb Darwood who owns the joint. I got a sleepin' room in the back. I heard you bangin' on the door but couldn't make it out quicker on account of I don't move around very fast on this bum leg."

"Sorry I sort of barged in, but we were pretty anxious to get in out of the snow."

"That's understandable enough."

"My name's Lew Torrent, by the way. This is Miss Victoria Wilson."

"Howdy." His eyes flicked past me to our snow-caked horses. "You lookin' to stall your animals?"

"You bet. They've earned it. A good rubdown, plenty of grain and hay, some warm, dry bedding."

Reese's gaze came back to Victoria and me. "Not much doubt you two will also be spendin' the night in town. Maybe a couple or three nights, dependin'. We got a couple good boardin' places, if you're interested. Or, if you'd rather, Leo and Madge Knudsen rent out some nice rooms upstairs over their cafe just up the street."

"You're certainly right about us needing a place to stay for however long it turns out to be necessary," Victoria said.

The old man eyed the two of us for a beat. Then: "If it ain't bein' too forward, mind if I ask what brings you to Fordham?"

"Not at all," I assured him. "You see, we've been scouring all through these foothills looking for Miss Wilson's missing brother. The last she heard from him ..."

So Victoria and I quickly went through our practiced spiel, complete with her showing the anonymous tintype supposedly of her brother. But this time, in recognition of having located the Greek Potion show, we added a new wrinkle: Victoria alleged that, in the last letter she got from her brother where he wrote of joining the Greek show as a means of building a grubstake, he also mentioned a man named Ambrose Tuttle, already a member of the troupe, who was mentoring him. This was why we were so anxious to catch up with the show since hearing it was broke down here in Fordham, we explained. Even if Victoria's fictional brother was no longer a part of it, we were hoping at least Tuttle still was and that he might have an idea where young Joe had gone to. By tossing out Tuttle's name—starting with Reese and expanding to others—we were hoping it would jar a reaction out of the man himself that would cause him to do something desperate enough to help reveal the evil depth of his true identity.

"Sure wish I could be of some help about your brother, ma'am," Reese responded once we ere done laying it out for him. "But I'm afraid I ain't got nothing to offer. It's true those medicine show folks are back in town, their wagon broke down and all like you say. But I've never had much truck with 'em, not when they was here before and not since they came back. Well, other than stallin' their pullin' team horses that is. I seen enough of 'em, though, to tell you there's only four in the group and none of 'em come close to matchin' that pitcher you showed me. On 'tother hand, two of 'em are older gents who maybe could be that Tuttle fella you mentioned. I never caught their names, 'cept one of 'em claims to be a professor or doctor or some such."

"Every little bit helps," I told him. "We appreciate your time."

"Like I said, wish I could help more. But what help I *can* be and oughta be, is to tend these horses of yours before all that snow and cold sinks to their bones."

"Yes, by all means go ahead take care of that," I said. "But one more quick question before we get out of your way ... Do you have any idea where the members of that show troupe are staying, or where we might be able to find them?"

Reese had moved to our horses and was beginning to cluck soothingly to them. He turned his head to look over his bony shoulder at me and answered, "Mostly, leastways when they was here before, I think that outfit sleeps in their own covered-over wagons. Might be different this time, what with the weather. Any case, the wagons are at the blacksmith's, up the street between the cafe and saloon. There's a lot of folks gathered at both places this mornin'—hunkered against the weather while they cuss and dis-cuss it. Could be you'll find your show folks in amongst 'em, or leastways probably somebody who'll know better where they are."

"Thanks for the information. And, again, for your time. We'll head up the street to try the places you suggest."

Chapter 29

The trip from the livery to the cafe was a short one but trudging back out into the wintry blast made it far from a simple stretch of the legs. On the other hand, ducking out of it once again and stepping into Knudsen's eatery made the steamy warmth and delicious aromas waiting there all the more pleasant.

Entering amidst a gust of cold wind and swirling snow flakes naturally caused the faces of those already present to turn in order to see who the new arrivals were. Spotting two strangers meant the looks took on some definite surprise and maybe a touch of suspicion that resulted in eyes lingering on us a bit longer than normal.

As far as the makeup of staring patrons, it was mostly men, a dozen or so in number, dressed in rugged work clothes and tending toward an average age crowding thirty. The most notable exception was a matronly, rosy-cheeked woman standing behind a lunch counter at the fare end of the room. She was wearing a frilly apron, had her silver hair pinned up in a bun, and the somewhat wary expression on her face promptly gave way to a welcoming smile.

Heeling the door shut behind Victoria and me, I flashed what I aimed to be an ingratiating smile of my own and proclaimed, "Boy, it sure is a lot nicer in here than it is out there!"

This generated some mutterings among the men seated around the room's various tables. There were a couple chuckles, but I also caught a "no shit" and at least two "what the hell ya expect?".

But the response I most appreciated and decided to focus on came from the rosy-checked woman, who said, "We do our best, stranger. But it's really not very hard to be more hospitable than a blizzard."

I traded looks with Victoria and we moved forward, weaving between the tables to advance on the woman at the counter. As we did this, we began unbundling some of our wraps and when Victoria once again shook out her long, lustrous hair she got a far more charitable reaction from the crowd of onlookers than my lighthearted remark had earned.

"Land's sake, girl!" exclaimed the rosy-cheeked woman. "What are you two poor souls doing out in this dreadful weather? Where are you from—did you get lost?"

"We rode in from Promise," Victoria answered. Then, smiling, she added, "No, we're not lost. Though you might well think we misplaced some wisdom by thinking we could make it here ahead of the storm."

At this point, a short, rotund man with thinning hair and a gray-flecked walrus mustache came through a door behind the counter that I guessed led back to the kitchen area. He was wiping his hands on an already stained cook's apron that swelled out over his belly. "What's going on, Mama?" he wanted to know, his voice touched with a slight accent.

"These impetuous children just rode in through the storm. Hurry and get them some cups of hot coffee," the woman said in an off-handed way that suggested her giving orders was not an uncommon thing. As further demonstration, she wagged a finger at Victoria and me and told us, "You two, sit. You look half frozen, but we'll fix you right up."

A moment later we were seated on stools at the counter with cups of dark, steaming brew in front of us. "I'm Madge Knudsen, this is my husband Leo," the woman announced. "May I ask who we have the pleasure of serving?" She waited for Victoria and me to introduce ourselves and then was ready with another question. "And what, pray tell, is it about our little town that made you so anxious to get here that you'd brave the nasty turn of weather we're having?"

"Mama!" scolded her husband. "You are too bold with your nosiness."

"Nonsense," Madge countered. "I can tell when folks are practically busting to get something off their chests, and these youngsters have got that look plastered all over them. Why else would they come riding in here on a doggone blizzard? So I'm just helping to cut to the chase."

I grinned. "You sure have us pegged, ma'am. We definitely are here to try and get some answers on a very urgent matter. I wish everyone would be so open and easy to talk to."

So once again Victoria and I went through our spiel.

As we did so, I was very aware that—in addition to Madge and Leo leaning eagerly into every word from their side of the counter—most of the patrons hunched over their tabletops behind us, were also bending their ears to what we were saying. That was fine. The wider and sooner word spread about what we were looking for, the quicker we stood the chance of getting our hoped for reaction.

"I'm sorry we have no answers to help you," Madge said sadly, handing back the tintype Victoria had passed her and Leo to look at. "You can pass your picture around the room if you like, but if neither Leo or I recognize that face then I'm pretty sure none of our regulars will either. However, you might still be in luck. Because two of the folks directly involved with the medicine show you're asking about happen to also be present. They" —she pointed— "are sitting right over there."

I turned my head and followed the line of her finger. Sure enough, though I hadn't noticed them upon making our blustery entrance, seated at a small table over against the side wall, somewhat separate from the other patrons, was a broad-shouldered young man and a slender girl with a scarf tied over her blonde hair. From the advertising posters I'd studied, I had no trouble recognizing them as the pair of performers billed, respectively, as Hercules and Aphrodite in the Greek Potion show.

Victoria and I wasted no time heading over to talk with them. Their eyes followed us as we approached their table and, from their expressions, it appeared they'd overheard enough to already have a pretty good idea what we had in mind.

Victoria spoke first, saying, "Please pardon us if we're

interrupting. But we would be very grateful if you could spare us a few minutes of your time."

"It's a free country," Hercules said, guardedly if not somewhat sullenly. "What's on your mind?"

Before either Victoria or I could respond, the blonde girl beat us to it. "We heard most of what you told Madge and Leo. We'll go ahead and have a look at your picture, I like you, but I doubt we can help you because there's been no other young man besides Leland as part of our show for all the time we've been with it."

"How long is that?" I asked.

"Since last season. We toured with the professor then and he invited us to join him again this spring."

"And that name you asked Madge about—Tuttle, was it?" Leland, the part-time Hercules, shook his head. "That's nobody either Elise or me has ever heard of either."

"There's only four in our whole troupe," Elise said. "Us, Professor Kropolaus, and John, our narrator. The professor and John are both in their fifties, so they're surely no match for your missing brother, ma'am."

"John?" Victoria echoed.

"John Sharpe. He narrates our show to link the performances of Leland and me and then the lead-in to the professor and his potion."

"How long has he been with the show?"

"Since we started out this spring. He answered an ad the professor placed."

"But he never, not even early on, had anyone with him? A friend or associate who might possibly have been my brother?" Victoria asked, playing our ruse to the hilt.

Elise gave a little laugh. "You don't know John. He's very much a loner. Apart from rehearsals and shows, he hardly mingles even with us. He keeps to himself, smoking his stinky old pipe, just reading and meditating."

Victoria sighed. "This is all very puzzling and distressing. My brother clearly wrote of a medicine show built around Greek mythology and a man named Tuttle who'd offered to mentor him ... I – I don't know what to think."

"Please don't take it that we doubt or dispute anything you've told us," I said to the young couple. "But you must understand that, after all our effort to catch up with your show, we don't want to give up without being thorough. For that reason, I think it's still worth talking to your professor and this John fellow. Do you know where we could find them?"

Leland grinned. "The professor's up the street at the saloon. He likes to sit in on a good poker game whenever he can find one ... and to also do a little drinking of stuff other than his own potion."

"As for John," said Elise, "you'll find him in his room."

"Room?"

"Upstairs. When it became obvious we were going to be stranded here for an extended time, what with the broken wheel and then the storm," she explained, "the professor went ahead and arranged for us to stay in the rooms Madge and Leo have for rent. John is in number three, second on the left when you get to the hallway."

Chapter 30

Leo Knudsen showed Victoria and I to the stair- well leading up to his rental rooms on the second floor. Once he'd gone back to his kitchen and left us alone at the bottom of the steps, Victoria clamped my forearm in a tight grip and gazed up at me with wide, excited eyes. In a barely contained whisper, she said, "This is it! Do you feel it? We're on the brink of seizing the fiend who has both horrified and captured the imagination of the whole world. All the groundwork my father laid, everything that's been propelling us through these mountains, it all comes to a head and ends right here!"

"Seems like," I allowed. I was experiencing my own quickened pulse and could sense a rush of what felt like unstoppable momentum. But I'd learned a long time ago that nothing is certain until it is completely done.

"The smug devil is even up to his old tricks," Victoria hissed. "Taunting everyone, though a bit more subtly, just like he did the London cops when he first started calling himself Jack the Ripper and Saucy Jack."

I frowned. "Not sure I follow you."

"Don't you get it? John Sharpe? The names John and Jack have always been interchangeable—and how many women has he sliced and slashed with a *sharp* blade?"

I felt an icy trickle run down my spine as I realized she was right. The cocky bastard *was* taunting everybody! Unbuttoning my parka for easier access to the holster on my hip, I lifted the .44 from its leather and dropped it instead in the side pocket of the heavy coat.

Victoria's eyes followed the move. "You can't shoot him! It's important we take him alive."

"I understand that. This is just a precaution for something I consider even a bit more important ... *us* staying alive."

We started up the stairs. Since they, like the rest of the building, weren't constructed with the greatest precision, they creaked with each step. But under the relentless battering of the howling wind outside, the whole structure creaked and groaned even louder.

We found ourselves in a narrow hallway, standing in front of a door with the number 3 painted on it. With a final exchange of somber looks, we took deep breaths and braced ourselves. I slipped my right hand into my pocket and closed it around the Colt. At the same time, my left raised to touch the small leather pouch dangling from around my neck—Sleek Turtle's medicine bag, that she'd insisted I wear to help ward off evil. It seemed like an appropriate time to call upon whatever power it might have.

Victoria reached out and rapped a hard knock on the door. After a slight pause, a voice from within said, "Who's there?"

"A word with you, sir," Victoria called back.

Another slight pause, and then the door opened. I'm not sure what I expected, but if the man standing there was Jack the Ripper then he was truly evil incarnate. And yet, appearance-wise, he projected no particular feature to convey that. Just a tall, trim man in his fifties clad in a long, loose, almost cape-like coat. In one hand he held a large-bowled pipe with a curved stem. A starched, strikingly white shirt collar hugged his throat and at the V of its lapels was a precisely knotted tie, maroon in color. Above that a long, narrow face framed by thick, dark hair showing no signs of gray. But despite the lines and faintly sagging flesh added by the intervening years, it was most definitely the same face as that of the young man pictured in the old newspaper photo standing beside John Wilkes Booth.

"What is the nature of this call? What can I do for you?" The question was spoken in a rich, smooth baritone.

I left it up to Victoria, and she answered in a strong, steady voice, saying, "We're here to see Ambrose Tuttle."

The man in the doorway was very good at masking any inadvertent reaction to the name. But I'm pretty good, too, at what I do. Years of dealing with liars and cheats and con artists of every stripe taught me good. And no matter how well masked, I saw a reaction on Tuttle's face. It was there in the ever so faint tightening at the corners of his mouth and the minuscule pinching of his eyes.

In a voice that remained smooth and calm, however, he replied, "I'm sorry, there's no one here by that name."

"Are you sure?" Victoria insisted.

"Very. Good day to you."

Tuttle eased back half a step and started to close the door. But I reached over Victoria's shoulder and slapped a preventing palm against it, saying, "How about a pal of his then ... calls himself Jack the Ripper?"

All the cool, imperturbable calm the man had been maintaining up to that point suddenly shattered and what burst through in its place was an intense, menacing, unmistakable madness!

"No!" Instead of a rich baritone, the single word came out in a raw, guttural roar. Simultaneously, the hand holding the large-bowled pipe thrust forward toward the face of Victoria, who was positioned slightly ahead of me, hurling ash and burning curls of tobacco across her eyes and nose. She emitted a short, startled scream and jerked back against me.

While Victoria and I were momentarily entangled in the doorway, Tuttle whirled and raced across the width of the room. Without hesitation, he launched himself agilely and went crashing out through the window!

I cursed at the sight of him disappearing into a cloud of furiously swirling snow, but at the moment my greater concern was for any injury Victoria might have suffered. I spun her around to face me and began frantically wiping ash and embers from her face. "Did it get in your eyes—are you okay?" I demanded.

In a ragged half-sob she replied, "I – I'm okay. It burned my cheek a little, but not my eyes."

I took her by the arm and tugged her gently but firmly into the room, searching for a wash basin and spotting one over against the wall. Leading her to it, I poured water from a pitcher onto a clean towel and began carefully dabbing her face. "Oh, that feels good. Yes, that's better," she murmured.

Bitter wind and clouds of gusting snow were pouring into the room from the broken window. Out in the hall I could hear voices and the clump of hurrying feet. Moment later, a scowling Leo Knudsen was filling the doorway. "What's all the commotion? What's going on here?"

"A madman just threw hot ashes in the face of this girl and then escaped out the window," I told him.

"Mein Gott!" Leo exclaimed as other faces crowded up behind him.

Victoria clutched my arm. "I'm okay ... Go after him! Don't let him get away!"

Easing back from her, I said to Leo, "Somebody get over here and help this girl. Keep flushing her face with cool water. I'm going after a killer—anybody wants to help, come on and follow along before the new snow covers up our tracks!"

I hurried to the shattered window and put one foot up on the sill, leaning out into the buffeting wind and eye-stinging snow. The drop to the ground wasn't as great as I expected. Down below, I could make out the disturbed ground cover where Tuttle had landed and then tracks leading off. But everything was being rapidly erased by continuously falling, blowing snow. I planted my foot more solidly and then shoved out and down ...

Fordham Mining Camp
Colorado Rockies Front Range
Friday, third week of Spring,
11:00 AM

How!?

How had they found him?

Who were they?

These were the thoughts racing, screaming through the mind of the man in the flowing coat as he ran stumbling and staggering through the slashing wind and boiling clouds of snow. Never before had he been forced to flee like this, feeling so desperate and so threatened by the thought of capture. Once or twice, back in the fogbound hellhole where it had all started, he'd had to hurriedly slip away from a scene where he'd done a deed. But that had been easy. He knew the twisting maze of streets and alleys so well ... and there was always the fog, the cloak of invisibility he could count on to envelope and protect him like an old friend.

But today there was no fog. There was only the biting cold and the pounding wind and snow. Not friends; far from it. Rather threats in their own right. Threats to numb him and grind him down and smother him into lifelessness.

But no, he would not allow that to happen! He must find a way to survive the weather and avoid capture. He had to! He had successfully eluded the most renowned police force in the world, he surely could outwit a pair of backwoods bumpkins who'd somehow stumbled onto his identity. But in order to do that, he first had to keep from freezing to death.

The trademark long coat the man wore was a fairly substantial garment, but never meant to protect against blizzard conditions. The man knew he had to quickly find some additional warm wrapping to protect his core heat. Damn! If only he hadn't panicked and bolted the way he did. He should have stood his ground and challenged those upstarts who appeared at his door. They couldn't have proven anything. How could they? Mere suspicions and accusations—however they'd acquired them—could never have brought him down.

But he'd played right into their hands by lashing out and then fleeing.

Now he'd have to make the best of it.

Having raced blindly away from the back side of the cafe, the man now stopped running for a moment and tried to get his bearings. It was difficult in the still-falling, wind-whipped snow, but one of the things the man prided himself on was always making a quick, thorough study of his surroundings, especially when planning to do a deed. Last night's event had been no exception. And although conditions then, even in the dark, were far better than now, he was still able to recognize some familiarity to the spot where he had halted his flight.

Fatefully enough, he was on the back side of the saloon from whose whore cribs—small, cramped tents crowded up close to the rear of the building—he had lured away the stupid cow needed to satisfy his demons.

For a brief moment, the man considered forcing his way into one of those tents to seek shelter and warmth. But no, he decided, the risk was too great for one of the bitches to cry out and reveal his presence. He might even get trapped within those folds of filthy canvas.

Thoughts of the cow he'd dragged away last night stirred another idea. She'd been a rather large woman wearing a heavy wool skirt and a jacket with a fur-trimmed hood. That skirt and the hood portion of the jacket, even if the rest of it was too small to fit—wrapped around him, those could provide some welcome extra layers of warmth. There would be some torn fabric as a result of his scalpel and some blood, of course. But blood had never bothered him and most of the clothing would be sufficiently intact.

It was something. A start toward surviving and staying ahead of the pursuit that was sure to come.

Maybe, just maybe, he could burrow into the depression under the body with its extra attire and just hold there. Wait for the storm to break and pursuit to lag, then hope a better opportunity would present itself.

In desperation, the man in the long, wind-whipped coat turned and hurried toward the evergreen growth where he'd concealed the results of last night's deed.

Chapter 31

I was following close enough behind Tuttle so that I was still able to make out his tracks before the freshly falling snow filled them in. His course was somewhat erratic—no doubt due to slipping and skidding as he ran, even as I was doing in pursuit—but for the most part he was sticking close behind the row of Fordham's downtown businesses. Without darting inside one of them, he had few choices as far as where he could go. Unless he continued on out of town and into the wilderness. Which, given the conditions, seemed damned near certain suicide.

As I ran, slipping and sliding in his wake, I tried to reason what he might try. My hat blew off and I cursed.

He'd been in town longer than me, maybe he'd spotted something about its layout that I'd had no chance to observe. All I knew for sure was that the livery—where he could grab a horse to attempt a mounted escape—was behind us. Possibly he knew of some other place up ahead where there were horses. But racing off into the storm, even on horseback, was still a huge risk. Not to mention the fact, whether he realized it or not, I was too close behind to allow him time to saddle a getaway mount.

Once or twice, I thought I saw jerky movement up ahead. But then a blinding swirl of snow would intervene and it was gone.

I kept running.

Until, abruptly, I reached a spot where the tracks I was following stopped continuing straight ahead. The markings in the snow were jumbled, as if Tuttle had stood shifting and shuffling his feet uncertainly for a moment. And then the tracks veered away from the buildings and went off toward the high cliffs and evergreen growth that ran all along the north side of the town and the valley.

The crazy bastard was doing it. In the midst of a raging blizzard, on foot, he was striking out to try and make his escape into the wilderness.

I hesitated a moment ... then went after him.

Three Hundred Yards North of Fordham Mining Camp Colorado Rockies Front Range Friday, third week of Spring, 11:40 AM

The man in the flowing coat tugged and yanked desperately, rolling the stiffened corpse one way and then another in order to position it for the removal of its attire. He was on his knees in the thick evergreen growth, bent forward to his task. He had the dead prostitute's skirt draped over his shoulders like a shawl as he tried to pry the corpse's unbending arm in a way that would allow being able to pull off the sleeve of the jacket.

The problem of being cold was temporarily solved. The man was sweating from his exertion. He knew that wouldn't be good in the long run as he would be damp and wet when he started to cool again. But otherwise this idea he'd hit upon showed promise of working out satisfactorily.

The higher branches of the aspen trees served to prevent much of the falling snow from drifting through and the ground-hugging bushes blocked a good deal of the wind. Yes, he began to truly believe that burrowing down into the depression where he'd originally stuffed the slain cow and then covering himself with the layers *of added clothing he was now laying claim to might very well give him the means to survive. By also pulling the corpse and some thick branches over him, he could create a pocket of protective warmth that may not rate as high comfort but would be sufficient to sustain him.*

At last pulling the jacket free, the man issued a grunt of triumph. A moment later, as he was getting ready to swing the garment around his shoulders and tuck his head into the fur-trimmed hood, he felt a heavy lump in one of its pockets. Rummaging with partially numb fingers, he pulled the object free and found it was a gun. A large caliber, over-under two-shot derringer.

The man hated guns. He hated their ugly appearance and the awkward way any he had ever handled felt in his grip; not to mention the stink of the oil they were always smeared with and the acrid smoke they released when fired. Worst was the flesh-ripping, bone-smashing damage done by the bullets they discharged. Not at all clean and precise like the work done by a sharp cutting tool.

The man's first instinct was to fling the gun away. But then he paused, reconsidering. Under the circumstances, distasteful though the thought was, the very purpose of a loud, vulgar gun might actually give him an edge he otherwise lacked and could find himself badly in need of before this was over.

Reluctantly, the man dropped the derringer into the pocket of his long coat. A moment later, almost like an omen to signal the necessity of that begrudged act, he heard the not-to-distant voice calling through the sharp wind.

"Over here, men! He came this way—into this thick underbrush ... Spread out in a line and keep moving

forward! We can flush him back out into the open!"

The man in the flowing coat shot to a standing position. He'd taken too long preparing his burrow. He hadn't expected his pursuers to be so close behind. But they were; the nearness of that voice proved it. And, by the sound of it, they were several in number.

The man in the flowing coat had no choice. Whoever was out there would be "flushing" through here any moment, leaving no time for him to get properly concealed the way he'd been planning.

There was only one thing to do.

He had to flee again.

Chapter 32

The evergreen thicket was dense as hell.

It started about a hundred yards behind the back of the downtown buildings, sparse and somewhat sporadic at first but then the ground level underbrush quickly thickening and soon becoming studded with tall aspen trees. I could see where Tuttle had gone in, but it didn't take long before any sign of his tracks was obliterated by tangled growth. The farther I went in, the lesser the amount of snow filtered down through the high, wind-tossed branches. So even when I came upon small patches of open ground, there was barely enough fresh dusting to show a footprint.

A couple of times I stopped and listened, hoping I might hear the sound of my quarry thrashing through the bushes in his flight. But while much of the snow was blocked from falling back in here, the moan of the wind high in the trees was still the dominant sound.

I forged on, cursing in anger and frustration. From the pocket of my parka, I pulled the .44 Peacemaker. I'd promised Victoria I wouldn't shoot to kill. But as elusive as Tuttle was proving to be, that didn't mean I wouldn't take the option to drop the sonofabitch with a leg shot if I got the chance, rather than risk him getting away.

Then I got an idea. It was a trick Col. Sam had employed one time in a forest engagement during the war when our depleted outfit was being advanced on by a much larger Rebel force. They hadn't caught full sight of us yet, but our forward scouts had reported back what was coming our way and coming in a hurry. Thinking fast, Col. Sam scattered what few men we had and instructed us to start shouting back and forth like we were several different companies ordering the troops under our commands into position for a counter assault. Hearing reports of this, but still without a clear visual on us through all the trees and brush, the Reb commander ordered his men to halt their advance and take up a defensive stance instead. While they were holding that way, waiting for the counter assault that never came, we slipped away and were in the clear before they ever realized what happened.

Not that I had any intention of slipping away on Tuttle. But what I hoped for was that, knowing I had to be somewhere close and he likely couldn't spot me any better than I could him, I might be able to create the illusion I had more men with me—enough to force him out of wherever he was hiding.

And damned if it didn't work.

Up ahead, I saw him pop into sight and once more start running, deeper into the brush and trees, headed for the high cliffs not too far beyond. I immediately broke after him, intent to catch up or bring him down with a bullet if I had to before he gained the open where he'd have the chance to lose himself in more clouds of boiling snow.

But his long legs worked in his favor for running and leaping through the thick brush. I was having trouble closing the gap on him. Plus, the numerous trees were blocking me from getting any kind of clear shot.

I chugged on, freezing gulps of breath somehow turning to fire down deep in my lungs.

And then, all of a sudden, we were out of the trees and brush and the high cliffs were looming over us. There was only a short span of upward sloping ground, no more than forty yards, some of it studded with boulders poking up through the snow, before it was all cliff face. Several vertical gouges and furrows were worn into it, some quite shallow, others reaching back deep to a pinched-off closure.

Curiously, while plenty of falling flakes were coming down out on the slope, the wind was somehow buffered across this stretch. It reached down from on high in staggered swirling gusts, but otherwise was largely diminished.

Reaching the edge of the clear area, I saw that I still had decent visibility as I watched Tuttle scramble up to the cliff face, aiming for one of the deeper vertical seams. He made an almost comical sight with some sort of shawl flapping around his shoulders and what looked like a lumpy, fur-trimmed hood pulled up on the back of his head.

"Tuttle!" I called. "Give it up! You're trapped, you got no place to go!"

When he spun to face me, there was nothing comical about the menacing, maniacal expression that twisted his face.

I walked farther out of the bushes, the .44 held at my side. "Give it up," I said again. "It's over for you."

What he did next was totally unexpected and out of character for him. But I should have been prepared for it, for *some* kind of desperation move, nonetheless.

Shouting, "No! It's you who it's over for!" he raised his arm and I saw, too late, the derringer he extended in his fist.

I threw myself to the ground, scrambling behind a nearby large boulder, as I heard the crack of the derringer discharging. I don't know where the bullet went. As far as I could tell it came nowhere close to me. But it didn't matter. The aim of Tuttle's slug turned out to be of no consequence at all compared to the damage brought on by the report of the shot.

Like I said, I heard the crack of the derringer go off. A second later, while I was still flattening myself behind the boulder, I heard another cracking sound. Much louder and sharper. And then a sudden, rapid series of growling and rumbling all mixed together like an enormous belch issued from a giant stomach.

I risked poking my head over the top of the boulder in time to catch a final glimpse of Tuttle before he entirely disappeared under a downpour of snow and chunks of ice and loosened rocks tumbling onto him from the high ledges of the vertical seam he'd partially backed into. After hitting the ground and filling the lower confines of the seam, the snowslide/avalanche continued to burst outward for a good distance before it was done. It was mostly out of steam by the time it reached me, but if not for the boulder I remained ducked behind it still would have given me a good battering.

As it was, all I could do was press myself tight against the rough, cold stone with clouds of billowing snow and debris rising up all around me and thank my lucky stars that I hadn't managed to close the gap on Tuttle any tighter.

Epilogue

I'd spent enough time in the mountains to know how avalanches can sometimes be triggered by a sudden loud noise. If there was any doubt that's what had happened to Tuttle, the Fordham locals removed it when I told my story. They all agreed that some older, partially melted and loosened layer of snow up on a higher ledge, already unbalanced by fresh accumulation on top of it, had only needed the shock of Tuttle's gunshot to jar it the rest of the way loose and bring it crashing down. As for the man at the bottom, it would be weeks, months— and only then if the summer was warm enough to completely melt the resulting heap of snow and ice—before his remains would ever be found.

Losing Tuttle and the ultimately incriminating testimony that hopefully could have been grilled out of him, drastically altered the series of articles Victoria was able to write about him and his killing spree. While the string of slain prostitutes scattered across the front range could be convincingly connected to the man (much to the horror of his fellow troupe members), the same unfortunately couldn't be said about the rest of it. His alter identity as Jack the Ripper, the John Wilkes Booth association, the London years and the time in New Orleans following Lincoln's assassination ... too much of it would be open to doubt and dispute lacking harder, more non-speculative evidence than Victoria could provide. Without Tuttle to back it up (either by admission or by supporting identification from those who had encountered him in some of those places) there was risk that doubters would resort to ridicule and counter-speculation that might result in smearing Russ Wheeler's good name.

It was for this reason, to guard her father's name and reputation even though she would have been willing to make a fight of it on her own, that Victoria decided to confine her reportage merely to the coverage of a mad killer who had been obsessed with and inspired by the work of Jack the Ripper. Numerous newspaper and magazine articles about the Ripper's exploits were found among Tuttle's personal belongings, along with a leather bound set of scalpels and other cutting instruments, supported this claim. (There were also numerous articles on Booth from his acclaimed acting days found among Tuttle's belongings, but no one paid any particular attention to what that might mean.)

In the end, the series of articles Victoria wrote were published to wide circulation and high acclaim by the same news syndicate her father had worked for. Additionally, they hired her to write full time for them. In a private aside, she confided to me her regret about not being able to present Tuttle's full story as so painstakingly pieced together over so many years by her father.

Still, she was proud of what "we" (her choice of words, although my name – at my request – had been largely kept out of her reportage) had been able to accomplish. The Ripper's killing days were ended, the fiend had met a harsh and final judgment. What was more, she added with a devilish smile, who was to say that in the months and years ahead she might not be able to unearth more conclusive details that would still allow her father's "story of the everlovin' century" to yet be brought forth in full?

* * * * *

It took a while for the whole "Tuttle, the Ameri-can Ripper" thing to play out and for all of Victoria's wildly popular articles to see print.

But in the midst of it, as soon as I was able to get back to Denver, there was a piece of personal business—somewhat peripherally related—that remained to be taken care of. It had to do with the two pieces of paper, the closely matching sketches, I had been carrying around in my shirt pocket. One was the map showing the sequence of mining camps Meadley had sketched for me just before Victoria and I were getting ready to head up into the foot hills. The other was an almost identical drawing, right down to the stationary and letterhead, I'd taken off Cherokee Farrow after the shootout in the Promise saloon.

When I silently laid them, side by side, on the desktop in front of Meadely in the O&PW Denver branch office, his normally pale complexion turned even whiter. And when his fear- and guilt-laced eyes lifted to look up at me, I knew with a sickening twist in my gut there was no longer any doubt about what I'd feared the most.

I only had one question. "Why?"

It took him a minute. He licked his lips, averted his eyes. I thought he was going to do some pleading, try to weasel out of it somehow. But instead, he abruptly squared his narrow, twisted shoulders and glared defiantly. "You ask why? Because for the better part of two decades I've hated your guts, that's why. At last I decided that, before I go, I wanted the pleasure of seeing you dead."

The statement caught me enough off guard so that I was momentarily at a loss or words.

Meadely spread his misshapen arms. "Take a good look, you sonofabitch. All of this, this twisted up human freak that scuttles around like a crab ... It's all thanks to you. Have you forgotten who was driving the munitions wagon that night when it flipped and crushed me into this?"

"It was the middle of a rainstorm," I protested. "The muddy bank gave way and the wagon tipped. Nobody in the driver's box could have prevented it."

"But it wasn't nobody—it was *you*! You jumped clear and came out fine. I came out like this. After months of agony and torturous rehab, I got told this was the best I was ever going to be and that's what I've been living with ever since."

"But why bring it up now? Why strike out against me after all this time?" I demanded.

Meadely's mouth twisted into a sneer. "Because, after living with this all these years—after watching you and other operatives ride in and out of here on challenging, exciting assignments while I was stuck in this broken shell of a body and this box of an office and living quarters I was confined to—Fate decided to drop one more shovelful of rotten luck on me. Last month I got the word: I have a cancer, eating me up from the inside out. I won't see the middle of Summer ... Hearing that was when I by-God decided that, before I went, what I *would* live to see was you go ahead of me."

A small twinge deep inside me almost felt sorry for him. But it didn't last long. I said, "So you sent Cherokee, Brocus, and Mungo after me to get the job done."

Meadely's gaze drifted off, as if seeing something far away. "I only hired Cherokee. I could afford to pay well, I'd saved up plenty of money over the years. What the hell did I have to spend it on? So who else the halfbreed brought in was up to him ... First those two up in Cheyenne because he wanted to use locals to try and avoid any ties back here to Denver. When that didn't work and he heard you were heading up into the mountains, he got the map from me and brought in Mungo and Brocus."

My gut clenched. "Cheyenne?"

"That's right. The attempt on you up there, the one that ended up costing Russ Wheeler his life, was set in motion by me too. I was genuinely sorry to hear about Russ getting caught in it."

Now it was my turn to sneer. "So, even though you knew Russ's daughter was traveling with me, you still sent those three killers. I could accept that. Hell, I've had killers sent after me by far better men than you. But did you ever stop to think what they would have done to Victoria if they'd succeeded and gotten past me?"

Meadely's gaze came back. It and the expression on his face were devoid of any emotion. "Sorry ... I got no pity left for anybody but me."

I expect the look on my own face was very similar to his. "So there's a doctor in town who knows about your cancer. Right?"

"Uh-huh."

"Good. Then he can tell everybody" —I said as I reached for the throwaway short-barreled .38 I'd brought specially with me, pulling it from my waistband at the small of my back and jamming its muzzle to his forehead— "how you must not have been able to stand the thought of all the upcoming pain your illness would bring." And then I pulled the trigger.

After pressing the .38 into Meadely's dead hand and wiping some blood spatter off my own with a hanky, I began formulating the details of the story I would tell Marshal Barton up in Cheyenne to convince him to lift murder charges against Everertt Byron, the embezzler. I'd explain how, before he died, Cherokee Farrow confessed to setting up the ambush that resulted in Russ's death. Nobody argues with the confession of a dying man.

As I got ready to quit the O&PW branch office, I paused in the doorway a moment to look back at the twisted form of Meadely slumped in his chair. I had two lingering regrets. One, that Russ Wheeler had died because of this little bastard ... and two, that there hadn't been a way to leave the spiteful wretch alive long enough to suffer the full agony of the cancer eating up his guts.

A Look At: The Bodie Kendrick Bounty Hunter Collection

AWARD-WINNING AUTHOR WAYNE D. DUNDEE
SPINS ANOTHER EXCITING YARN OF GRIT, GUN-
FIRE, AND GALLANTRY IN THE BODIE KENDRICK
BOUNTY HUNTER COLLECTION!

Bounty hunter Bodie Kendrick makes a living
bringing in wanted men, sometimes face down across
a saddle. In this tenacious, hard-edged collection follow
Bodie on his countless journeys through the Old West.

AVAILABLE NOW ON AMAZON

About the Author

Wayne D. Dundee is an American author of popular genre fiction. His writing has primarily been detective mysteries (the Joe Hannibal PI series) and Western adventures. Born in Freeport, Illinois, he graduated from high school in Clinton, Wisconsin, 1966. Later that same year he married Pamela Daum and they had one daughter, Michelle. For the first fifty years of his life, Dundee lived and worked in the state line area of northern Illinois and southern Wisconsin. He sold his first short story in 1982.

His work in the mystery field has been nominated for an Edgar, an Anthony, and six Shamus Awards from the Private Eye Writers of America.

Made in the USA
Coppell, TX
10 June 2021